AN ENGROSSING SAGA FI
FAMILY THEATRICS, EX
MONUMENTAL CHARACTERS .... ONE THAT BRINGS
AN UNFORGETTABLE AND GRATIFYING FINALE

Set around the renowned and historical homestead at the center of the drama, *Ship Watch* weaves together six intertwined relationships that extend from the gentrified city of Savannah and into the wealthy enclaves of Sea Island, Highlands, and Atlanta's Buckhead. The novel's characters are drawn in the loom by the family's elegantly formidable matriarch, Grand Martha, and form a multi-generational tapestry that includes the misfortunes of divorce and betrayal – but in more and even better measure opportunities for redemption, rediscovery, and the rarified gift of 'second love.' By combining an encompassing setting having a solid sense of place along with characters that are captivating and rather extraordinary, *Ship Watch* is a sometimes bittersweet, yet often comedic, Southern tour-de-force debut novel.

Editorial Reviews

Come peek inside the kimono of Savannah's bluest of blue-blood families. When ownership of Ship Watch, the family's long-owned grand plantation on the banks of the Savannah River, is contested, proverbial long knives are brandished. Much of this engrossing tale depicts place — Savannah, Highlands, and Sea Island – where the wealthy make merry and hold court.—**Jameson Gregg, Georgia Author of the Year,** *Luck Be A Chicken*

"Storyteller extraordinaire, raconteur, and old-school bon vivant Johnathon Barrett celebrates the most glorious aspects of Southern life in all four of his wonderfully written books"—**Janis Owens, award-winning and bestselling author of** *American Ghost* **and** *My Brother Michael*

"Ship Watch is the closest you'll come to breathing the rarified air of the Southern aristocracy. Grab your cocktail of choice and settle in for excess and exes, second chances, and at least one epic Julia Sugarbaker-style setting-things-to-right takedown.—**Jeffrey Dale Lofton, award-winning author of *Red Clay Suzie***

"Ship Watch, a stately Southern mansion built on the coast of Georgia in the 1800s, is only one of the intricate arrays of characters in this debut novel by Johnathon Scott Barrett. Readers will be transported into this down-home Southern story about April Anne Adams, a small-town Georgia girl, who finds getting everything she ever dreamed of doesn't guarantee happiness, and Tripp Randolph, who is set to inherit Ship Watch if his soon-to-be ex-wife doesn't win the mansion in their nasty divorce. April Anne and Tripp converge together and sparks, A page turner until the end."— **Ann Hite, 2012 Georgia Author of the Year and author of the award-winning *Haints On Black Mountain: A Haunted Short Story Collection* and *Ghost On Black Mountain***

"In the vital tradition of the Southern saga, Johnathan Barrett creates a splendid story of three generations headed by a powerful and fascinating matriarch. Readers will keep turning pages to find out how ·friends and family work through long-held frictions, while Grand Martha ultimately determines the future of the titular Ship Watch, the Randolph family's majestic estate."—**Susan Beckham Zurenda, award winning author of *Bells for Eli* and *The Girl from the Red Rose Motel***

"Readers will clutch their pearls--and then devour this deliciously dishy, multi-generational peek into the manners and mores of the Savannah, Highlands, Sea Island, and Buckhead moneyed elite. — **Mary Kay Andrews, *New York Times* bestselling author of *The Homewreckers* and *Hissy Fit***

"Meet Johnathon Scott Barrett, the literary first cousin to Fannie Flagg and Mary Kay Andrews. He joins their rank as he comedically writes about Southern life and Southern strife in this debut novel." — **Jackie K.**

Cooper, Host of *Entertainment Rundown* and *author of The Wisdom of Winter*

"Remindful of the works of Dorothea Benton Frank, *Ship Watch* is a charming, fun, and entertaining read. With characters that sparkle and dialogue that crackles, Johnathon Scott Barrett has crafted a Southern tale that is not to be missed. Pour yourself a glass of sweet tea – or three fingers of bourbon – and savor this wonderful novel.— **Michael Morris, award winning author of *Man in the Blue Moon, Slow Way Home*, and *A Place Called Wiregrass***

"With *Ship Watch*, gifted storyteller and cookbook author Johnathan Scott Barrett mixes up a delightful brew of Southern eccentricities and serves it with dash of romance, adventure and intrigue. Although family drama is nothing new to the illustrious Randolph family of Savannah, when the colorful matriarch known as Grand Martha sets out to save Ship Watch, their magnificent ancestral home, the stage is set for a rollicking good read!"— **Cassandra King, award-winning author of *Tell Me a Story: My Life with Pat Conroy***

"Few areas of the country dazzle and intrigue the way the Low Country does. Barrett brings it to life in an epic tapestry of Southern culture that will leave you wanting more. "— **R.J. Lee, author of the *Bridge to Death Mysteries***

"Set amongst the sumptuous backdrop of Savannah Georgia's elite, Johnathon Scott Barrett's debut novel, *Ship Watch*, is a compelling Southern saga of unyielding women and the alluring men they love, family tradition, and second chances."— **Robert Gwaltney, Georgia New Author of the Year, *The Cicada Tree***

"*Ship Watch* sings with expansive details about the dramas of a genteel Savannah family. It's obvious that author Jonathon Scott Barrett intimately knows this world, and he provides a fascinating birds-eye view into a stratum of society abundant with colorful characters and a culture of their very own. A must read for anyone who loves Southern fiction."—**Karin Gillespie, author of the *Bottom***

Dollar Girls series and co-author of *The Sweet Potato Queen's First Big-Ass Novel*

SHIP WATCH

Johnathon Scott Barrett

Moonshine Cove Publishing, LLC

Abbeville, South Carolina U.S.A.

First Moonshine Cove Edition Dec 2023

ISBN: 9781952439711

Library of Congress LCCN: 2023921166

Cover illustration supplied by the author, cover and interior design by Moonshine Cove staff.

.

About the Author

Described as 'the epitome of a Southern raconteur and gentleman' as well as 'reveling bon vivant,' Johnathon Scott Barrett is a seventh-generation Georgian with a deep appreciation of both the literary and culinary traditions of the South. A renowned host, he is the author of

three widely- acclaimed cookbooks, which critics hail for their content of entertaining stories as well as extensive recipes. Besides those works – *Rise and Shine!*, *Cook & Tell,* and *Cook & Celebrate* (Mercer University Press publications 2015, 2017, and 2022 respectively) his writings have also been included in periodicals such as *Okra, Deep South,* and *Shrimp, Collards & Grits.*

In addition to writing, Johnathon is a CPA and has worked as a nonprofit executive for the last three decades; currently he is the director of development for the State Botanical Garden of Georgia at UGA. He loves traveling (his father once said, "John is like a hound dog; just whistle and he'll jump in the back of the truck, ready to go) fishing, good bourbon, and his bevy of wonderful friends and family.

He splits his time with his husband, Thomas Eugene, and their dog, Maximillian, between homes in Winterville, Georgia, and Savannah. Please visit him at:

www.johnathonbarrett.com

Ship Watch is dedicated in loving memory of my mother, Joyce, and her baby sister, my Aunt Beatrice — from whom I inherited my love of the written word as well as many, many other of life's treasures.

Acknowledgment

Sincere and humble appreciation is extended to those who have been a part of my writing sojourns and that have made *Ship Watch* a possibility:

Joyce Dixon, my high school literary and drama teacher, who saw in me a talent of which I was unaware. For more than forty years she has been a dear friend and supporter.

Janis Owens, my favorite 'cousin' from the Panhandle and one of the finest writers the South has ever produced. Her Florida Cracker wisdom – and love – has been a treasure to me personally and as an author.

Monica McGoldrick, and the Girls on the Grill Supper Club in Savannah, whose encouragement was the catalyst for my first book, which led to a second, third, and now finally, *Ship Watch*.

My buddy since seventh grade Alphus Christopher Spears who, as with all my books, provided his extensive knowledge of the King's (and formerly the Queen's) English with edits and guidance.

Haywood Smith, the talented Georgia author who lent her editing wisdom and guidance.

Gene Robinson and the team at Moonshine Cove Publishing, Inc. who took a chance on this 'culinary storyteller' and brought my dream of a fiction novel to print.

Thomas Eugene and Max, who patiently tolerated my intense weekends and nights at home when I sequestered myself away to write.

The authors and reviewers that graciously took time from their abounding and teeming schedules to read *Ship Watch* and then provide their kind thoughts and praise: Mary Kay Andrews, Jackie K. Cooper, Karin Gillepsie, Jameson Gregg, Robert Gwaltney, Ann Hite, Cassandra King, R. J. Lee, Jeffrey Dale Lofton, Michael Morris, Janis Owens, and Susan Beckham Zurenda.

To the city of Savannah, whose beauty and allure provided the magical backdrop for *Ship Watch*. How fortunate to have had the Hostess City of the South as my home for more than thirty years.

Preface

In the tradition-laden South, surnames are often passed down through the generations and across family branches as given names, denoting a person's maternal and paternal lines. Nicknames are also prevalent and particularly helpful in distinguishing family members with similar first and last names. The reader will find both of these cultural practices in *Ship Watch*. Included herein is an alphabetical listing of main characters with brief descriptions as a guide when reading the novel.

April Anne Adams, a South Georgia bestselling author and attorney, late of NYC

Frank Adams, April Anne's father

Joyce Adams, April Anne's mother

Eloise Calhoun Baylor, a descendant of one of the First Families of South Carolina and wife of Judge Brantley Baylor

Brantley Allison Baylor, federal judge and eldest of the Baylor siblings

Whittaker "Whitt" Allison Baylor, Atlanta attorney and brother to Brantley and Lily

Leigh Anna Baylor, wife of Whittaker

Adam Bedford, Baylor Randolph's first love

Lachlan "Lachy" Campbell, cattle farmer, Scotophile, and Lovey MacGregor's fiancé

Melissa "M'liss" Ray Chandler, Jana Randolph's late mother

Anthony Darlington-Smythe, Martha Randolph's British cousin

William Joseph "Billy Joe" Dozier, Atlanta realtor and Lovey's gay ex-husband

Stephens Gamble, deceased ancestor of Martha Randolph

Eulalie and Eurelia Gamble, daughters of Stephens Gamble and Martha Randolph's great aunts

Patrick Collin Steward Hogan, a former Special Ops soldier, he is Lovey's cousin and personal driver

Bebe Frank Kahn, Savannah pediatrician and Jana Randolph's friend

Bernie Lischer, renowned photographer and cousin to Bebe

Dr. Jackson Lockwood, Atlanta psychiatrist and hopeful paramour of Lily Randolph

Louvenia "Lovey" Steward MacGregor, Savannah interior designer, best friend to April Anne, and a cousin of the Randolph family

Buckner "Buck" Pearson, Savannah businessman and serial predator

Mary Nan Bishop Pearson, Buck's late wife and childhood best friend of Bernie

Addison Peyton Randolph, Sr., late husband to Martha Randolph

Addison "Add" Peyton Randolph, Jr., son of Addison and Martha

Addison "Trip" Peyton Randolph, III, son of Add and Lily Randolph, husband to Jana Ray Chandler Randolph, and father of twins Peyton and Ray Randolph

Baylor Stephens Randolph, younger brother to Trip and son of Add and Lily

Elizabeth "Lily" Baylor Randolph, widow of the late Add Randolph, sister of Brantley and Whittaker, mother to Trip and Baylor

Jana Ray Chandler Randolph, an Atlanta native and soon-to-be ex-wife of Trip, mother to twins Peyton and Ray

Martha "Grand Martha" Stephens Randolph, family matriarch, widow of Addison, Sr., and mother to Add, Jr.

Peyton Chandler Randolph, son of Trip and Jana, twin brother of Ray

Ray Addison Randolph, son of Trip and Jana, twin brother of Peyton

Augustus "Auggie" Gamble Stephens, Savannah barrister and second cousin to Martha

Thomas Trotter, President & CEO of Randolph Shipping

Jenny Lynnette Wilson, April Anne's sister

Stuart Wilson, Jenny Lynnette's husband

Part I

May

Chapter 1

April Anne had just finished the last touches of her makeup routine, which was rather minimal, when a knock came on the door to the bedroom. "Yoo-hoo, hon. You 'bout ready?"

"Yes, Lovey, come on in," she said as she turned sideways in the dressing chair towards the door.

Her friend of more than twenty years, Louvenia Steward MacGregor, known fondly as 'Lovey," entered in her typical swoosh of movement. While not a large woman, she nonetheless always seemed to fill up a room due to her expansive and garrulous personality. Her thick mane of blonde, wavy hair was pinned high on her head, crowning her round, cherubic face. She was wearing one of her signature safari inspired dresses; tonight's ensemble featured bold white and black zebra stripes. Lovey bent down, gave her friend a quick kiss on her left cheek, and placed a glass of wine on the dressing table.

"Here, hon, have a little something to help get yourself together."

"Thanks, Lovey, but it's too early for me to start, even with wine," she replied.

"Nonsense. Here in Savannah, it is a tradition to have some libation when you are getting ready to go out for the evening. It's called a gettin' ready drink."

"I'm beginning to think there is always a tradition involving libations in this town, regardless of the occasion. And is it a 'getting ready drink,' singular, or can there be more than one? I spy two slices of lime in your glass," she answered good naturedly, pointing a finger toward the crystal tumbler in her friend's hand.

"Nothing gets by you, does it, Nancy Drew?" Lovey sat down at the foot of the bed. "I just like a lot of lime, thank you very much, so there," she answered, sidestepping whether it had been one or two

13

cocktails poured into the glass. "And before I finish this gin and tonic, and get all sentimental, you know how I am, let me tell you again just how grateful I am to you for coming down and being here. This past year has been, as the late Queen so eloquently put it, "annus horribilis."

April Anne reached over and took Lovey's free hand in hers. "You have nothing to thank me for, good Lord, you've been through enough. I can't imagine how painful it was to watch your Mama get so sick, and her passing away so quickly. And then your own horrible cancer scare. Now are you sure you're going to be OK? There are no more lumps, are there? The prognosis is clean you said."

"The specialists assured me that there were only two — listen to me, 'only two,' like one is not enough — and that all were removed. Everything was fine at my annual physical last month, thank the good Lord. I'll tell you what, though, my titties will never be the same. Those crazed doctors have cut, pushed, pulled, mashed, and yanked so much on these babies that for a while there they looked like a couple of eggplants."

Lovey giggled at her attempt at humor, and April joined in. "And fortunately, my hair all grew back. My thick hair has always been hot, but let me tell you, hon, a damn wig will roast your head." Again, the friends joined in a bit of laughter. "I do have to admit having a time of it, though. Being an only child has some blessings, but it also can be a bitch. Luckily, my sweet, sweet cousins were godsends. Trip and Baylor made all the funeral arrangements while I was trying to keep myself healthy. And now you're here, and we'll have a grand old time. I'm going to love having you with me this summer."

"It's a blessing to be here. I've wanted to move back to Georgia for a long time now and have just been waiting for the dust to settle from the divorce. I'm lucky at this point in my life and career my editor comes to me, and not the other way around. I'll only have to go back to New York a couple of times this year. You just don't know how grateful I'm for you taking me in and letting me lick my wounds, so to speak."

Lovey took another sip of her drink and looked fondly at her friend. "You stay here as long as you want; I'll love the company. I don't care about wandering around in this big old pile by myself. You'll have plenty of room; we can set up your computer in that connecting bedroom," she motioned toward a doorway with her cocktail, "and you'll have your own sitting room, bathroom, and bedroom. And think about it, April Anne, it'll be even more room than you and shithead had in your Manhattan apartment."

April Anne laughed; Lovey had never cared for her ex. And space would not be a problem here. With its six bedrooms and baths, and a multitude of family spaces, the MacGregor house was enormous. Located in the city's first streetcar suburb, Ardsley Park, a neighborhood with streets lined with live oaks draped in Spanish moss, the home was set on over an acre. "Thanks, Lovey." She reached over and squeezed her friend's hand again, "you're absolutely right."

Lovey stood up. "Let's head downstairs; Patrick is always spot on time and will start blowing the horn if we're not ready although he drives like molasses on a cold day. It'll take us a good half hour to get to Ship Watch."

"OK, let me grab my purse." April Anne picked up her evening bag and walked over to put her arm around Lovey's waist. They went out into the wide upper hall and down the ornate staircase to the formal entranceway leading into the house. April Anne marveled at Lovey's skill at design and understood again why she was in such high demand for her craft. "Lovey, all this turned out to be so beautiful," she said as she gestured with her free arm around the room. "It's like walking into an *Architectural Digest* dream home."

Hugging her close, she answered, "you're so sweet, April Anne Adams. I just love you. It was all Mama's idea to redo the house after Daddy died, though. She said she wanted to brighten this place up and get rid of some of those humongous Edwardian pieces that had been Grandmama Mac's. The furniture was excellent quality, but this Mediterranean house just didn't call for that particular type. We kept some of the more sentimental items, but the rest were sold to a client in Buffalo who bought a big old pile of a Tudor House on Lake Eerie. I decided the new decor should be in the spirit of 1920s Palm Beach chic. Most of the furniture came from an auction house down in Boca Raton." The two ladies had been walking through the living room and dining room, and Lovey led them back to the bar in the library. "Here, I'm gonna put another little splash in my glass before our ride gets here."

"Not to worry, I'll just go ahead outside." April sat her wine glass on the bar, walked through the multi-paned French doors onto the side veranda and took a seat on a wrought iron bench. She was looking forward to seeing Ship Watch; she had heard about that grand plantation for years, having read articles about it in *Preservation News* as well as *Southern Accents*. It had been in the Randolph family since it was built by the first of their ancestors who moved to the new world in the late 1700s.

George Randolph had been sent to Savannah to expand his family's shipbuilding and iron businesses, which proved to be very successful ventures in these new United States. Commerce and shipping were booming, and the family prospered with it. In 1814 Randolph sent four of his most skilled workers to Philadelphia for three years to study the art of building construction and furniture making. He entrusted these master carpenters to carry out the design and building of the family homestead, and according to the photos she had seen, the result was a unique combination of Georgian splendor, inspired by the architecture found in the City of Brotherly Love, and low country style that the hot, humid southern summers required for comfortable living. The mansion's exterior walls, constructed of famous Savannah grey brick, were covered with a smooth surface of pale stucco, scored to look as if the house had been built of limestone blocks. Floor-to-ceiling windows, which allowed cooling cross breezes throughout the house, adorned the parlor and second stories. Cast iron lintels and balustrades imported from the Randolph iron works in Liverpool added to the ornamentation. Verandas, held up by 16 perfectly proportioned Doric columns, framed the house on all four sides. A pitched roof made of Welsh slate hosting eight multi-paned dormers topped the second story. In the 1870s George Randolph's grandson crowned the house with the addition of a Victorian cupola surrounded by a widow's walk. From this perch, he could gaze eastward and watch the building of his ships along the broad Savannah River, giving the house its name.

Many of the home's furnishings had been designed and custom built on site by the four expert craftsmen. They had brought home drawings and specifications for some of the finest sideboards, highboys, rice beds, and dining tables and chairs being made in Philadelphia during the early 19th century. Using local Georgia pine and ash, and supplementing with rich veneers made from imported Barbados mahogany, the men fabricated pieces on par with those made by the artisans in Pennsylvania. The family still owned these highly valuable pieces. According to a quote April Anne had read in an article featuring a curator at Winterthur, the Randolph furniture included "*the* most extensive, important, and valuable collection of fine American Southern furnishings in the world."

As she thought of how impressive these Randolphs and their home sounded, Lovey came through the doors just as her two-toned silver and grey Bentley pulled up front. April smiled at the vanity plate the classic car sported "LUVYMAC."

"There's Patrick now," Lovey pointed out as she turned and locked the doors behind her.

The young man got out of the car and opened the rear doors as the two ladies walked down the flagstone pathway. "Hey, Pat. Let me introduce you to my very best and dearest friend, April Anne Adams. We were roommates at UGA, and she is staying with me this whole summer. I'm *so excited.*" she gushed, giving her friend another hug around the waist.

"Glad to meet you, Mrs. Adams. I've read several of your books, but my Mother, she's read them all." April extended a hand, which Patrick warmly shook.

"It's nice to meet you. Please tell your Mother I would love to meet her, too, one day while I'm here," April said with a smile, and sat herself inside the car.

As Lovey was about to get in on the other side, Patrick said in a whisper to Lovey, "Hey, you didn't tell Miss Adams this was a theme dinner tonight?" as he motioned his head towards the car.

"Whatever do you mean, Pat? There is no theme tonight, just a simple family dinner," she asked back, looking puzzled.

"Oh, my bad. I just saw you were head to toe in safari gear and thought maybe you all were going to be having a *Jungle Book* supper." He smiled and then added mischievously, "Or something to do with *The African Queen*."

"You are awful, and I'm ready for you to get your smart mouth back up to Athens as soon as this summer is over."

"What was that all about?" April asked as Lovey slid in beside her on the leather seats.

"Oh, he's just a pain in the derriere, and thinks he is a stand-up comedian," she said as Patrick started the car. But there was a twinkle in her eye as she spoke.

As the car pulled onto the street, Lovey looked over at April. "Let me give you a little background about tonight. All should be fine, but it may have some, let's just say, awkward moments."

Giving a dramatic sigh, as she was sometimes prone to do, Lovey continued. "Before we get there, the family is having some pow-wow, all of which has to do with my cousin Trip's divorce from his wife. We all figured that they would part ways once the twins were old enough to handle the trauma — they're rising seniors at the University of Virginia— but no one would have guessed that there would be so much contentiousness and ill-feelings."

"Well, as I know from experience, no part of a divorce is easy," April stated, shaking her head slightly.

"You're right, absolutely right, but instead of just splitting assets and going their separate ways, it seems that my dear lovable bear of a cousin, whom I just love to death, has been having an ongoing affair with a woman over in Hilton Head, and it has changed the whole situation. Now Jana, his wife, is threatening to go to court, and take him for every dime he has, including the deed to Ship Watch. It's just too much for words." Lovey sang out the last sentence in her well-practiced exasperated voice, and fanned her face, as she was flushing from the gin and tonics along with the emotions of the discussion.

April looked puzzled. "I just can't imagine anyone losing a home with such family history attached to it just because of an infidelity, can you?"

Lovey replied shaking her head for emphasis, "No I can't. Honestly, it is just a much bigger mess than I would have ever thought. And another thing that has them all in a tizzy is that everyone knows about Trip's affair now; it's all over town."

"Sure is," Patrick interjected as the car glided down palm-lined Victory Drive. "I heard it the other day from some fellows at the Golf Club. They were wondering why anyone would cheat on someone as as pretty as Jana Randolph."

"Stop listening in on our private conversation," Lovey said, a bit irritably. "And, quit gossiping. I swear, men are worse than women when it comes to running their mouths."

"I can't help but overhear, Lovey, since you, as always, are talking with your outside voice," he quipped back, good naturedly.

Lovey kicked the back of the driver's seat with one of her black leather dress boots, hard.

"April, don't pay any attention to him at all." Rolling her eyes and motioning towards him with her head she added, "I can't believe we're kin; something got mixed up on his end of the gene pool."

"I didn't realize that the two of you were related. I did think you all were going at one another at full tilt to be just a regular employer and employee. You were starting to sound like Karen and Rosario off *Will and Grace*." April laughed. "You remind me of Karen just a bit, anyway. I'm just saying."

"Ha, ha. You are not as good a comedienne as you are attorney and author, sweet pie." Lovey reached over and pinched her friend's cheek. "But yes, we're cousins on Daddy's side of the family. I'm related to the Randolph's through Mama."

"Ouch, Lovey," she laughed while she slapped at her friend's hand, "but I don't think you need to be worrying too much about Trip. In my humble opinion, and I'm not that well-versed with Georgia divorce or property laws, but if the children are grown, and there is an adequate separation of assets otherwise, it's unlikely to have a judge or jury awarding such a unique and historic family home to an ex-wife. If I were her lawyer, the only strategy in this sort of petition would be to stretch out the case in hopes the more difficult and lengthier the proceedings, the more willing the other party would be to come up with more concessions, i. e., money."

"Yes, I suppose you're right." Lovey stared down at her cat's-eye and onyx bracelet, giving it a twirl on her wrist. "Jana is probably angling to get as much out of this marriage as possible. But she better be careful, too."

"What do you mean?"

"Well now, you know I'd rather walk a mile on my lips than criticize someone."

Patrick, looking into the rearview mirror at the two friends, deadpanned, "If that's the case, Miss Lovey Mac, your odometer is about to turn over another hundred thousand any minute now."

"Now that was just plain mean, mean, mean. I swear I do not know why in the world I put up with you," she said heaving another sigh. "Now hush and let me finish."

"Anyway, April, lately word around town is that Jana is having her own little *liaison amoureuse*, and from what I hear, with one of the most unlikable fellows in all of Chatham County."

"Yep, our paper lady reports that Buck Pearson has been telling everyone in town that he and Jana were, 'going at it," Lovey's cousin chimed in, and April laughed out loud as she looked up to see his reflection in the mirror, eyebrows raised and wiggling up and down.

"Sweet Jesus." Lovey exclaimed. "Even the people who deliver the paper know about this."

"Mrs. Grayton isn't just any paper lady, Lovey. She is like Savannah's own version of the *National Enquirer;* she knows all the dirt. She could write a book about this town."

"Book's already been written, and John Berendt made millions," Lovey said, referring to the famous novel *Midnight in the Garden of Good and Evil.* She waved her hand toward the young man in a gesture of impatience. "And I told you to stop gossiping already. It is a very unattractive trait."

"OK, next time Mrs. Grayton shares some juicy news with me, mum's the word, so don't blame me because you don't know the latest scoop."

"I hate to interrupt this ongoing exchange of familial affection," April said, patting her hand on the seat of the car to get their attention, "but tell me more about the supposed affair of Jana's and this Mr. Pearson."

"I'm sure that Patrick and Mrs. Minnie Grayton, the Liz Smith of Savannah, could tell you more than I can," Lovey said, speaking to the back of Patrick's head, and then continuing on to April, "though word has it through Buckner that the two of them are, as he puts it in his plebeian way, 'going at it.' Why in the life of me, if she were going to choose someone to shag with, would it be that a-hole? Lord, I cannot bear that man. You know the type, April, one of those men so absolutely full of himself, with such a big ego, he doesn't even realize no one else wants to even be in the same room with him."

"He's rich, but the guy is certainly a jerk," came a response from the front seat. "The only reason the men golf with him at the Club is because he buys all the drinks after their rounds, and those fellas can really put away the single malts, particularly when it's on somebody else's tab."

Lovey sat forward in her seat. "I *told you* to stop listening in on our conversation. I'm trying to talk to my friend whom I have not seen in two years, so can you just keep your comments to yourself? I swear, I have a good mind to fire you."

"Fine." The young man answered with a little hurt in his voice coming through. "You won't hear another word. It's not my fault you don't have a driver's license anymore, so don't take it out on me."

At these words, Lovey blushed from her neck up, her face aflame. April took the opportunity to gaze out her window and give the moment time to pass, not wanting to pry.

"Well thank you, Patrick Hogan. I appreciate your airing my business out." Turning to her friend beside her, she continued, "April, it is not big deal, but I did have my license suspended, and I would have told you, but I'm just absolutely, totally, totally embarrassed about it."

"What happened, hon?"

"Well, you know I've never been a good driver. I'm constantly running over a curb, backing into cars in parking lots. I even rear-ended my own Mother on our way to bridge club one night." As she spoke, she became more animated and agitated, her arms waving about her as she relayed her story. "I racked up so many tickets my auto insurance has been cancelled by two companies in the last four years. I just don't have the attention span to drive; my mind is always on four or five topics, and you know, I even talk with my hands when talking to myself," she continued, nodding her head in agreement to her own story. Her large, dangling, zebra-striped earrings waved back and forth as she spoke. "Anyway, a couple of months ago, I got, yes," she closed her eyes and shook her head slightly, "a DUI. But April, I swear, it was not what it might seem."

"Lovey, it is fine. I'm not judging you, don't think a thing about it," she answered with sincerity.

"Seriously, it was the most damn awful thing ever, and just my luck. I had taped the last four episodes of *Downton Abbey,* and settled in upstairs, all propped up on the bed in my nightgown ready to watch TV. In the spirit of the show, you know all this British pomp, I served myself a few gin and tonics while watching. Well, in the third hour or so I put the TV on pause to get up and go to the bathroom and heard the street sweeper rumbling a few blocks away. I remember thinking, "Oh shit, I parked on the wrong side of the road; I need to go move the car, so I don't get another ticket for blocking the sweeper." I threw on a robe, ran barefooted downstairs, grabbed my keys, turned off the alarm, and scooted across Washington Avenue to my car. I got in, in a hurry 'cause I still had yet to pee, put the car in reverse, and BAM. I back into a two-hundred-year-old live oak, and off goes the car alarm full blast." She paused for a quick breath. "Well, the fellow in the sweeper sees all this, and being a *concerned city employee,*" Lovey said with sarcasm, "he calls the police, who appear in record time. Two patrol cars pull up, and the officers ask me to "step outside of the auto." So, there I was, midnight, in the middle of the avenue, with no shoes, no makeup, hair down, dressed just in a robe and my granny flannel nightgown."

April had to grin just a bit. "Yes, I'm sure that you probably made quite the impression."

"Snarky remarks are expected from the smart-ass in the front seat, but not you," she said, raising her left eyebrow slightly. "But seriously, I explained to the officers what I was trying to do, and at the same time was just about to wet my undies. You know from college days I can't control my bladder — you didn't hear that, Patrick — particularly when I get worked up. I finally told the older cop, I know his daughter, she teaches at St. Vincent's, "Mr. Fawcett, if you don't let me go inside, I'm going to have *another* accident."

"Well, this young cop from the other car piped up and asked me if I had been drinking. Not thinking, I said, "Well yes, that is why I have to pee so bad." And you know I would *never* have said the word "pee" in front of grown men otherwise, but I just wanted to get the hell off of the street and out of view of all my neighbors who were out on their front porches, and taking their dogs for a walk as an excuse to see what was going on. I was just *humiliated,* April hon." She was close to tears at this point, and the hands had never stopped moving.

"Anyway, they made me take one of those breath tests." She mimed the gesture, blowing her cheeks out. "I registered just over the legal limit. It was just too much for words. Too much for words. Mr. Fawcett didn't make me go downtown to the precinct, but he did give me a ticket. The next week I was back in Judge Hunt's court, with another citation, and this one for DUI. He was as nice as he could be, given the situation. Lord, I'd seen him more in court than at Mass this past year, and bless him, he threw the DUI charge out. But he did charge me with reckless driving and "failure to this" and "failure to that" along with one helluva fine, $ 5,000 thank you very much. With that, my license was gone, and it can't be reinstated until September, which will be two long years." She fell back against the leather seats, fanning herself, exhausted from telling her story.

"So *that* is why I have the red-headed worrywart," she said, pointing forward, "driving me around while he is home from grad school this summer. End of sad, sad Lovey story."

April had been listening intently through the whole monologue, and her heart went out to her friend who was one of the sweetest people she had ever met. "It must have been very difficult. I can only imagine. Don't be too hard on yourself. You've had enough to deal with."

Patrick, who was making a left turn now onto the Old Augusta Road leading to the estate upriver, added with a grin, "When we stop the car, I'm going to give you a big, fuzzy hug and sweet kiss on the cheek to make you feel better."

"I want neither a hug nor a kiss from you, Hobbit Boy. I don't want you getting near me." She answered teasingly, smiling now and her spirits making their way back to her usual cheerful norm. Turning toward April, she said, "As kids we used to call him 'Bilbo Baggins' because he has big, fat, hairy feet."

"Fine. But I bet you'd welcome a fat tongue kiss from Lachlan Campbell." Her cousin perfectly imitated Lovey's sing-song voice with eyes widened in mock seriousness.

Lovey blushed again, and before she could answer in a retort April cocked her head toward her friend and asked, "Who is this Mr. Campbell, pray tell?"

"Honey, we haven't had enough time yet to catch up with everything, and when we get out of earshot of someone who is a loudmouth, I'll give you all the scoop. But I think this one may be a keeper."

Patrick glanced in the review mirror. "Considering Lachlan is about one hundred years old you might not get to keep him for too long."

"Sweet Jesus, you annoy me." Lovey rolled her eyes and turned to April. "Lachlan happens to be just 55, only 15 years older than I. He owns a big cattle farm up in Effingham County." Just as she finished those words, Lovey suddenly remembered the box of Godiva chocolates she had bought to take to Lily as a hostess gift for the evening; she had left them sitting on the dining room table. "Patrick. We've got to go back to the house. I forgot to bring Lily's truffles. Shit and damn fire."

Patrick chuckled. "I'm happy to, but that's going to make you a good half-hour late in arriving."

Lovey shook her head and leaned back heavily with resignation into the rich leather seats of the Bentley. "Being late is the story of my life. They wouldn't expect me to be on time, anyway. "All three laughed at the truth of the matter as Patrick did a U-turn on the rural stretch of highway and headed back into town.

Chapter 2

As the black BMW 650i cruised down the Tybee Road leading into Savannah, it passed miles of palm trees and oversized oleanders which were about to burst into bloom in the May sunshine. The late afternoon provided a perfect opportunity to have the top down, and the breeze carried with it the distinctive smell of salt marshes that bathe coastal Georgia. The driver, as stunningly handsome as his car sleek and expensive, was not thinking about the magnificent beauty of the scenery as he headed inland. Instead, his mind raced with thoughts about family, ranging from love and fondness to total exasperation. He hated confrontations and made all efforts to avoid any unpleasant situation. He knew, though, that tonight would most certainly be an evening filled with both drama and angst.

He was looking forward to visiting with his grandmother, whom he had affectionately nicknamed "Grand Martha" when he was a child; she was an imposing woman in many ways yet also possessed a rich sense of humor and had a heart the size of Atlanta. He had not seen the striking, larger-than-life lady in over three years since she had moved to England, and he was thrilled to have her back home. But along with Grand Martha came the family "meeting" which would include his brother Addison, III, known as "Trip," and Trip's soon to be ex-wife, Jana. The divorce, which should have surprised no one in coming, at least not in the immediate family, had turned acrimonious as well as tedious in Baylor's humble opinion. While he loved his older brother beyond measure, he was also extremely fond of Jana and didn't want to be caught in the middle of their troubles. A straightforward dissolution had turned into a battle of wills since it came to light that his sibling had indulged in an affair with another woman. Jana had decided to sue in the divorce proceedings not only for half of Trip's assets, but also for the family's historic home, Ship Watch. When Grand Martha had

26

caught wind of the situation, she was on the company jet bound for Savannah the very next day, and thus tonight's pow-wow.

Baylor thought, given some of the recent town gossip, that Jana had way overstepped herself with these demands of ownership of the plantation, but he would not share that opinion. All the dirty details would have to be between her and Trip; Baylor wanted nothing to do with it at all. God only knows what his late father would have thought of this mess. Add, Jr. hated family matters being aired in public. At least his cousin Lovey would be joining them for dinner after the family corporate melee, and she always brought a bright spot to any gathering. Thank God she was coming.

He reached over and gave his dog, a golden Labrador retriever, an affectionate rubbing between her ears. "Thank goodness for Lovey, don't you say Tammy sweety?" Tammy gave her owner a big woof of appreciation for the attention and turned her head upwards to get more of the warm, southern air in her face.

Pulling up beside Baylor at the first traffic light just off the island was an SUV filled with five sorority sisters from nearby Georgia Southern University. The girls had spent the day on the beach working on their tans while drinking Skinny Margaritas and were all still a little buzzed from the sun and libations. The driver, a perky and mischievous gal named Mindy, was the first to notice the black sports car and the tall, blonde athlete driving just ahead of them. "Girls. Girls." She yelled over the chatter of the other four who were talking about their upcoming shopping trip to Atlanta to get ready for the last of the spring Greek socials. "Absolute hunk of man in a Bimmer coming up."

The sisters turned and let out squeals of delight and appreciation as they pulled alongside the convertible. "Oh. My. God. He looks like Adonis," Nancy, the group romantic sighed. "Can you imagine wrapping your arms around those big, broad shoulders and running your fingers through those golden locks?"

"Is your last name Kardashian? All you ever talk about is sex." Mindy teased, but they all were admiring the scenery as the light turned green and the two cars took off.

"Speed up, girl." Celeste urged as the BMW pulled ahead. "Don't lose him. I want to blow him a kiss."

"Oh hell, Celeste, you don't want to blow him a kiss. You just want to *blow* him." Mindy retorted, and the car erupted in laughter. "God doesn't like ugly, Melinda Kaye, thank you very much" came the reply from her childhood friend, who didn't bother to turn around to deliver the admonition; she was still admiring the fellow in the hundred-thousand-dollar convertible.

A moment later, another light was turning red, and the Escalade pulled up next to the hunk and his dog, who were still unaware of the attention.

"Seriously, you all, that man is H-O-T." Nancy commented, and just as she let out the "T" in "hot", Baylor noticed the five faces peering down at him, all in states of animated excitement mixed with slight inebriation. The big Cadillac was rocking with the girls' laughter and squeals.

Amused, Baylor nodded upwards towards the SUV with his deeply dimpled chin and gave the girls a short wave of his left arm, which had been resting casually on the doorframe.

The man's cool attention added more fuel to the girls' playfulness, who were now hanging out the windows, blowing kisses, whistling, and letting out wolf-calls. Worried about the attention her father's Caddy, with the state senator license plate on the rear bumper, would get if this carried on, Mindy made a swift turn into a Wendy's for a pee stop and a few choice words for her sisters to "calm the hell down."

The Labrador sitting in Baylor's passenger seat, excited by all the activity, barked several times at the waving girls in the retreating SUV. "What is it, sweety?" Baylor laughed at his dog as she cocked her head at him. "Are you trying to tell them something about barking up the wrong tree?"

Pressing the control key to the Parrott Head station, the handsome driver turned up the volume as *Love and Luck* started playing. Singing along with Jimmy "*...better days are in the cards, I feel it in the changing wind, I feel it as I glide....*" he drove on into town towards Ship Watch.

Chapter 3

In 1885, when his twins Eulalie and Eurelia reached the age of 30, Stephens Gamble finally realized neither of the daughters would ever marry. Not particularly caring for the company of females under foot, he took a portion of the money he had set aside for their dowries and built them identical, side by side townhouses facing the city's most prestigious park, Monterey Square. Both ladies were fond of European architecture, so he had the four-story structures designed in an Italianate style. The only discernible difference between these imposing homes was the color of the exterior trim; the egg and dart lintels, tall doorways, and side verandas of Eulalie's was a celadon jade green, while Eurelia's a robin's egg blue

These two spinsters of Savannah society were Martha Randolph's great-aunts, and she inherited the houses after their deaths. Martha and Addison, Sr. had moved into Eulalie's house the year after Baylor was born, allowing their son and his family to move out to the plantation. After the twins were born Trip and Jana, Add and Lily followed suit and moved to town, taking residence into Eurelia's next door, giving another new generation of Randolphs residence at Ship Watch

It was within the blue trimmed townhouse that Elizabeth Baylor Randolph, known to family and friends as Lily, had spent the day trying to organize her thoughts for tonight's dinner. Regardless of what she was trying to do, or whom she was talking to on the phone, all she could think about was the situation between Trip and his wife, Jana. Then, to top it all off, here was Martha, back home, demanding an audience as though she were a sovereign returning from her trip abroad. And truth be told, Lily was not enthusiastic about having her mother-in-law back living next door.

Trying to collect herself and her thoughts before leaving for dinner, Lily wandered about her parlor floor library, looking over silver framed photos of family and friends placed throughout the room. Seeing all the smiling faces and recalling pleasant memories seemed to give her some peace of mind. She had picked up a sentimental favorite, one of her husband and their two grandchildren, Peyton Chandler and Ray Addison, that was taken at Christmas not long after the twins were born. When the phone rang, she walked over to answer, and instinctively reached to first pluck off her right earring. "Damn" she said aloud. She had forgotten to put them on, which meant she'd have to make another trip upstairs.

"Hello," she said into the phone after the fourth ring.

"Miss Randolph, this is Benny. Are you ready for me to pick you all up, ma'am?"

"Oh, yes, thank you, Benny. Give me five minutes, and I'll collect Martha and we'll be out on the side veranda."

"I'll see you in a few moments then."

Lily put down the receiver and walked to the elevator at the rear of the house. She rode up two floors to the top and stepped directly into her dressing room. Before she and Add Jr. had moved into the townhouse and given up the plantation to that difficult beyond words daughter-in-law, he allowed her to convert the 1,500 square foot fourth floor into one large, exquisitely designed space to house her wardrobe. It was, by reputation, the largest and most elaborate room of its type between Washington and Palm Beach, and although Lily tended to shun notoriety of any kind, she accepted this distinction with quiet pride. She looked around the room to see where she had left her jewelry; she did remember having taken the pair out of the safe. Finally spying them on one of the tables on either side of her damask covered recamier, she clipped on the Mikimoto pearls and went over to the triple set of full-length mirrors. Since she had been so absent-minded throughout the day, she wanted one last look just to make sure she'd not forgotten something else.

Her reflection indicated all was in place and showed she still looked presentable even 4 years after her 60th birthday. Never considering herself especially pretty, she did feel graced with good features, and learned to accent them to their fullest. Because of her thin frame and height, she chose clothes with refined and classic designs that complemented her 5'8" stature without calling particular attention to it. To the envy of her friends, Lily was the same size 4 as when she married and could still wear the outfits from her wedding trousseau.

She had chosen for the evening one of her favorite suits, an Oleg Cassini original that her mother had worn to a cousin's christening in 1964. The material was a rich, soft beige silk that set off Lily's hazel eyes and perfectly coiffed hair. She smiled as she thought how often Baylor teased about her hairstyle, describing it as "yellow helmet." Although it had started turning white right after Add Jr. died, her hairdresser had kept it the same shade of blonde with which Lily had been born. With a final look, she went back downstairs to gather her purse, Martha, and she thought to herself hopefully, a little bit of patience.

Chapter 4

Being back home was not nearly as painful or emotional as Martha thought it would be. To her relief, the pictures, paintings, and other personal items she saw as she walked through the rooms of the townhouse brought back joy and tender memories rather than sorrow and distress.

On the return to Savannah the previous day, she had been surprised at the feeling of anticipation when the Gulfstream jet circled the countryside on its descent. Goosebumps tingled her arms as she gazed out her window upon the vast expanse of green salt marsh cut through by fingers of blue, with tidal creeks and rivers flowing into the Atlantic. And whether the salty, earthy fragrances below floated up to her, or they were only from a memory, it didn't matter. She was home.

Settling down into a comfortable chair in the front parlor to wait for Lily, she thought back over those years of her absence, what had led to her departure, and all which transpired during that time.

Losing Add, Jr. had been a blow that staggered her to the core. Her only child had been an exceptional son, father, and businessman. He had his father's hearty laugh, Martha's good looks, and both his parents' sense of love and loyalty. A freak accident during a quail hunt in South Carolina extinguished that light on his 60th birthday. Luckily, she had her two grandchildren and two great-grandchildren to help ease some of the pain. She could look at them and see her beloved son in each of their faces.

She and Addison, Sr. had leaned on one another as never before. Both were strong people, but it seemed the loss affected Addison more than it did Martha. He became quieter, intensely introspective, and reserved. A little over a year following his son's death while in New York on business, Addison suffered an aneurism as he walked through the lobby of the Pierre. He was dead, the attending physicians said, before he reached the hotel floor.

Martha still could not remember taking the call and learning of his passing, attending the funeral, or any details from that week. What she knew of that time she learned from her family and friends. Evidently, she fulfilled her role as the grieving but proper widow, accepting with grace and dignity the sympathy shown by the scores of people who came to pay their respects. Lily told her that over 1,000 people were gathered for the visitation at Fox & Weeks, and the register books showed signatures from people of all walks of life, including the current governor of Georgia, three past governors, and two senators. She was just as touched, or maybe even more moved, though, by the names of all the employees at Randolph Shipping who attended. Almost every retired employee that could physically attend the ceremony came. It was a testament to the man she had so dearly loved.

The news articles, all which Lily had kept for her to read, described Addison with terms such as "the last of a breed," "the epitome of what corporate America should be," "a great and respected steward of our community." Reading through these items for the first time, Martha wept with both grief and pride.

During the few weeks following the funeral, Martha lived in a haze of pain and sorrow; she felt the grief so strongly, so physically, that she thought she might die herself. Each waking moment in the city of her birth, in the home she loved so much, brought back memories so strong that they would literally cause her to have to sit down, or grip a nearby wall to keep from falling.

To keep what little sanity she felt she still possessed, she knew she needed to be somewhere that would not be a constant reminder of her late husband and son. Fortunately, before leaving to go back to London from the funeral, her cousin, Anthony, had asked more than once that Martha come for a visit. "My dear, I would dearly love to have you come and stay with me. The flat in London is a lonely place now that Lenora is gone; you'd be most welcome. You could stay into the summer, too, if you'd like. Chipping Camden is splendid during the

34

season, and the gardens there, my sweet cousin, will just simply take your breath away."

Martha had taken him up on his offer and a month after Add, Sr. was buried, she was flying into Gatwick. Anthony proved to be a wonderful host, unobtrusive but accommodating at the same time. He gave her the space she needed for the first few weeks, and then they grew into a familiar routine of companionship. Her cousin introduced her to his priest, Father William, a wonderful young Anglican who specialized in grief counseling. She spent many hours each week with this man of the cloth, slowly coming to grips with her losses. The weeks in England stretched into months, and Martha comfortably stayed on at Anthony's urging. The two of them spent that first summer, as they did the following two, in the Cotswolds. Martha, a master gardener herself, became immersed in the gorgeous grounds around Anthony's small but elegant estate, which had been neglected since Lenora passed away.

They also spent a great deal of time entertaining guests in from the city for long weekends, and she filled other days assisting at the local infirmary and with the altar guild. The time in England with her cousin, the friendship of the vicar, and her volunteer work proved to be meaningful therapy as she emerged from the three years more relaxed and at peace. In Martha's opinion, Anthony was a saint for letting her stay for so long. He had been a devoted and loving husband and declared after Lenora's long bout with cancer and death that he would never remarry. Having Martha in residence was a godsend for her gentle cousin, and they both found great comfort in each other's company.

The news of Trip and Jana's divorce, though, made her decide it was time to go home, no matter how difficult it might prove. Divorce to her was a last resort, regardless of the circumstances. Although she obviously had no power over whether the couple stayed together or not, she did have a great deal to say, and a great deal to decide, on matters that would affect the entire Randolph family in the years to come.

And so, she sat in the late afternoon thinking over her decisions, awaiting Lily's call to pick her up, and to take her to Ship Watch.

Chapter 5

Augustus Gamble Stephens, known since he was in grade school as "Auggie," slowly drove his vintage midnight blue Mercedes roadster through the entrance gates of Ship Watch. On each visit he marveled at the impressive mile-long drive to the mansion, which was made of crushed oyster shells and lined on both sides with ancient oak trees draped in Spanish moss. The silver-haired attorney was asked to be a part of the family gathering by his cousin, Martha, as Auggie had handled all of Martha and Addison's legal matters since the early 70s. Parking his auto in the drive turnaround in front of the historic home, he took off his leather driving gloves and glanced into the rear-view mirror and straightened his bowtie. He thought to himself that while he wasn't thrilled to be included, at least the night should prove to be rather interesting.

Chapter 6

After April Anne was introduced to the family gathered in the main house, she and Lovey strolled through the extensive gardens down to what the family dubbed "The River Club," a low country styled cottage built for casual get togethers and dinners. Supper would be served there after the family "conference" in the big house.

April found this turn-of-the-century folly fascinating with its wide-planked cypress floors, chandeliers made of oyster shells, and the enormous fresco painting of the Savannah River that covered the entire wall above the ballast stone fireplace. "This place is simply intriguing. I don't know that I've ever seen 'rustic' done up so comfortably," she said as they nibbled on cheese straws and roasted pecans that had been placed out in anticipation of their visit.

"I know, isn't this just a perfect place for having a party? You can seat 16 at the dining table with ease." Lovey opened the door for the two of them to walk onto the porch. The coffee colored, swirling waterway that divided South Carolina from Georgia lapped on the shore just in front of them.

April leaned on one of the porch rails. "Lovey, I'm flattered to have been asked to join tonight, but honestly I feel rather awkward. It would have been easier on all of us if I had been able to meet everyone when things weren't so, well, emotional."

"I know, hon, but seriously, Lily asked me to bring you along to help ease the tension. She said it would guarantee everyone's best behavior. And trust me, she was as surprised as I was when Auggie came in and announced himself; he wasn't on her guest list. Lawyers that come to a party with a briefcase can make folks a bit wary, even those you are related to. But don't worry, we'll get through the night. You'll see that all my relations are charming, I promise."

Chapter 7

Jana and Trip came downstairs from their separate master suites in the Randolph mansion just before April Anne and Lovey started out for the River Club. Tensions were running high given the circumstances, and even though the room was large and spacious, almost everyone chose to keep physical distance from one another. Trip sat at the antique card table, while Jana chose a corner of one the library's immense couches across the room. Martha was seated in one of a pair of tartan-plaid, wing-backed chairs, nursing a martini, while Auggie sat across the fireplace from her in its mate. Beside him on the mahogany side-table was his Brooks Brother valise. Lily stood almost like a sentinel, ramrod straight with her hands behind her back by the double doors that led into the entrance hall.

Baylor arrived last, kissing Lily on the cheek as he entered the room. Pulling out a chair next to his brother, he tried to share a bit of humor. "Well, it looks like we should be on the sound stage for the movie *Clue.* Grand Martha did it in the library with an olive pick," he said, letting out a little chuckle. No one found his attempt at easing the air amusing. Lily let the remark pass by and turned her attention directly to her cousin-in-law. "Auggie, it's so good to have you here tonight, but I have to admit I didn't know you were coming. I've had an extra place setting arranged; I hope you'll join us for dinner." Her tone was polite, but the trained ear of a genteel Southerner would have picked up the bit of steel in the invitation. Looking over the top of her martini glass as she took a sip Martha answered from her chair. "I asked Auggie to be with us in an official capacity, not for a social visit."

Lily gave a slight smile. "Well, Martha, pardon me, but you requested we all get together for dinner and to talk through a few family matters beforehand; we certainly didn't expect to discuss any business or legal affairs tonight. While I don't mean to be impolite, particularly

38

with you having just returned home after such a long time away, I think you'll understand that we're all a bit surprised you've brought your solicitor along." The slight inflection of the word "long" was not lost on her mother-in-law. The relationship between the Randolph matriarch and the wife of Addison, Jr., known as "Add" to his friends, had been a complicated one from the beginning. The two women respected each other and if push came to shove would admit to a degree of affection. They clashed, though, in several ways and often. In their case, the similarities of strong personalities and opinions, as well as family position, often led to an open disagreement. Such would be the case tonight.

Martha placed her martini glass on the side marble-topped table and looked directly at her daughter-in-law. "Yes, Lily, I have been away for a long time; as a matter of fact, three years, two months, and a few days; we all know that. But I'm here now and, yes, there are some legal matters to go over with each of you."

Lily narrowed her eyes a bit and counted to three. She didn't want a confrontation, but it irritated her to no end that Martha had the gall to scoot back home at a moment's notice and expect the entire family to stop whatever they were doing and bend to her demands. A legal discussion at a time like this. What was the woman thinking? There would be plenty of litigation to deal with in the following months with this horrible divorce. "Perhaps you want to talk legalese tonight. I for one do not. While you've been away enjoying the English countryside and taking in the London theater, I've been dealing with enough issues, legal and otherwise, to last a lifetime. I've worried myself sick for the last few months of how this," gesturing with a slight turn of her head in the general direction of the room where Trip and Jana were seated, "will play out with the whole city talking about this family."

Martha twirled her engagement ring, an impressive nine carat diamond solitaire, back and forth on her finger as was her habit when agitated. Try as she might, she could not help but become misty eyed. The remarks from Lily were meant to hurt, and had hit home. "I now understand the chilly ride out here tonight, Lily. Barely a word from the time we left until we arrived. Obviously, you have something to get off your chest. But yes, I left town. To be brutally honest, I thought I was losing my mind with grief. Everyone thinks I'm some hard, tough old bird, but when Addison died, it was like losing young Add all over again. It was just too much for me to bear." With the last few words, she choked and reached into her handbag for a handkerchief. All was silent in the library except for the ticking of the antique clock tucked into one of the many bookshelves.

Almost immediately, though, the octogenarian composed herself, leaned forward with both hands resting on the arms of her chair, and brought back to the conversation her renowned Grand Martha personality, green eyes flashing with sparks. "In regard to all the issues and matters you have had to deal with, you have a whole firm of lawyers at your disposal that the company has on retainer. And last I remember you still don't have to cut the grass or wash the clothes. So, while I was in the Cotswolds at garden parties, as you said, I'm not aware of anything that has kept you away from your rounds of parties on the Savannah and Highlands social scenes."

The rest of the family took in a short, collective gasp almost simultaneously. While they had all witnessed the two ladies disagree and clash, those occasions never included such strong words or biting tone. Jana, who was extremely reserved and kept her own counsel, let a bit of dry wit and irreverence by softly drawing out "meow" just loud enough for Baylor to hear. Unable to contain himself, he let out a short snort of a laugh, which he tried to cover as a sneeze. All heads swerved to look at the youngest Randolph son, who blushed several shades of red.

Before the exchange became more heated, Auggie stood and addressed the group in his best mediating tone. "I think we need to get along with the matters so we can go about our business. I have a dinner engagement in town at 7:30."

From the corner of the library, Jana agreed. "Yes, thank you, I'd like to get this over with as soon as possible." With that she stood, ready to exit. "I honestly have no idea why you want me here, since before too long I will no longer be a part of this family."

Martha gave a slight shake of her head in exasperation. Glancing quickly at Lily, she said, "I'm sorry, dear. We've both been through more than we'd like." Lily gave a slight shrug of her shoulders and an eased expression that said, "all was OK" and nodded. She didn't want to spar any further and had already said more than she should.

Speaking to Jana, Martha continued. "Honey, a lot of what I have to say does involve you. Indulge me just a bit." She then looked at Trip. "You both are determined to go through with this divorce? You've exhausted all efforts to try and make things work?"

"With all due respect, Grand Martha, I really don't want to air out our personal problems. They are just that. Personal." Trip answered, looking at a point somewhere above his grandmother's eyes, not wanting to meet her searching gaze.

"My dear boy, from what I understand everyone in town is talking about this dissolution, so let's not play the "personal" card." As Martha spoke, Jana noticed her husband was showing the familiar 'deer in the headlights' look he often had when confronted by one of his parents or Grand Martha. "Typical," she muttered to herself.

Martha pressed on and waved a hand back and forth twice between Jana and Trip, her wide gold bangles jingling together. "Let me ask you both another question. Do you not take your wedding vows seriously?

"What exactly do you mean, Martha?" Jana inquired.

"Exactly what I asked, sweetheart. I remember very clearly the two of you stood before the altar at the Cathedral of St. Philip and swore before God that you were bound until death do you part. Jana Ray Chandler of Atlanta and Addison Peyton Randoph, the third of Savannah, made a promise and contract before God that day. One that you both seem intent on breaking."

Jana kept her composure but inside she was beginning to seethe. She had long put up with the interference of her in-laws, telling her what to drive, where to go to church, how to raise her children. Such continuous interjection was one of the main reasons driving this divorce. Before she could answer, though, Baylor spoke up with a small grin and eyebrows raised. "Wow, Grand Martha. You sound like some sort of Pentecostal evangelist. Keep talking like that and they'll take away your pew at St. John's Episcopal." As before, no one laughed along with Baylor, though both Lily and Trip did find the remarks rather amusing.

His grandmother rolled her eyes a bit as she looked over in his direction. "And you, dear boy, are sounding like a failed comedian on *America's Got Talent*." She held out her half empty martini glass toward Baylor and gave it a slight swirl. "Here, take your mind off our conversation for a moment and put a few more ice cubes and another olive in this for me. And bring me an ash tray, too."

Lily sniffed in irritation. She hated people smoking indoors.

"Please don't be tedious, Lily. I allow myself only four Virginia Slims a day. And right now, it's either a cigarette or a valium, and I don't need to take medicine with this martini." Lily rolled her eyes and prayed again for patience. If there was a bubble over her head holding her thoughts, the family would learn that she wished Martha would take three valiums, and then Lily would gladly take her right to the airport and put her on the next plane bound for London before the 'old bird' as she referred to herself woke up.

While Baylor dutifully refreshed the cocktail and fetched a crystal ashtray off his late father's desk, Martha spoke again. "What is it, then, and give me a straight answer. There is no reconciliation or mediation in the works?"

Jana stood stock still and worked to keep her composure. "Regardless of what Trip has in mind after this line of biblical instruction, I have no intention of staying married to him one minute longer than necessary. "All efforts, as you called them, Martha, ran out when he started sleeping with his Hilton Head girlfriend."

Trip looked at his wife, who was still as stunningly beautiful as the day he met her. He had seen men stop dead in their tracks as she walked by. Tall, lithely built with skin the color of cream, azure blue eyes, and long thick hair that looked like a honey in the sunshine, she was prettier than any model gracing *Vogue*. But inside that lovely exterior lay a personality so reserved, and so guarded, it was impossible ever to fully know her. "No, Grand Martha, we do not plan on staying married. It's finished." He then said to his wife, "the affair is finished as well. It has been over for more than a year. And I'm sorry, Jana. I truly am."

Jana refused to respond to his apology, not now at any rate, and remained silent. Lily, ignoring her daughter-in-law, took a chair at the card table with her two sons. She reached over and squeezed Trip's hand and gave him a look that told him she loved him. She certainly would not miss having Jana as a part of their family. The girl was an excellent mother, she would give the she-devil her due, but that was the only kind thing she could say about the ice princess who had scooped her son up at the tender age of twenty-two.

During this short exchange, Auggie removed several files from his briefcase and neatly stacked them atop Add's desk. Martha took a long, final drag off her cigarette, wishing she could have another, and savored the last sip of her martini. Placing the glass back down on the table, she raised herself up and turned to gaze at the life-sized portrait of Addison Steward Randolph that hung over the fireplace. She stood collecting her thoughts for a minute, a diminutive but determined woman in a pink St. John outfit. Her hair was upswept in a chignon and held together with a pearl and gold clip, a style she had worn for the last thirty years. Turning around, she appeared to Auggie even more weary and tired than she had just a few minutes before. His heart went out to her because he knew how difficult this was. And because he had been in love with Martha since they were teenagers. Given that they shared a set of great-grandparents and were second cousins, such a match was unacceptable for the Gambles and the Stephens. Augustus was forced to sit on the sidelines while Addison Randolph played the role of winning suitor decades earlier.

"So, the marriage is indeed over. That makes the decision here clear cut. But let me ask you one thing, Jana. I understand that you are suing

Trip for ownership of Ship Watch, besides more than half of his assets and then alimony as well. Is that correct?"

"My attorney can answer any questions about the details of what I may or may not be asking for. If that is your line of inquiry, I will excuse myself." She turned to leave the room.

Martha spoke to Jana's back. "Hon, we've had a very congenial relationship all these years, one close enough where I felt as if you were my own granddaughter. So let me rephrase this question and ask simply why. Why would you try and take Ship Watch away from this family? With all the money and extensive properties you'd receive otherwise, you'd still be a wealthy woman without a financial care in the world. That isn't to mention all that you've inherited from your own family. The Rays and Chandlers left you extremely well off."

Outwardly Jana showed no signs of nervousness, but her voice rose an octave. "I'm suing for ownership of Ship Watch precisely so that it will stay with the Randolphs. Do you think for a moment that I'd allow this birthright to slip through the twins' fingers?" She pointed at her husband and continued. "Oh yes, let Trip keep Ship Watch, and then see him marry his South Carolina tramp, or some other gold digger, who'll give him another set of children. New wife, new kids, new inheritance plan. Have you thought of that possibility, Martha?"

"Yes, Jana, I have considered such a scenario. I, and others before you, have given it great thought. That is why we're here tonight. But I've also taken into consideration that if you were in possession of our home nothing would keep you from selling off this land, part and parcel, to the highest bidder. I'm sure there are any number of developers who would like to throw up a few hundred McMansions on this property." Martha closed her eyes and shuddered at the horror of such a thought.

Lily joined back in the conversation, appraising her daughter-in-law with a cool, smug smile. "For goodness' sake, Jana, quit playing the martyr. I'm tired of hearing about your supposed honor being stained. Please. Everybody in town is saying that you've been sleeping with Buckner Pearson. Oh yes, wouldn't Buck just love to get his hands on Ship Watch."

Jana spun around, hands on her hips, showing a stunned expression. "What *in the hell* are you talking about, Lily? Me? With Buck Pearson? Whoever told you that? I have *never* slept with that arrogant oaf." Her cool composure was gone, replaced with a flushed face and neck.

Trip nodded and looked up at his wife, who was standing just a few feet from him. He could tell she was shaking slightly, and he could not remember ever seeing her so upset. "Jana, I haven't confronted you about it because my lawyers said not to say anything." Turning to his mother, he said a bit sarcastically "Thanks, Mama." And looking back at Jana, he went on. "Buck has told several folks that you all have been an item, and that you all are, well, intimate."

Baylor sat silently, shaking his head. He could not process the thought of Jana and Buck. What a prick that man was.

Jana looked at each person in the room and between almost locked jaws stated "I don't care what people are saying. I have never slept with that despicable man." Still trembling a bit but with a steadier tone she then turned to her husband "Trip, I know that I can be impossible in your eyes, and life with me has been difficult from the start. But I have never, ever lied to you, and I'm not lying now. This vile rumor is not true. I swear to God."

Trip looked into her eyes and saw the woman he fell in love with more than twenty years ago. She was right. For all her faults, she was always truthful, even to the point of hurt feelings. "OK, I believe you, Jana. But you just need to know what is being said. And you or your lawyers need to get him to shut his mouth. Peyton and Ray don't need to hear that their mother may be seeing someone like that sleezebag."

"I certainly hope that it isn't the case, Jana; I would be sorely disappointed if it were indeed true," Martha said.

Jana started to answer, but Martha waved the girl off with an impatient gesture of a bejeweled hand. "Whatever you or Trip might or might not choose to do with the plantation does not matter from this point going forward, anyway." She walked over behind Add, Jr.'s massive desk and, taking the chair Auggie offered her, sat down, and continued, "You will never own Ship Watch."

Everyone stared at Grand Martha in silence, wondering what she had done to ensure such an outcome. Baylor and Trip exchanged questioning glances, while Lily stared straight ahead at her cunning mother-in-law. *What's she up to?*

Jana looked down at the assertive lady in the expensive suit and her confident expression. "Well, Martha, this decision will rest with the courts. I'm suing for possession of this property, like it or not."

"No, you are gravely mistaken. When your attorneys learn the facts, you won't be adding Ship Watch to your list of demands. I'm no psychic, but I can assure you of that fact." Auggie noticed the ring twirling back and forth continuously as her hands stayed in her lap. "Because you see, this house and this property is not something you can sue Trip for. It does not belong to him. It all belongs to *me.*"

Lily let out a short, exasperated breath. "Whatever do you mean, Martha? We all know the terms of the will. Trip inherited the plantation and Baylor the two townhouses. It was all signed off on and probated."

"You all have conjured up some scheme and signed over ownership to keep it from the divorce proceedings." Jana angrily pointed a finger back and forth between Martha, Lily, and Trip. "I see now, I see exactly what the three of you are up to. But it won't work. If you made a transfer of those deeds to avoid this divorce, the courts will overturn it in a heartbeat. Bring it on, we'll settle this with the judge and jury."

Martha rolled her eyes and looked squarely at Jana. "We have not conjured anything between us. Nothing has changed regarding the deeds or court records for this property. Measures to protect the plantation were put into place long ago, just in case of such a distasteful scenario as this."

Immediately Lily and Jana began to speak at the same time, each louder and with even more animosity than before. Trip, who for the last couple of moments appeared as if daydreaming, slammed his right hand down, hard, onto the wooden table, his college class ring making a dent in the polished surface. Baylor and Lily jumped at the sound. "Enough. For God's sake would you two be quiet for a moment. You sound like a couple of mad cats." Both women stopped talking, but the air was still full of electricity. "This apparently is between me and Grand Martha. Not either of you. So, would you let her speak? I'd like to hear what she has to say." With that he rose from his seat, stood in front of the fireplace, and folded his arms across his chest. "Grand Martha?" he asked, cocking his head a bit to the right.

His grandmother looked up at him and thought to herself how very much he favored his late father. He was not handsome like Baylor, but good looking in a solid way that spoke confidence. He was tall like the Randolphs, just over six feet two inches, and had broad shoulders and an athletic build, though he was starting to get a bit of a middle paunch, just like his dad. And like his dad, his sandy hair was starting to recede and was laced with strands of grey on the sides. The wide, Randolph chin with the large dimple was there as well. Standing as he was, it was almost as if Add, Jr. was back in front of her. Looking on, Lily was having the same thought.

Clearing her throat with a short cough, as she had become emotional thinking about her late son, she began her answer. "Let me start by saying that nothing would please me more than you as sole owner of this heritage, and that it would continue in our family for perpetuity. But things are so different today than they were when I was your age. Even before your father passed away, God rest his loving soul, Addison and I had discussed how couples no longer stayed together; divorces became the norm and not the exception. Marriages were coming to be seen simply as business contracts, and not holy ones that were made to be taken seriously. We saw so many people go their separate ways, and families divided, as were properties and assets. You remember what happened with Allison and Scott Finley's divorce. She was awarded half the family bank, then sold her part to an investment group who ran the place into the ground. Those bank shares were selling for pennies on the dollar just before they went under, a fortune and a legacy lost. And not just the Finley's, but the shareholders and people that worked for them.

Anyway, your grandfather and I decided, with Auggie's counsel, to protect this property from such a tragedy. What this family has built over the last two centuries is an integral part of Georgia's history, as well as the entire history of the Southern east coast, and we were determined to make sure it stayed intact in the years to come. Auggie can explain the legal details, but to put it simply, yes, you were left the plantation. But there is a section in your grandfather's will making the inheritance provisional as long as I'm living, one that allows me to regain ownership. No reason need be given, the document is straightforward in that with a stroke of the pen the house and all the property are mine to do with as I see fit. Addison and I struggled with this decision, but I believe what we did, and what I'm doing now, is the only recourse. Auggie has a letter from your grandfather that was signed, notarized, and sealed, only to be opened if we came to this point." Looking up at Auggie, she asked him to read it to the group.

While Martha was speaking, Trip walked over to one of the large, floor to ceiling windows, hands clasped behind his back, and stared out at the gardens below. Martha's cousin took out a sheet of paper, cleared his throat, and read the following:

Dear Family,

Some decisions are difficult to make, and oftentimes those close to you won't understand the prevailing reasons behind them. I do hope that, in time, you will see what your Grandmother and I have put into place was done with grave consideration and love for each of you, as well as our steadfast concern that the Randolph legacy with Ship Watch be a constant for generations to come.

Part Nine, Section 3, clause vii gives Martha Stephens Randolph full authority and power to regain title of the plantation (the legal description is provided therein) at her discretion. She and I promised one another that this action would be taken only if deemed absolutely necessary. If you are in possession of this letter, it would appear such a time has come about. I leave it to her and Augustus, or his designee, to decide what will happen when transfer of ownership occurs. Options discussed at this current time include donating Ship Watch into a foundation that will be privately held and managed or making provisions with an organization such as the National Trust for Historic Preservation to be used as a museum and place of study. With much love to each of you, I'm

Forever yours,

Addison Peyton Randolph, Sr

Shock clear on their faces, no one spoke for a moment. Martha looked around at the stunned faces and said "There is a provision for all of you, including you, Jana, and of course the twins, to each have 15 acres with a portion of water frontage. We also retain rights to ownership of the River Club, which will be open to family use only. Auggie has the details and will share the documents with you in due time. But the bulk of the property including the main house, outbuildings, gardens, all will be transferred to the National Trust."

Trip turned around to address his grandmother, his voice hoarse with emotion. "I can't believe what you've done. You simply took it on yourself to make such a grave decision that will affect this entire family going forward, and you didn't consider consulting me? That says a hell of a lot of what you think of me, Grand Martha. While I love you and welcome you home, you'll have to pardon me. I simply can't be in the same room with you for another moment."

Trip strode through the wide doorway without saying another word. Jana hesitated a moment, and followed behind him, not looking back. Hands on hips, Lily was next to speak. "Amazing. You'd separate the rightful heirs to this property and place it in the hands of a group of people who have absolutely no ties or love of what we have here? My God, woman, you've tried my patience for decades, and I've done my best to accept your domineering and demanding ways. This just exceeds what I can bear. You'll hear from my attorneys. I'll fight this and we'll drag it out until you are too old and feeble to fight it any longer." Picking up her purse and tucking it under her arm, she added, "Find your own way home, Martha. I'm leaving, now."

Martha calmly answered, "Lily, my dear, I know you're angry and don't blame you. But I think you'll come to your senses and see I really had no choice. Too, let me add here, if you try and stop this in the courts, I'll cut you from my will and I'll also stop your annual income from the family trust. Remember, I'm still at the helm writing the checks. And yes, I can do that."

Before turning and heading out the door, Lily closed her eyes, sighed, shook her head, and said "You bitter old bitch."

Baylor went over to his grandmother. "Well, you sure know how to make an entrance when coming back home." He bent down and kissed her on the cheek. "I don't have a dog in this hunt, as you know, and love you whatever happens. But this was high-handed, even for you, Grand Martha. You might want to lay low with The Lil and Trip for a while." Glancing out the window toward the River Club, he added, "Anyway, we were supposed to have company for dinner tonight. It would be bad form for us to all walk out on Lovey and her friend. I'll head down to the River Club and entertain them solo."

Martha took her grandson's face in her hands and gave him a quick peck back. "You are an angel, Baylor. Thank you. Tell Lovey I send my apologies and that I'll make it up to her sooner than later."

Then looking at Auggie, she sighed, gave him her hand to help her stand, along with a wry smile. "Well, I guess you get to drive this 'bitter old bitch' home, cousin."

Chapter 8

April and Lovey were deep in conversation when they heard eight large paws tramping up the wooden porch stairs.

"Tammy. George. Sit." Baylor shouted out as he followed behind the two yellow Labradors. Both dogs stopped directly in front of the two ladies, tails wagging in excitement.

"Hey there, Handsome," Lovey said as Baylor bent down and gave her an affectionate kiss on the cheek. "You *finally* get to meet my bestest friend. April Anne, this hunk of burning love," she said with a twinkle, "is my second cousin once removed, Baylor Stephens Randolph."

"Yes, three last names all at once. Mama was a Baylor, and Grand Martha a Stephens" he explained, taking a slight bow. "So nice to finally meet the famous April Anne Adams. Thrilled to have you in Savannah, Miss Adams."

"Thrilled to be here and thank, you, Man with Three Last Names," she answered with a teasing smile. "I never thought we would ever actually get to meet in person; the last time I was supposed to see you was at Mrs. MacGregor's funeral. That blizzard had flights delayed all up and down the northeast coast. Was so sorry I missed being here." She reached over and patted Lovey on the shoulder. "And who are these two beautiful babies? Did I hear correctly, Tammy and George?" At the mention of each of their names, the two dogs thumped their tails and twitched on their haunches.

"Yes, this is Tammy Wynette, my girl, on the left, and Trip's Lab, George Jones, on the right." Noticing the look on her face, he continued on. "I know, strange names for dogs, right?"

"Well, yes, I'd say so, particularly when their owners have such auspicious Georgia names."

Laughing, Baylor said, "Yep, there's the custom of naming all our family after one another, and truthfully, we even get confused who is who sometimes. Then my father loved old style country music and started the tradition of naming his dogs after stars from the Grand Ole Opry. And usually in twos, so they keep one another company." On his fingers he counted off "First was Johnny and June, after Johnny Cash and June Carter, then came Porter Wagoner and Dolly Parton, and next was Loretta Lynn and Conway Twitty. These two are the latest in the line."

Giving the dogs a rub on the head, and the command to stay, Baylor held open the screen door and motioned the ladies inside. "I need to fix myself a drink. God knows I need a good strong one." Walking over to the bar, he scooped ice into a rocks glass, poured three fingers of bourbon from the decanter, and took a big, long sip. "Ahh. My nerves are just about shot." He reached over and plucked up a printed menu from the dining table, which was set for 8 guests, each with a place card embossed with the Randolph crest. "Lord, will you look at this feast Chef Nick has made this evening," and read off the list. "Spiced cucumber soup, a baby beet and chevre salad, shrimp cakes with Savannah red rice, succotash, rosemary and parmesan biscuits, followed by one of those fabulous peach tarts. All Grand Martha's favorites. Guess it was his way of saying welcome home." He took another sip and shook his head. "Shame she'll miss out on it."

"She isn't joining us? And where is everybody anyway?" Lovey knew there'd be fireworks in that family gathering.

Baylor swirled the glass in his hand. "I'm not exaggerating when I say that they are all madder than wet settin' hens and not fit for company. Except Grand Martha. She just seems tired."

As Lovey was about to ask what he meant, he held up his hand to stop her. "What plans do you all have tomorrow night?"

The two women gave one another a puzzled look and Lovey answered, "Nothing. Why?"

"I'm way too wound up to sit through a four-course dinner right now, even though it's probably the best meal being served in Chatham County tonight. Let me have Chef pack all this scrumptiousness in a cooler, and you two come out the beach house tomorrow evening and have supper with me and Trip. It'll keep." He took the final sip of his drink. "What your favorite cousin here would like is another bourbon, and to have Patrick drive us over to Miss Ruby's and let me work my way through a rack of barbequed ribs and a platter of onion rings. My psyche is calling for serious comfort food."

Looking over at April, Lovey explained, "Miss Ruby's is a hole-in-the-wall diner left over from the speak easy days, but she has the best barbeque in town."

"That's totally fine with me. I'm game. But aren't we a bit overdressed for a juke joint?"

"Nah, hon. We're fine. There's always a mix of folks there, from bricklayers to barristers." Lovey looked over at Baylor. "You're buying, though, sport, and go grab a few bottles of wine to take with us. I love Ruby's food, but her wine is rot gut."

"Sweet. I'll let Chef know about the food and raid the wine closet while I'm back there in the kitchen. Will fill you all in on what happened up at the big house on our drive over to Ruby's. But let me warn you," he said as he walked by, "it ain't pretty."

Chapter 9

In her upstairs suite Jana had a Keurig machine, small microwave oven, and mini fridge so she could enjoy the privacy of a cup of tea or glass of wine in her nightgown without having to make the long trip down to the kitchen. With some steaming chamomile in hand to calm her nerves, she spotted a note that was slidden under the door. Picking it up, she walked across the room to her favorite corner chair, one that caught the soft cross breezes through open windows.

J, hope you know tonight's announcement caught me as off-guard as it did you. I'll be in touch after I've had a chance to think things over. In the meantime, I'll be at the beach house and will stay there until I head to Highlands for the summer. Call me if you need me or want to talk. Yours, T

Lord that man got on her last nerve sometimes, but he was so damn nice and considerate it was hard to stay mad at him, even when she was divorcing him. She could detect slightly the scent of a cigar, one of his few vices, and a hint of his Old Spice aftershave, on the note card. Those smells took her back to childhood, and memories of her father.

She knew one of the first things that attracted her to Trip was the fact he reminded her so much of her late Dad. Both were tall, broad-shouldered men who carried easy smiles and had the same shade of hair that turned bright blonde in the summer sun. Stirring her tea, she remembered back when she first laid eye of her future husband. It was the summer of her debut year, and she was on Sea Island with her Mother for the season. She had spied Trip across the room at the first of the summer's dinner dances at the Cloister, leaning against the bar looking as though he wished he were somewhere else. He had glanced up from his drink and saw her staring, smiled, and walked over to introduce himself. They were inseparable for the rest of the summer.

Trip was living at Grand Martha's house on East 5th Street, along with Baylor, and the brothers worked at the Club, with Trip serving as a fishing guide and Baylor giving golf lessons to the members' kids. Both Jana and her new beau liked solitude and quiet. They swam in the sage green tidal creeks that coursed through the island, took Trip's sailboat over to Little St. Simons for picnics on the beach, and shared intimate dinners huddled over a glass or two of red wine. Through the course of that wonderful, lazy summer they fell in love under the tall pines and spike leafed palmettos of the Georgia coast. It came as no surprise to her at all when he proposed, and it was done in a romantic manner so like Trip.

They were at Bennie's Red Barn, an old St. Simon's institution famous for its steaks and seafood, sitting at their favorite table tucked away near the fireplace. The restaurant was also known for its singing waiters who serenaded guests with spirituals, blues, and rock classics. As the last bites of their desserts were taken that August night, Calvin, one of the waiters, appeared at their table, on cue. Bowing slightly, he said "Excuse me, Miss Jana. Mr. Trip has asked me to sing you something special tonight." He then belted out a soulful rendition of Paul McCartney's love song, "Maybe I'm Amazed." The entire restaurant stopped to listen as the deep baritone voice echoed off the rafters. When the last of the lyrics were finished, Trip moved from his chair and dropped on one knee as Calvin placed a baby blue ring box in his hand. Trip snapped open the container to show a five carat Tiffany diamond solitaire, and asked the magic words, "Jana, will you please marry me, and be my wife?" When she said 'yes,' the patrons stood, cheered, and toasted their happiness with a several dozen bottles of champagne Trip had ordered special for the entire restaurant.

As the fall semester began, they'd said their goodbyes and gone back to their respective universities to study finance, Trip at UNC, and Jana at UVA. As business geeks who loved numbers, both were excellent students and while missing one another, they enjoyed being in school.

The first extended time back together since the summer came at Christmas, when the Randolphs invited Jana and her mom Melissa to join them at the Greenbrier for the holidays. Mother and daughter rented one of the historic cottages next to their future in-laws and the plan was for 7 days of meals and celebrations together. All started fine, with M'liss, as her mother was known, and Lily sharing many of the same friends in Atlanta. All of Trip's family were welcoming and warm, though it became apparent early on that Lily and her husband were accustomed to having things go their own way. Jana and Baylor already enjoyed each other's company from their time together on Sea Island, and both Grand Martha and Addison, Sr. were extremely cordial and shared with them their congenial sense of humor.

As the days progressed, however, Jana noticed more and more Lily's tendency to take control of a room, and from there the entire day. The bossy attitude didn't seem to bother M'liss, but then she was the type that saw only the very best in everyone. She was also very fragile; she'd always been rather shy but became even more so after Jana's father died. Traveling down the Cashier's Road from a day of golf at the Wade Hampton, he swerved to miss a doe and her fawn and crashed head on into a tree. He died instantly. M'liss sold their vacation home and refused to go back to Highlands. It seemed as each month passed by, she withdrew a bit more into herself. Jana, who was of a stronger and more definitive personality, like her late father, became very protective of her mother. It was this sense of sheltering that brought about her first of many clashes with Trip's Mom

It was just after dinner on Christmas Eve, and everyone had gathered in the living room around the fireplace and the huge, decorated fir tree that the resort had provided for the Randolphs. M'liss was at ease for a change and glowing with a few small sips of sherry. She spoke to everyone in the room. "I'm so very, very happy that we were able to join you all for the holidays. Christmas for Jana and me has been a rather lonely affair these past few years. You've made us feel so at home, and such a part of your family." She hugged Jana, who was standing next to her, around the waist. "And I was hoping before we left for Mass, that we could each open one of our presents. It was a tradition my Charles and I had together while he was with us." She looked up and smiled at her daughter, who stood several inches taller than her diminutive five feet.

Everyone murmured in warm agreement except for Lily, who stood up from her chair and crossed over to stand by her husband. "Well, M'liss that sounds lovely, but Add and I always like to get to the church early so we can get good seats. It fills up so quickly; if we arrive late we'll end up sitting in the choir loft."

There was a bit of an uncomfortable silence in the room. Jana glanced over at Trip who chose the moment to notice the twinkling lights on the tree. She tried to choose her words carefully. "We shouldn't take long, Mrs. Randolph. Daddy was so anxious to see us open our presents; we always did this as a little gesture to appease him. He was like a kid himself at Christmas."

"Jana, honey, we really need to leave the cottage soon if we want those seats. We can open a gift or two when we return." As if the matter was settled, Lily patted Add's shoulder and turned to pick up her purse. Jana looked pleadingly at her fiancé, who instead of returning her gaze and speaking up for her, fiddled with his cufflinks. This avoidance was to prove to be habitual, and one that Jana grew to despise.

Determined to stand her ground, Jana hugged her Mother a little closer, whose big blue eyes were already glistening. "Well, Lily, I tell you what," leaving off the respective Mrs. Randolph, "you all go on to Midnight Mass. Mama and I will stay here and open two of our gifts. We're fine worshiping from the loft seats." Looking over, she said, "Trip. When you've finished straightening out your cuffs, would you please call and arrange for another car for my Mom and me?"

At that point Grand Martha rose from her seat by the tree, where she had been watching the back and forth, and gave a little chuckle. "Lord, Lily, you and Add are always in such a hurry." She glanced at Jana and gave her a half wink. "Jesus won't be upset that we aren't the first people at his birthday party tonight." Baylor covered his own chuckle by clinking the ice in his glass.

Martha crossed over to Jana and her Mom, and placed her hands on theirs. "I think this is a fine tradition that we need to continue as this family grows. We'll be happy to stay and open some gifts. What fun."

Jana was glad to have gained an ally that night, and after the brief exchange of presents, they were off to St. Thomas Episcopal, the small church which catered to the resort's wealthy guests. Thank goodness there were a few pews left open in the back upon arrival; otherwise, she was sure she would not have heard the end of it later. And while the service was lovely, and all were in high spirits when returning to the cottages, Jana had been unable to sleep. She kept thinking the engagement might be a mistake. Throughout their time on Sea Island, Trip was carefree and easy going, and always forthcoming with his thoughts and feelings. Around his parents, though, he became a different person. He was quieter, rarely shared his opinions, and would not make a decision without first consulting Add or Lily. If he wasn't willing to speak up for his soon to be wife now, what would the future bring? The more she dwelt on it, the stronger she felt the need to call off, or at least postpone, the wedding. However, the next morning before she could state her fears, M'liss had talked on and on over their breakfast about how she was the happiest she'd been since Jana's father had passed away. Jana remembered well her Mom saying, "Nothing in this world could make me more content right now than to see you married to that wonderful young man."

With her Mother's enthusiasm for plans for the wedding, and talk of parties and honeymoon, and of course the possibility of grandchildren, Jana let her reservations slip away. When she did bring up her dislike of Lily and her feelings of hurt by Trip's seeming lack of attention where his new wife was concerned, M'liss gave gentle counsel. "Oh, darling, I know Lily is strong willed, but honey, so are you. It's all a dance, and you'll learn how to find a place in their family soon enough. And I'm sure Trip is caught up in the middle. He's accustomed to trying to please his Mama, and now he must make his fiancée happy as well. He's learning the dance, too, so be easy on that dear heart. He reminds me so much of my Charles; he's going to make a fabulous Daddy to your children."

Fortunately, there weren't any other instances that holiday, as the family settled in to enjoy the snow and brisk weather in the West Virginia mountains through New Year's. Good luck stayed with her as all the parties, planning for the nuptials, and finally the wedding itself all went off without a hitch that June following Jana's and Trip's college graduations. But as soon as Jana had moved to Savannah, that all changed. Lily was a constant and she seemed determined to run every aspect of their lives. And while he was not around nearly as often, Add was just as bad. M'liss's wedding present to the couple would be their first home, and Jana had found a charming waterfront cottage on Wilmington Island that she and Trip fell in love with on the first trip out to see it. When they shared their news with the Randolphs, Add stated, "The place sounds nice but that really is too far of a drive from the plantation. We'll need you to live closer into town." He had gone back to reading his newspaper with no thought of further discussion. Trip had answered something along the lines of "we'll keep looking, Dad." But Jana, who was already pregnant with the twins — that happened unexpectedly on their honeymoon — was in no emotional state to keep her temperament under control. It was only after she threatened to move back to Atlanta, with the soon to come new Randolph grandchildren in tow, that the house was purchased.

These sorts of episodes happened repeatedly, and with each one, the love for her husband chipped away until laid bare. Sleeping with him came to a halt; she had no desire to share her bed with someone who would rather please his parents rather than his wife.

Sitting in her chair, the tea finished, Jana realized some of those arguments in those early days could have been avoided, and that she probably did make too much of trivial matters which occurred along the way. That was water under the bridge, though. While Trip was a tremendous father, and at heart a good man, she stopped loving him years ago. And regardless of whether he did or didn't know of Grand Martha's plans, she'd be damned if she sat idle and allowed the twins' inheritance to slip through her fingers. She'd be in touch with her attorneys first thing in the morning.

With the thought of the twins, though, came the unbearable realization they were under the impression she was sleeping with Buck Pearson. Putting down the cup and saucer, she headed into the bathroom thinking she might be ill. She turned on the hot water, undressed, and stepped into the shower. She needed to bathe and clean herself, yet again. That bastard had come so very close to raping her. Her shoulder continued to ache from the wrenching of her arm, and she could still feel his wet tongue on her neck as well as the erection on her thigh. Overwhelmed, she threw up into the shower drain. When it washed away, she sat on the marble bench and wept. It took a good ten minutes, but after the crying jag she composed herself. Jana's innate, strong sense of self came forth in spades. She shut off the water with a determined and firm turn of hand, and promised aloud to herself, "I will make that bastard pay."

Chapter 10

After breakfast the following day Lily started the morning with phone calls. The first was to her younger brother, Whittaker, a managing partner at the venerable Atlanta law firm of King & Spalding. He assured her he would contact Auggie and the attorneys for the National Trust as soon as possible and stall any action for the time being. When she told him about Martha's threat to cut her out of the Randolph trust, he laughed. Both of them knew Lily had more money of her own than she could already spend, and Martha was tight as a tick anyway with her annual distributions. It would be fun, though, to tie her up in some additional litigation, for simple aggravation's sake, so they decided to play that one by ear. The main concern at hand was stopping the transfer of deed to the plantation.

The next call was to Lovey to apologize for Lily's absence the night before. To repay the young ladies, she'd told them that they'd simply must come spend the season with her in Highlands. She had actually already decided to invite them, as Lily wanted to do some updating in the main house, and needed Lovey's help. Plus, having the renowned April Anne Adams in residence would make several of the ladies in her bridge club and tennis team jealous. She could also use the company. When Trip wasn't behind his computer working, he was outdoors fly fishing or hiking. Baylor stayed booked all summer giving golf and tennis lessons at the Club, and when he got home, he was usually too tired for decent conversation. Lovey said that they'd let her know soon, but Lily was pretty certain they'd accept. Who in their right mind wants to stay in the heat and humidity of Savannah for the summer when they could be at 4,000 feet of cool mountain splendor?

The final call that morning was well-planned and calculated. It was to Vincent Judson, who had been her interior designer long before Lovey was born. Vincent was on the executive committee of the National

Trust board, and one of the biggest drama queens who had ever graced God's green earth. The man simply could not keep a secret, but people put up with his pretentions and over-the-top behavior because he was the very best decorator in the States. He and his wealthy husband, one of the heirs to the DuPont fortune, were two of the largest donors for the arts and preservation on the east coast, which explained Vincent's position on the board.

"Well Lily Randolph, I haven't seen or heard from you in ages." Vincent answered directly into the iPhone, seeing the caller ID. "What are you up to this fine Saturday morning? How are things down in quaint Savannah?"

Lily rolled her eyes. Vincent always referred to Savannah as quaint, indicating all was bigger and better in the Hamptons and Palm Beach. The way he talked you'd think his father had been an English baron instead of a barber from the tiny town of Irmo, South Carolina. Vinny had married way, way up the social ladder. "Oh, Vinny, things are fine here, I'm getting ready to head to Highlands for the summer and am in the midst of closing the house down here for the season. Where are you? Are you already ensconced in New York?"

"Darling, no, Peter and I are still in Palm Beach. We had some water damage at the cottage from the last storm, and our god-awful cretin of a contractor up there is taking his slow, sweet time to get things patched up. We hope to be back on Meadow Lane by the end of next week. Everyone else has left and we're just camping out here by our little lonesome selves."

"Tsk, tsk. Poor Vinny. Having to camp out in such a magnificent place as yours."

"Darling, it's just so terribly boring and tedious with everyone gone. The only people left in the city are the maids and lawn boys." Vincent knew that Lily always had a purpose and was not one to call just to chitchat. Tired of the idle back in forth, he changed gears. "So tell me, my Georgia Peach, what is on your mind and what did I do to deserve this delightful surprise today?" Looking down and admiring his new pair of embroidered house slippers, he waited for her answer.

"Vinny hon, I've missed you. It's good to hear your voice." She paused for a moment. "But there is something I wanted to ask you about. And to tell you the truth, you've hurt my feelings, keeping such a secret from me."

Uh-huh. Here it comes, thought the decorator. "Lily, whatever do you mean? What have I kept from you?" He could not think of what she was talking about.

"Well, Martha flew back from England yesterday, and called the entire family together for a meeting. Then and there she dropped the bomb that she was deeding the plantation to the National Trust. To say we were shocked and dumbfounded, and even outraged, would be a total understatement."

Vincent choked a bit on his tea but recovered. "Lily, my goodness. Why, we thought all the Randolphs agreed for this transaction. Her attorney just asked us to keep this quiet and not go public with the transfer until the legal work was finalized. He said that the family wanted the matter private." Now this was interesting. What a bit of family drama and intrigue.

"No, we were totally taken off guard. The first we heard of it was last night." Then, she planted the bait. "But now that I think about it, it doesn't surprise me."

Vincent knew he was being led down a path; Lily wasn't nearly as clever as she thought. He decided to play along, and feigned concern. "What do you mean, this doesn't surprise you? If I were in your shoes, I'd be floored."

She hesitated a moment, then continued as if she were thinking her words through carefully. "Well, it's Martha. You know she just has not been herself since Mr. Randolph passed away. Don't tell a soul, Vincent, but I think she was even suffering from the onset of dementia before he died. Don't ask me how I know; I don't want to betray her trust in such a way. She is, after all, my mother-in-law." She sighed for effect.

He saw where she was going with this and asked, as he knew she hoped he would, "Nooo. You don't mean you think Martha is, well, mentally unstable?"

"I cannot bring myself to say such a thing at this time, but I'm just looking at the patterns. Memory loss, acute depression, and loss of motor skills. Martha stopped driving more than three years ago. And she just moves to England without so much as an explanation and hardly a goodbye. She shows back up unannounced, saying she has given the Trust title to the property this family has held for more than two centuries. You don't just give away that kind of heritage, let alone one that is worth tens of millions of dollars."

While he figured Lily was exaggerating about the memory loss and depression, he agreed that the transfer of Ship Watch from that old Southern family, one that still had heirs, wasn't easily explained. "Well, Lily, I completely understand your consternation and alarm. This whole situation has to be terribly upsetting to you. Is there anything I can do for you? Just name it."

"Vinny, it is just enough having you as a friend to turn to. Please don't say anything to anyone about this call. The last thing I want is to bring attention to this matter, or for people to think that our family is in such dire emotional stress. And of course, I want to protect Martha. While I'm puzzled and hurt, I just have to think her actions are something she simply can't, at this point in her life and health, understand or comprehend."

"Lily, no worries. Mum is the word here. I'm just so sad that you all are going through all this turmoil. Call me anytime you want to chat and come see me this summer in the Hamptons. Peter and I would love to show you off."

"You are too sweet, dear boy. I may just take you up on that. Give that dashing Peter a hug for me and keep in touch. Safe travels, my friend."

"Ta-ta, darling. Hugs back to you." Clicking the phone off, he hurried outdoors, where Peter was having a late breakfast and reading the newspaper by the pool. Sitting down in a chair next to him, he excitedly told him about his conversation with Lily, repeating it almost word for word. Peter shook his head and looked at Vincent. "Darling, you know she is just trying to get you to 'stir the pot' for her so to speak. She wants everyone to think that Martha has lost her mind." Knowing it was a useless request, he went on to add, "My advice would be to stay out of this and don't say a word to anyone."

Vincent clapped his hands together and laughed. "You know you need to stir the pot so that the stew won't stick to the bottom. I don't give a fig about Martha, or Lily Randolph, for that matter. Lily dropped me like a hot potato once Add Randolph's cousin finished design school. But it will be fun to make a few calls, get some tongues wagging, and sit back and watch the show. Stay tuned for coming episodes." With that, he and his complement of corgis sailed back into the house. He needed to charge his phone. It would be a productive afternoon in his gleeful mind, though he would need to call the Trust President first and tell him about this development. Who knows where all this might lead.

Chapter 11

Trip sat out on the screened in porch of the family beach house, a classic 1930s shingle-sided cottage crowned with a pitched tin roof. The view looked out onto the sand dunes covered with sea oats, over which he could see the waves rolling in as high tide approached. The calm, soft breeze carried on it the sounds of shore birds settling down to roost for the night. It was a relaxing, welcoming setting after last night's family row.

He rocked in one of the old chairs, lost in thought as he waited for his brother, Lovey, and Lovey's friend to arrive. While he didn't think he'd be much company, he was glad to have some distractions. Lovey always made him laugh, and having Brother, the affectionate name they called one another, around would be a comfort. He'd learned a good bit about April Anne from Lovey, and of course from hearing her name mentioned in the entertainment news; she was apparently a very popular author, and he seemed to remember that one or two of her mystery novels had been made into TV movies. He hoped the comradery would make a nice way to spend the evening, and, since they would be having one of Chef Nick's famous low country dinners, the food was guaranteed to be excellent.

Looking down at his watch, he noticed that it was already after six o'clock. They were supposed to have arrived by 5:30, but God love Lovey, she was never on time, and would keep the undertaker waiting at her own funeral. He walked back inside and poured himself a short glass of bourbon, then unwrapped, cut, and lit a 70-ring Patron cigar. Lovey hated his cigars, but they'd all be sitting on the porch, and she could sit upwind; plus, he could tease that her being late had driven him to drink and smoke. Settled back in the rocker, it was another 10 minutes or so when his cousin's Bentley finally pulled into the drive with Baylor at the wheel. Tammy and George flew out of the car and charged up the broad wooden steps; Trip stepped out of the way to let them bound onto the porch. Baylor followed, carrying two armloads of luggage and baskets of food. Lovey emerged next and gave him a big hug. "You are stinking up the whole beach with that damn cigar of yours." She moved aside to allow her visiting friend in through the screen door. Trip was immediately entranced by the petite beauty standing in front of him. He caught himself staring at her large, brown, doe-like eyes and perfectly formed lips that were half-parted into a smile. Flushing a bright red from his chest all the way to the small bald spot that crowned his head, he finally found his words, and stammered out a hoarse "Please come in." He offered his hand as a welcome. Momentarily blinded from walking in from the bright afternoon sun onto the darkened porch, April felt his grip before she actually saw him. His hand, warm and incredibly masculine, seemed to be the size of a catcher's mitt, and the touch sent an electric ripple through her entire body. She looked up at his 6'2" tall frame and had an immediate mental vision of wrapping her arms around the broad shoulders and kissing his tanned, dimpled chin.

They sensed Lovey and Baylor staring at them with knowing looks, and both quickly moved away from each other in embarrassment. Lovey came to the rescue and took charge with a flurry of words. Pointing at Baylor she said, "Put our bags away, Handsome, and place the food in the kitchen. I'll put the goodies out later." She motioned Trip towards the front door. "Make yourself useful, Addison the Third, and fix us a blender of Margaritas. I'm parched. There's fresh squeezed lime juice, agave, and tequila in the Yeti bag. And you, Miss South Georgia, let's go freshen up a bit. We'll meet you boys back out here in a few minutes."

A half hour later, the foursome found themselves sitting outside on the porch, sipping on their second batch of frozen libations, and munching on a tray of hors d'oeuvres, which included some of Lovey's homemade pimento cheese, bite sized tomato sandwiches, and spears of pickled okra.

April's nerves calmed down some as she sipped her drink, but she and Trip still avoided eye contact. She didn't know what had come over her; she'd never had such an instantaneous attraction to anyone in her entire life, and certainly never thought she could just jump a man's bones right on the spot. She flushed again, and rubbed the cold cocktail glass against her cheeks, trying to cool off. After some small talk about how lovely the day was, and what a great dinner they had waiting for them later, Trip decided it was time to be the gracious host and apologize for abandoning the dinner party the prior evening. "Look y'all. So sorry about last night. I feel like shit for leaving and not joining you for dinner. April Anne, Brother and Lovey can both tell you that isn't like me. While we've had our moments before in our family, this one topped them all. Combining that with my current predicament with another legal matter, I was not fit for nice company. I just needed to be by myself. Hope you all forgive me."

April smiled and answered but avoided his eyes. *God he is so damn attractive* she thought. "Don't worry about it on my end. Please. I decided this morning if I ever get stood up for a party, I want it to be by the Randolphs of Savannah. You all know how to make it up to someone. I mean, goodness." Counting on her fingers, she continued. "First off, here we are spending the weekend at this incredible cottage, which I just love by the way. Then your grandmother sent over a certificate for the two of us that includes a full day at the Westin spa, the night in the Presidential suite, and unlimited room service. Not too shabby by my standards. Then, to top that, if you can, your Mom phones and invites me and Lovey to spend the entire summer at y'all's place in Highlands. I mean, seriously? No apologies needed on my end." She raised her glass in a gesture of a 'thank you' toast.

Baylor said looking at Lovey, "Wait. You all didn't tell me that The Lil had invited you to stay with us this summer," Giving her a conspiratorial half wink that only she could see, he then turned to April. "But that's great of course. You'll love it. We usually spend all of summer there and sometimes right up until Thanksgiving. And the Motel 6 is really nice. The Lil always puts her guests there. It's clean, very convenient to Mama's house, and the owner is a local." He then nonchalantly took a sip of his Margarita and popped a tiny tomato sandwich in his mouth, looking expectantly at April.

Lord, Brother can be such a tease at times, Trip thought. But since he knew Baylor didn't waste his humor on folks he didn't like, he kept quiet to see how this would play out. Lovey waited, too, as she watched her best friend get initiated into what was the cousins' ongoing game of pulling one another's leg.

April gave them all a wide eyed, blank look. She knew she was a bit buzzed from the tequila, but surely to goodness he didn't just say what she thought he did. Thinking carefully, she answered back very politely. "I'm sorry, but I thought we were staying at Mrs. Randolph's house. I didn't realize we'd be at a motel. I mean, that is fine, I just didn't understand the arrangements."

Lovey chimed in, waving an apologetic hand that clinked with her bangle bracelets. "Oh, hon, sorry if I wasn't clear. We always stay at the Motel 6 when we go to Highlands. Like Baylor said, it's a nice place with a pool out front, and the wi-fi works pretty well, even if the place is on a dirt road." Trip looked at the spinning ceiling fans and took a couple of puffs off his cigar to keep from laughing. April was speechless and next to having a small anxiety attack. She had a novel to finish this summer, and there would be no way she could do so in a cut-rate motel that was bound to have see-through sheets and little bars of Cashmere Bouquet soaps. *What I'm going to do? How do I get out of this predicament?* She unconsciously fanned herself with her cocktail napkin and tried to clear her throat, stumbling a bit over her words. "Well, y'all, really, you all are so kind to include me, seriously, I'm flattered. But see, ah, I..." she paused for a quick second, trying to think through the Margarita haze. "I promised my Mama and Daddy to accompany them on a couple of their excursions over the summer, and well, that the first one is out west to the Grand Canyon. I said I'd drive. In thinking this over a bit more, I better not commit to staying the entire summer, and just come up for some quick trips. I hope that's ok with you all?"

The three cousins looked back and forth at one another rather seriously for a second, and then all at once they burst into laughter. Lovey was squealing "stop, stop, stop, I'm going to have to pee" while Baylor sank back onto his chair and whooped out a string of laughter.

Their guest was stunned and wished for a moment that the floor would open up and drop her onto the sand below. What in the world was going on here?

Trip, always gallant, came to her rescue. "You two stop it. That's enough. You've had your fun." He then added, "And Lovey don't pee on that chair. I just had all the cushions cleaned," which sent Baylor and Lovey into more hysterics. Trip stood up and motioned with his cigar to his two cousins, still laughing. "April, see what I have to put up with? They are like this all the time when we're together. A regular Laurel and Hardy." He smiled and shook his head. "Come on, Baylor, come clean with this young lady."

"Oh April, honey, I'm sorry. I couldn't help it. You won't be staying at an actual "Motel 6" with Tom Bodett leaving the light on for you." He slapped his thigh and hooted again. Trip glanced down at the pretty brunette, who was looking bewildered. "It's kind of a long story. See, my Dad liked peace and quiet in the house. To be honest, while he was a great father, he was pretty intense and rigid. After one particularly rowdy summer up there with a bunch of our high school friends and a scattering of cousins running around, he built a separate wing onto the house with six bedrooms and six baths, all lined up in a row. He didn't tell The Lil about his plans, though, and she showed up the next summer to see this new building jutting out from the side of the house like a crooked finger. Anyway, she was steaming mad, and when she got out of the car, she gave him this withering look that only she can give and said "Dear God in heaven. That looks like a damn Motel 6." And the name has stuck all these years."

"Yeah, as a joke Brother and I even had a custom carved wooden sign made for the place a couple of years back. It is an exact replica of the motel logo, and at the top we had the designer put in Mama's name, so it reads "Lily Randolph's Motel 6." We hung it right out front

70

by the driveway. I thought she was gonna give us hell about it, but she actually thought it was funny and let us keep it up. Guess it reminds her of Dad in some way," Baylor said as he got up to refresh his drink. April looked at each of them, shook her head, and started laughing herself, feeling relieved. "Goodness, you all really had me there for a minute. And by the way Lovey, you will pay for this, and soon."

Lovey let out another giggle. "Oh sugar, we all could read that bubble over your head that said "How in the HELL am I going to get out of this? "The look on your face was just priceless."

"Well, I'm glad that you enjoyed the laugh. Haha." April answered good-naturedly. "The Motel 6 is then actually a guest house?"

Trip, who had a hard time keeping his eyes off his cousin's friend, gave her a description. "Well, it's more like an attached guest lodge. Dad had it built in keeping with the same style of the house, which is traditional native stone and cedar shingles. Each suite is about 400 square feet, with its own private bathroom and sitting area, as well as a tiny kitchenette. The walls and ceilings are knotty pine, and the furniture was made in Asheville. What style do you call it, Lovey?"

"Arts and Crafts. It sort of feels like a small version of the Grove Park Inn. And each room opens up onto a screened porch that runs the length of the building and overlooks the mountains and the lake. Trust me, you'll be very comfortable there, sweety. The three of us love staying in the motel. We still hang out hats there when we visit, even though Lily now asks us to stay in the main house since we've all grown up."

April raised an eyebrow. "Oh, I don't know about the 'grown up' part. I think you three still might be caught in your high school years."

Trip smiled at her warmly. "April, I'm sorry we had fun at your expense. But thanks for the laugh. It's the first one I've had in quite a while. It has been a rough last couple of months," he answered, sinking back into his chair, and taking a sip from his cocktail. "Then Grand Martha's announcement last night came as a total surprise and shock. I'm still reeling from it."

"What are you planning, cousin? Do you think Martha can legally do what she's claiming?"

"Lovey, I'm not sure. I spoke with Spears this morning." Pausing and looking over at April, he said, "Spears Moody is my attorney, a high school chum of mine," and then continued on to the group. "He said he'd review the paperwork as soon as Auggie sends it over. You know, I'm not nearly so mad about the prospect of no longer owning the plantation as I'm that my Grandmother, who I love with my entire being, didn't confide in me. She just took it upon herself to do what she felt like doing." He drew on his cigar, looked at the smoke, and shook his head in disappointment.

"Well, Brother, it isn't unlike her, you know. She was always the real force behind Grandpops. She let him think he ruled the roost, but nothing happened in this family without her approval. She's even more protective of the family name than The Lil, and that is saying something. Speaking of Mama, have you talked to her today?"

Trip rolled his eyes. "What do you think, favored brother?"

"Don't get all sarcastic with me. I can't help it that I'm better looking than you," was the answer that came with a laugh. "Yes, I'm sure she was on the phone with you, Uncle Whitt, and anybody else she thought she needed corralling. And man, when she called Grand Martha a 'bitch' last night, I almost fell out of my chair. I've never seen Mama so mad."

Trip was very glad for the company that night, but he was bone tired. He hadn't slept well in quite some time, and last night he tossed and turned until long past midnight. "The more I think about it, the more I believe I'll step out of the way and let Mama take this on with Grand Martha. Lily Randoph won't rest until she gets some real answers, and I have my own legal battle to worry about right now. I can't handle them both and come away with any semblance of sanity."

"But doesn't the ownership of Ship Watch come into play with your divorce proceedings? You'll have to worry about it, at least from that perspective," Lovey said.

"That demand from Jana was a bluff; there's no way a judge will give her title to our property, I'm confident of that. Her argument about protecting it for the twins just doesn't hold water. If that were simply the case, I'd sign ownership over to them now. No, she is trying to draw this out and make me as uncomfortable as possible. She knows I hate controversy. And I've offered her plenty, more than half of what we're worth. She'd get the island house, which appraises at a cool couple of million. Plus, the condo in Atlanta, the apartment in New York, and enough cash, stock, and securities that she'll never have to worry about a thin dime in her lifetime. Besides, she's rich as hell in her own right. She was the only grandchild on both sides, and the Chandlers and Rays were loaded with all that Atlanta railroad stock, kaolin mines, and Trust Company money." He shook his head and let out a deep breath. "I'll still be comfortable when the decree is final, but just to get this divorce over with I've tried to be as generous as possible."

Lovey stood and offered Trip the tray of hors d'oeuvres. "Here, sugar, eat a couple of these little tomato sandwiches. I made them just the way you like, with plenty of black pepper, mayo, and crispy bacon. You need something in your tummy. I'll finish heating up the food in a bit, and we'll have supper at about seven thirty." When Trip took a couple of the canapes, she sat back down and looked at her older cousin. "Well, Trip, you know I love you like a brother, and I'd jump in front of a bus for you. But you have to admit that you pretty much well complicated matters by your..." searching for the right words, she fanned herself with a cocktail napkin. "Well, you know what I mean. If you'd kept your pants zipped, you might not have such a problem on your hands as you do right now. I'm just saying."

Trip took a long draw off his cigar and blew the smoke toward the ceiling. "Lovey MacGregor, of all folks, I thought you'd be a little more understanding about this. Jesus Christ."

April peered out toward the sea and sand dunes, and Baylor walked over to the ice bucket for a refresher, both uncomfortable with the turn in conversation. Lovey blushed red at her cousin's raised voice but continued on. "Granted, you hate controversy. You are a big, huggable, gentle giant who only wants peace and harmony. That's one of the reasons I love you so much. But by having an affair, one that was bound to become public, you poked a stick into that hornets' nest that we all know is Jana Ray. And I can't say that I blame her. I know how bad it feels to be betrayed. There. I said it. Get mad if you want to." She sat back and stared back at him with caring but challenging eyes.

"Well, m'dear, I love you, too. But apparently you don't know me as well as you think you do. Or rather you just haven't given me benefit of any doubt at all." Exasperated, Trip stood and began pacing the wide front porch. "Let me fill you in on a few things, Miss MacGregor. And it may be way too much information for polite company." Glancing at April he said, "Excuse me, but your friend and my supposedly devoted cousin has asked about why I dirtied the laundry, and I'm going to tell her."

Turning back to Lovey, he put his hands in the back pockets of his khakis, a habit of his when his temper was up, and pushed on, lowering his voice. "I have not shared the bed nor the affections — and you get my drift here — of my wife since Peyton and Ray were born. That's almost twenty-two years. Twenty-two long, lonely years. The first reason she gave was that she was physically unwell after the birth, which I understood. She'd had twins and I can only imagine it would take a while to heal. I was then told that she had a hormonal imbalance which kept her from having sex, and that lasted a year or so. Next, and I remember this well, we were down at her Mama's Sea Island house. The excuse at that time was the heat made her nauseated. That hadn't been a problem when we dated. Afterwards, she just simply stopped making any excuses at all. We haven't been in the same bed in over two decades."

He took a handkerchief out of his pants pocket, and wiped his forehead before continuing. He was so frustrated and mad that he had started to sweat. "And y'all know what? It wasn't the sex I missed as much as just having someone next to me. No intimacy on any level. It has been a cold, loveless marriage for way too long. Don't get me wrong. I know part of it is my fault. I never could manage making

Mama happy and keeping Jana pleased at the same time. God knows I tried. Mama always, always felt she had to have her way, and Jana has the thinnest skin of any one woman I've ever met. Even at times when the Lil wasn't purposefully trying to provoke Jana, Jana'd find fault regardless. She'd get furious at me for not taking up for her, or for not telling Mama and Daddy to butt out of our lives. I swear, though, half the time there wasn't anything to defend. Whatever. It's over and no going back. What's done is done."

Baylor, April, and Lovey sat there, looking at him in silence as he poured himself a glass of ice water and sat back down. "Anyway, there you have the reason I 'didn't keep my pants zipped' as you said, cuz. I was simply lonely. So very, very lonely." He then closed his eyes and rested his head against the back of the old rocker. April thought that Trip looked both incredibly sad and tired, and it was all she could do not to reach over and squeeze his hand for comfort.

Without opening his eyes, he started speaking again. "So you don't have to ask, let me tell you, too, about Regina. She and I were introduced at a cocktail party during the Masters a few years ago at Merry Stiff's house. Baylor, you came along, too. Remember, you said it was like all of Augusta was there that night? Anyway, Lovey, you and Brother know Merry loves connecting people with one another. While I was doing my best to hide out in a far corner of the terrace to escape the crowd and idle cocktail chatter, here comes Merry with this pretty lady in tow. Without preamble she says "Addison Randolph, I want you to meet a fellow tree hugger, Regina Compton, who lives down near you on Hilton Head. She's chairing a fundraiser for the Sea Turtle project up in Pawley's Island, and I just know that your foundation should be a part of those efforts." She then high tailed it and left the two of us alone."

"Well, we started talking, and, like me, she'd rather be anywhere but in a room full of rabid golf fans who were stoked on too many martinis. We made an appointment to meet for lunch the next day to discuss the fundraiser, and then I drove to Pawley's with her the following Saturday. The project she was working on actually was fascinating and I wanted to see what they were doing firsthand. It was all business and conservancy talk, but we eventually found we really enjoyed one another's company. She was lonely, too. Her husband died in an automobile wreck, hit by a drunk driver one night on his way home from his office. Left her very well off; he was part of some tech company that made computer software. Her only child, a daughter, was busy in school back at Cal Tech. Regina had come for an extended visit with her parents; they'd retired over on Hilton Head and had a big pile of a place in Sea Pines, and within two months both her Mom and Dad had died. One a stroke, the other heart attack. It was really hard on her, as you can imagine. She decided, though, to stay in the area to settle the estate and see about trying life on the east coast. Over time we became companions and eventually, yes, we developed an intimate relationship. But it's all over now. We came to realize that while we were fond of one another, and good for each other in a way, it wasn't love. When her daughter, who just finishing grad school, announced she was getting married, and going to have a baby to boot, it was an easy decision for Regina to move back to California. Now I'm alone. Again."

Lovey teared up and had to take a moment to dab her eyes. "I'm so, so sorry, Trip, honey. I had no idea. I mean, we all knew you weren't happy. But I didn't realize you and Jana were so miserable together. Please forgive me for judging you like I did. I'm sorry, too, that things didn't work out for you and Regina. She sounds very nice." Lovey stood up and went to give her cousin a kiss on the top of his head. "Let me get your supper together. You need something more in your stomach than tequila and a little bitty tomato sandwich." She then motioned with a finger to the younger of the two Randolph brothers. "Come with me, Handsome, and help dish up the soup and salad. We'll eat here on the porch; the breeze is so nice and balmy. I'll stick the crab cakes in the warming oven, and we'll have them afterwards. Won't take but a minute."

As Lovey and Baylor made their way into the house, Trip opened one eye and looked at April. "Sorry for the tirade. It was all pretty personal. But if you're going to spend the summer with us, I'm sure you'll get another dose or two of family angst along the way. Seems like we've had more than our fair share these last several years."

April shook her head slightly and gave him a small, sympathetic smile. "That's quite all right. No worries on my end

"Thank you. I'm glad we didn't scare you off. First with the Motel 6 silliness and then my extended tales of woe. I wouldn't be surprised a bit an Uber driver wasn't already waiting for you on the street right now."

Shaking her head again and speaking softly she answered. "I understand the feelings only too well about being in an unhappy relationship, and all the emotional baggage that comes with a divorce." She took the remaining sip of her drink. "My situation is somewhat similar to yours, actually. From what you said, it sounds as if you and your wife feel abandoned by one another. In mine and Eric's case, I take the blame in leaving him for my work and career. He, in turn, left me and found solace and affection in the arms of a long list of other women. Plus a good bit of nose candy." She blushed at the remembrances.

Not knowing exactly what to say, Trip stood and offered his hand out. "Here, let me take that glass and get you some water, or would you rather have white wine? I was going to open a bottle for the first course."

"I'd love some ice water right now, if you don't mind, thanks. And here, let me help you with the wine. I've been sitting so long I'm getting stiff. This rocker is so comfortable, though." She stood, took a step, and her right foot caught on the antique sisal rug covering the porch. In doing so, she bumped directly into Trip, who grabbed her around the waist to keep her from falling. April instinctively threw up a hand to keep balanced, and it landed squarely on his chest, right where the shirt opened at the second button. She felt the heat of his skin and a swath of thick, curly hair. Without thinking she let out a breathy "oh my."

At the exact same moment, Baylor and Lovey walked onto the porch with trays of food in their hands, catching the couple in what looked like, and sounded like from April's comment, an intimate embrace. April jumped back from Trip like a shot, who turned the color of a ripe, red cherry. Both became too flustered to speak. Lovey broke the silence, acting as if they'd not just witnessed the seemingly amorous scene. "Y'all sit down, and Baylor open that Pinot Grigio over there chilling. Actually, go ahead and open both bottles; we'll want more when the seafood comes out."

When they were all seated, and enjoying the delicious dinner, the awkwardness eventually gave way to innocuous subjects ranging from national politics to the weather. As Lovey cleared away the dessert dishes at the end of the meal, Baylor pulled out a bottle of champagne from the ice bucket. "I thought we needed to celebrate having Lovey's best friend with us for the summer. Lovey told me you had a real fondness for Veuve Clicquot," he said, holding out the bottle for April's inspection.

"Yes, indeed. Madame's vintages are my favorites. That's very thoughtful of you, Baylor." When he popped the cork and topped off the flutes of bubbly, April looked around at the other three. "It is extremely kind of you all to let me tag along for a summer at the very exclusive Highlands Motel 6." They all laughed and clinked their glasses together. "In all seriousness, I really appreciate the invitation. When Lovey asked me down to stay with her in Savannah, it was a godsend. I'm very much ready to move back South, but still not exactly sure where to eventually settle. I don't want to rush into making any decisions until I'm absolutely certain of the right spot."

Lovey clicked her tongue in irritation. "I still can't believe you gave up that wonderful condo in New York. You had that stellar view of Washington Square, and all the convenience of the Village. I swear."

"Well, yes, it was a prime property, but I'll never live in New York again. When I first moved there, I was living my absolute dream, being a published author and working in The Big Apple. But then, after my books started being a commercial success, I was hardly at home anymore. The publishing world is incredibly hard on an author in this day and age of the internet and social media. For years I was so scared that my next publication would not sell, I did anything and everything

Houser & Penn asked me to do. The speaking and engagement tour for each book would last almost three months, and I'd be everywhere from London to L. A. and all spots in between. During the promotion of my last book, I literally spent only four nights in my own bed for two months straight."

April paused to take a sip of her champagne while Lovey said, "I know that you've been crazy with your schedule. I've hardly seen you at all over the last five or six years."

"And neither had my husband, or rather, ex-husband. That was part of the problem." She glanced over at Trip. "Since you bared your story earlier, I'll tell mine. 'Misery' and 'company,' that sort of thing." She tipped her glass in his direction. "At the beginning of our marriage, Eric and I were very happy together, even though we hailed from different backgrounds; his family is Main Line Philadelphia while mine is Main Street, Quitman, Georgia. The biggest obstacle, though, was his extreme possessiveness. He always wanted control of our relationship, which I dealt with at the beginning. Then when my work became demanding, and my schedule intense, I chose more often than not to make my publishers happy rather than my husband. If they wanted me to fly to Seattle for a talk show, my derriere would be on the plane while Eric stayed home and stewed. After a while, we just stopped arguing about it. I suppose I should have suspected something at that point."

"How did you find out about his drug problem and all his women friends? You never told me."

"Sorry, Lovey, I've not meant to hold out on you. It's simply that I wanted to push it all out of my mind and think about the future, and what's next, instead of what's behind." April put down her champagne and continued. "I had worried for quite some time that there was an affair going on, but honestly never imagined he was using cocaine as well. It all came to me, though, when researching my last book, *Numbers Don't Lie.*

The other three people at the table all nodded their heads; they'd each read the bestseller.

"I spent a lot of time with a forensic accountant learning the intricacies of embezzlement and tax fraud. In the novel, the murder victim stole money from his company as well as his wife and hid it in offshore bank accounts. Well, a portion of the accountant's explanation was pretty straightforward regarding how this sort of theft is discovered. In an audit, IRS agents look at a tax return and take note of how much money is reported as income. They then compare that number to how much money is spent. The bottom line is you can't spend more than you bring in. On the flip side, if you don't spend all your earnings, there should be some left over.

The accountant showed it to me in a simple way. You draw the letter "T" on a piece of paper. On the left side, you write in all of your income and sources of money, including loans and inheritances. On the right, you list out all of your expenses, such as mortgages, groceries, charitable donations, trips, etcetera. If you have more money than expenses, then those excess funds should be sitting somewhere, say in an IRA or a CD. It was that flip side which caught my attention."

She stopped for a moment, took a deep breath, and continued with her explanation. "We had paid off the condo mortgage four years earlier with the sales of *The Good, The Bad, and The Dead* so that outlay was out of the picture. And in terms of personal expenses mine were rather low since I was too busy writing or promoting a book to shop or take a vacation. Eric worked long hours at the investment firm, and I wasn't aware of any expensive hobbies he had. Key word here is "aware." It all made me start thinking we should have a pretty decent size nest egg built up. My fees and royalties were substantial, and I knew he made a good salary plus bonuses at his firm. Well, I looked online at our accounts, and to my surprise, there was not nearly as much money in them as there should be. After more digging, the more convincing it became something was amiss. I then hired that same forensic accountant to look at our personal financial records, and within just a few hours she found that my husband was diverting about half of our income into accounts in his own name. When the records were subpoenaed in the divorce proceedings, we learned he was paying more than ten grand a month for an apartment on the Upper East Side from one of his accounts. In the other, there were multiple, periodic cash withdrawals. Those transactions were what he used to purchase the cocaine. The real kicker, though, was learning that in the apartment I was unknowingly paying for he had installed a girlfriend." She held her hand up in front of her. "Wait. Let me clarify. The one living there when all this came out was actually the *third* mistress that had occupied the love nest."

"Three mistresses and coke. Lord, honey, how much did he milk you for? I certainly hope you got it all back in the divorce."

"A portion of it came back, but not all. It was simply spent. Eric's earning power dropped to zero when he entered rehab, and he has just returned to work. His parents had to pull some serious strings to get him installed back at the investment house." She let out a little laugh. "Apparently money managers frown on their brokers snorting nose candy."

"I don't mean to get up in your business here, April, but are you OK financially? You know I'll be glad to help out in any way I can."

April smiled across the table. "Thank you, Lovey, you are one of the most caring people I've ever met. But I'm fine with money. Eric can't touch the royalties on any of my prior books, and from the court order he has no rights to any future income I may earn. The condo sold for ten times what we paid for it fifteen years ago and I pocketed all the proceeds. And I just signed a new TV movie deal that is pretty lucrative. All is good, promise." She crossed her heart with her right hand. "Emotionally I'm pretty broke, though, and just plain embarrassed."

Turning on a dime, Lovey rolled her eyes and gave a small 'humph.' "Embarrassed for what, pray tell? Your story doesn't hold a teeny-weeny candle to mine."

Trip thought that his cousin had a heart of gold but also the annoying habit of turning the story around so that she was center stage. "Lovey, what are you talking about? Everybody in the four corners of Georgia knew your husband was gay. He wasn't a flamer, as you call some fellows, Baylor, but folks figured it out sooner or later. No one was surprised when you all split. What is so embarrassing about that? And for the record, why did you marry Billy Joe Dozier in the first place?"

Before Lovey could answer, April interjected. "More true confessions here. I'm the guilty party who introduced Bill Joe to Lovey. We grew up together in Quitman and the two of us left for UGA the same year. That's where I met Lovey MacGregor, and she in turn my bigger than life friend, Billy Joe.

"Lord that boy was a mess, but so good-looking. I remember the first time he came to pick me up at the Kappa Delta house for a date. He was driving a brand new, candy apple red Trans-Am with a sunroof. Right out of his mouth he told me his Daddy was a rich, good-old boy who owned a big hog farm down in South Georgia. I made the remark that a hog farm must smell pretty bad. He looked over at me, let out a Rebel yell, and said, "Hell no Lovey Dovey. It smells good. To my folks it has the sweet aroma of lots and lots of green money." He was a hoot." Lovey launched a big laugh and slapped her hand down on the table for emphasis, rattling the glasses.

"Lovey you're going to break my stemware," Trip said, grabbing a flute that was about to topple over. "We all know Billy Joe was a hoot. And a redneck, although a totally likable one. But he was a homosexual. Why marry him?"

"Because you uptight blueblood, son of Elizabeth Baylor Randolph, he was F-U-N. He made me laugh, and he was attentive, kind, caring, and so easy to look at. Some of the best times of my life were spent with Billy Joe. When I was around him all my cares and worries just disappeared." Lovey got a bit quieter. "I know looking back he really married me to please his die-hard Baptists of a Mama and Daddy. But we adored one another, and in his own way, he loved me."

"Excuse me, Miss MacGregor, for the record, I'm *not* 'uptight.'" Lovey and Baylor both gave him looks with raised eyebrows that indicated, "Yes, you really are."

Trip pressed on anyway. "There're a dozen couples in Savannah we all know who have stayed together even though the hubby likes to swing the other way. What made the two of you divorce, and what was so embarrassing? We're clueless here."

Lovey answered slowly and matter-of-factly to the group. "Because he got caught. We had an unspoken understanding that I was *not* to see or hear of any hanky panky on his part."

April asked, "So when did he get caught? And how?"

Which was all Lovey needed to dive straight into one of her drama scenes.

"Oh, honey, it was too much for words. Too much for words." She fanned herself some more, this time with both hands, the bangles clicking out a staccato beat. Pausing for effect, she added dramatically, "Let me set the scene: We decided to treat ourselves to some R&R; I had finished up a project over on Palmetto Bluff, which almost put me into an early grave, and Billy Joe had finally sold the old Butler estate. We booked a suite on a sleek, new Oceania ship for a two-week cruise through the Southern Caribbean. On Oceania they employ these hot Russian, Czech, and Croatians as their butlers and wait staff; the men are these ruggedly handsome fellows that grunt when they smile, and the women are all six feet tall with cheekbones that look like carved ivory. Well, Boris from Bulgaria was the assigned butler for our suite. Keep that point in mind and follow along."

She reached for her champagne and took long sip. "We had two days in St. Barts, and one of my clients from Chicago had asked us to have lunch while we were in port. She and her husband have a magnificent winter home overlooking the bay of Gustavia, and they wanted me to do an inspection for a redo. Now normally Billy Joe would jump at the chance to see this type of property, particularly if he thought he might get the owners to consider using him as an agent. Besides, he just loves hobnobbing with the rich and famous.

Instead, he tells me he was just going to sit by the pool and maybe read a book, and for me to go ahead and send his regards. Excuse me?

Billy Joe Dozier hadn't read a book since he left the University of Georgia. That piqued my little gray cells, as Poirot would say."

I said "Fine, I'll go by myself, and be back in time for cocktail hour." I get dressed and leave Son of the Rich Hog Farmer sitting on the balcony terrace in only his underwear and a gold chain, drinking a Budweiser. The Donaldsons, the couple I was going to see, had sent a driver to pick me up, and when getting into the car he reminded me my passport would be needed to get through the Customs gate. Which, of course, I had totally forgotten. Back to the ship I go. Given the time it took me to get off the boat, down the terminal to the car, then back on board, it was about 45 minutes or so. I get to our stateroom, open the door, and just what do you think I find walking into the room, pray tell?"

Before anyone could answer, Lovey again slapped both bangle clad hands down on the table, shaking the old wood and the glassware, and exclaimed, "Billy Joe Dozier, AND Boris the Butler. *Naked as jay birds*, sitting in the Jacuzzi bath, and *locked* in a big ol' tongue kiss."

The three other dinner guests sat quietly for a moment, and then burst out laughing. "Y'all, this is NOT funny. I'm totally upset and just absolutely next to tears." Lovey came out of her chair and stomped her foot, hard, which made the others laugh that much more. She remained there, in an indignant pose, hands on hips, for about a count of three, and then doubled over herself, having a laughing fit. "Y'all stop. I can't laugh like this. Oh Lord, I've got to pee." And she bolted into the house to the guest bathroom.

When she returned a few minutes later, April was wiping tears from her eyes, and Trip was commenting about how his sides hurt he'd laughed so much. "Well, I'm glad you all got a laugh at my expense tonight." Sitting back down, she continued her story. "At the time, I was mad enough to spit. I made that South Georgia tart get off the boat and fly home. I finished the rest of the cruise by my little lonesome. I never told anyone about that episode until tonight." She looked a little wistfully at her champagne glass. "We did go our separate ways, but I couldn't stay mad at that sweety pie forever. He needed to go out on his own and find a life that would be a forever happiness. Now that his Mama and Daddy are both gone, he is full out of the closet, and getting married this summer. I've met the fiancé, and he reminds me of you, sort of, Trip. Kind of buttoned up and reserved, but Billy Joe needs that. It'll give him balance. They've even invited me to the wedding."

"Are you going to go, Lovey?" April asked. "If you do, let me be your date. I'd love to see my old friend. And he certainly has found his niche in real estate. You see his photos all over the society and business magazines in Atlanta."

"That boy could sell ice to the Eskimos in winter. He's made a bundle in that Hotlanta market, and he and Wallace, that's the boyfriend, have a penthouse in one of those Buckhead high rises. I'm sure he's going to invite you, hon. The wedding is going to be over the top, as only Billy Joe would have it."

Trip remarked to Lovey, "Tell him this uptight former cousin-in-law sends his best regards, as does the other former kin, Brother here." Trip looked over at his younger sibling and noted to himself that Baylor had been very quiet for the last half hour as all these stories had been told back and forth. Lovey was thinking along the same lines; Baylor usually was in the thick of any conversation, and always quick with the one liner. Lovey reached over and patted Baylor's arm. "You all right, sweety? You're awfully quiet. I guess you can't relate to these sad, sad tales of love gone wrong. As the sexiest damn man in Savannah, you have to beat both the ladies and the men off like flies, and none of them have yet to catch this big hunk-a-hunk-a-burnin' love, have they?"

Baylor sat stock still, staring off as if saddened by some far away scene. Then, to everyone's shock and surprise, huge crocodile tears rolled down his two exquisitely sculpted cheeks. "Brother, what's wrong?" Trip went to his brother, stooped by his chair, and placed a hand up on Baylor's shoulder. It was rare that Brother cried; the last time he'd seen tears from this one was at Grandfather Randolph's wake.

Lovey was visibly upset. "Oh, sweetheart, did I say something to upset you? If I did, I didn't mean to; you know I run my mouth without thinking sometimes. I'm sorry." While she loved Trip to the ends of the earth, Baylor was like her baby brother, and she was extremely protective of him.

Baylor wiped his eyes with the back of his hands as Trip handed him his handkerchief. "Thanks, Brother." He blew his nose and took a deep breath, relaxing back into chair.

"I'm OK. Just give me a second." Trip filled Baylor's glass with fresh iced water and set it beside him. His brother took a big gulp and said, "Love you, man."

Trip squeezed his shoulder. "Love you, too," and went back to his chair.

"Lovey, stop crying or I'll start back again. It wasn't anything you said, not anything in particular. It's just that I *do* know how it feels to be hurt by someone you love, and to be left behind. Oh hell, here I go again," he whispered as more tears fell.

Lovey dipped her dinner napkin in her own glass of water and handed it to her cousin, who wiped his face with the cold cloth. "Baylor, honey, tell us what's bothering you. Please. Seeing you like this is killing me."

April spoke up quietly. "Baylor, I can excuse myself if you want to talk to Trip and Lovey alone." She went to stand, and Baylor put his hand up toward her in a gesture to stay seated. "No, April, it's fine. You've opened up to us like family, and I can do the same in return. It's something I should have gotten off my chest with these two years ago." He motioned with a nod of his head at Lovey and Trip. "But I've never felt like there was a right moment. Hearing what each of you all have gone through, well, it's given me a bit of courage."

"Take your time, Brother. We're not going anywhere." Trip scooted his chair back a bit from the table so he could cross his legs. He wanted to look relaxed so to set Baylor at ease.

Baylor began his story softly, "It started just after my graduation from Emory. You remember, it was the first summer since I was born that I wasn't with you both either on Sea Island or in Highlands for the season."

"Yes, we missed you a great deal. It wasn't the same at the Motel 6. Sure was quiet without you underfoot," Trip said.

Baylor gave a small, affectionate smile back. "I had met someone very special earlier in the year, a fellow named Adam Bedford. He had finished law school a few years earlier and was practicing in Atlanta. We were paired as double partners in a charity tennis tournament at the Driving Club. After the match that day, Adam walked with me back to my car and gave me his card. He told me to call him later in the week and that he'd love to take me to dinner. To be honest, I was definitely attracted to him, but still very new to being 'out' and dating any guys. The few times I did go out with someone, it had not turned out too well." Shaking his head in frustration, he added, "It's complicated."

"What do you mean, Brother? You don't have to share anything you don't want to."

"How do I put it?" He thought for a moment. "First, coming to realize I was gay wasn't easy, not at all. I was trying to find my way and figure out how I wanted to live my life, which would be so different than what Mom and Dad had. As I ventured out, meeting other men, it became obvious that a lot of fellows out there wanted me just for, excuse me ladies, sex, or if they found out I was a trust fund baby, they wanted me for my money."

April and Lovey gave one another knowing looks, and April spoke up. "Not to be rude, Baylor, but you were sipping from the cup we women have been drinking from for generations. If you're good looking, or rich, that's all a man sees."

"I get that and understand, totally, but in the gay world of Atlanta, Georgia, I think that scenario was even more prevalent. Don't get me wrong, I've met a lot of really solid, incredible men over the years, but back then the ones that chased after me were pretty shallow. They were looking for 'between the sheets' action, or someone to treat them to a four-course dinner at La Grotta. I just became very cautious and guarded."

"It was hard to downplay my looks, though I purposefully avoided trendy, designer clothes. I talked Dad out of his relic of a Jeep

Wagoneer, the old green one with the wooden sides, and left my sports car back home. That way I wasn't buzzing around town in something so flashy. If anyone asked about my family, I didn't lie. I just didn't give all the details. Told everyone I was from Port Wentworth, which is the truth, that's the closest town to the plantation. And I said that my Mom was a housewife, I mean, she didn't work, right? And that my Dad worked on ships. That's the truth, too." Trip and Lovey both gave him a questioning look. "Well, he did work on ships. I just didn't tell everyone that he owned the company. And the companies that made the parts for the ships."

Trip added in, holding up one finger after the other, "And the docks, and the tugboat companies, and the local bank that specialized in marine business, and the diesel fuel company. I could go on and on, Brother."

Baylor got a sheepish look on his face but was determined in his answer. "I know, I know. I didn't mean to be misleading, but I promise it was self-preservation. Bottom line is I didn't call him back. But he somehow got my number, I'm guessing from the Pro at the Club, and gave me a ring. I reluctantly met him for dinner a couple of weeks later, and we hit it off with one another in a big way. He was smart, well read, enjoyed jazz and the blues, loved to fly fish, and was a seeded tennis player. We ended up spending the weekend together and were inseparable for the next six months. He practically moved in with me in that little cottage in Grant Park. He claimed he loved me. We even had a Christmas tree we bought together and decorated that year. I honestly thought that I'd found my soul mate." Baylor stopped for a moment, and rubbed his eyes with his hands, as if to wipe clean the memories.

"In my mind, we were a 'forever couple,' and I assumed he felt the same. Late that spring, though, he took a couple of trips home to visit his parents up in Dalton. His father had a law practice there. Both times when he came back, he was moody, and distant. It would take several days for us to get back into our routine. Then I had to travel to Savannah for cousin Margaret Faye's funeral, and when I got back home after four days away, he had moved out of the house. Left me a note on the dining room table. It read that he was moving permanently to Dalton to take over his Dad's practice, and that while he enjoyed our time together, he 'really wasn't gay' and needed to get on with his life. Oh, and yeah, he wished me the best of luck."

"Oh, honey, I know that had to hurt like hell," Lovey said, reaching over again to pat his hand.

"Yes, it did. He claimed over and over again during those months we were together that he loved me. We had made a home together. We held each other in our arms at night in the same bed. I mean, I could not figure out what happened." He closed his eyes for a moment and tried to control his emotions.

"The result is that I became severely depressed and had no one to talk to. We really had kept to ourselves, and our social life had been limited." At this Trip and Lovey both started to speak, but Baylor raised his hands to stop them. "Yes, I could have called on either of you, but at the time I still wasn't ready to tell you I was gay. You can't imagine what all was going on in my mind."

"To make matters worse, and this is what literally put me over the edge, a month later, who is sitting at the kitchen table when I come home from work one afternoon? None other than Mr. Bedford. I didn't know whether to punch him out or pick him up and carry him into the bedroom. I just stood there, while he explained to me in lawyer speak that he was sorry, missed me, and needed to be with me again. My head was spinning and, fool that I was, believed him. He stayed the weekend with promises he'd be back the next Friday. Well, that Friday came and went, and then Saturday passed, and I was still curled up in my bed that Monday morning. Alone. And with no phone call. A few days later, there was a letter in the mail, his modus operandi. This one told me he had made a mistake, and hoped maybe we could 'catch up with one another' sometime in the future. Fucking psychopath."

Lovey let out a small cheer. "Woo hoo, Handsome. To hell with him. Hope you wiped your hands clean after that."

"I tried, cuz, I did. But I couldn't get him out of my mind. I became more depressed and anxious. Stopped eating, stayed in bed all day, and resigned my post as assistant tennis coach at Emory. I didn't talk to anyone, wouldn't answer the phone. Then one day, it must've been about two weeks later, there is Mama knocking on the front door. Hers were the only calls I'd take, and even through me trying to fake it with her, she knew something was wrong."

Lovely said, "I'm surprised it only took her two weeks. Lily has one heck of an intuition and is a Mama Bear when it comes to her two cubs."

"Luckily, she came in and took over. Made me shower and put on some clean pajamas while she cooked up my favorite meal, breakfast at supper time. Those eggs and grits were the first things I'd eaten in days. She knew better than I did that I was really, and truly, sick. The next day she bullied me into the car, which was pretty easy. I mean, even when I'm feeling 100%, I don't argue with the Lil. She drove me all the way down to Florida and checked me into Charter-by-the-Sea. I was there for just under two months. Mama took a suite at the Ponte Vedra Inn and stayed there the whole time I was recovering.

Trip was shocked. "Brother, what in the world? How the hell did I miss all of this? I never knew. Mama never said a word to me. We all thought you were having surgery on your elbow. That's what she and Dad told everyone, and that she was going to be with you through the physical therapy. I remember at the time thinking it sounded odd. Brother never mentioned anything about one of his elbows bothering him. So now we all know where you really were that summer."

"Hey, it wasn't all a ruse. I did have a procedure on my left elbow at the Mayo Clinic while down there." He gave a small smile and folded his hands out on the table in front of him. "I'm fine now. Really. They have a great program there for depression. And it didn't take long to figure out part of why I was so upset. Apparently, those of us who have always gotten in life what we expect, or want, have a hard time accepting loss. We're not accustomed to it. Brother, you and Lovey know I'd always led a charmed existence. I don't deny my looks, and fortunately I'm pretty intelligent. Hell, there isn't a sport I haven't excelled at." Turning to April, he cocked his head slightly and said, "I lettered in football, basketball, baseball, track, golf, and tennis in high school. Plus got a full tennis scholarship to Emory. I even took up boxing and wrestling on the side."

April listened to him list off his accomplishments and realized that the young man was not bragging. There was no hint of arrogance in his tone. Baylor was simply stating the facts.

"You're right, Handsome. Things always came easy to you. And everyone has always just adored you, even when you were a brute on the football field or in the ring. You've always been a golden boy." Lovey looked at Baylor with great affection and with moist eyes. "I just hate that you had to go through all of this unhappiness.

"It's all good now. The depression is under control and has never really come back. I now know how to handle loss and rejection. It's been a long road, but I've stayed the course." He paused for just a second and added, "And you know what? I'm feeling like it's high time for me to get out there and find someone. I've denied myself a personal relationship for too long. I deserve a special fellow to share my life with." He smiled again, this time without sadness, but with his usual confidence and charm. Lovey had thought on more than one occasion, like the present, that Baylor had enough wattage in his grin to light up the entire city of Savannah.

Lovey clapped her hands and whooped, "That's the spirit, Handsome. I'm going to start match making as soon as the sun rises tomorrow."

Before Baylor could give out his protest, Trip hopped up and addressed the group. "OK. We all unloaded a whole helluva lot of drama tonight. We need to get past some of this seriousness. Let's go dancing. The Tams are playing at the pier tonight. Tickets are on me."

Lovey squealed in delight and the spirit of the outdoor room swung 180 degrees. "That's a great idea, and I get the first dance. April Anne, you are in for a treat. Even though cousin Trip is a bit uptight, he can tear up the dance floor. You haven't shagged until you get twirled around by that big lug."

Baylor was all in, too. "I agree with Brother. We need to leave these heartaches here on the dining table. I'm game for some beach music. Whatcha think, Miss Adams?"

April was more than ready to trade in the morose talk of lost love for something uplifting and fun, and how she loved to shag. "Y'all just point me to the pier, I'm totally game."

They hurriedly filed down the porch steps to Lovey's Bentley with songs of beach music, dancing, and love in their heads. It was a welcome change for each of them, one that they hoped would last for the entire summer ahead.

Chapter 12

The next morning Lovey and April lounged underneath the shade of an oversized beach umbrella a few feet from the water's edge. The outgoing tide gave off small ripples of sound that lulled them to sleep not long after their arrival. Lovey, the first to wake, tried to read a magazine while April continued to doze. Impatient, though, to talk about last night, she finally rolled up the *Vanity Fair* and popped April, rather hard, on her leg.

"Ouch. What did you do that for?" April sat up, startled, and pulled off her sunglasses. "That hurt."

Lovey looked at her innocently. "Horse fly. Nasty creatures. Was gonna bite you."

"Ha. Tell me about nasty creatures," she replied with a grunt, giving Lovey a gimlet eye before replacing her shades and lying back onto the chaise.

"Lazy pants don't go back to sleep. I'm lonely and want to talk." Lovey dug into the small Yeti cooler next to her. "Here, Trip dropped off these off from Bojangles before he and Baylor left to go fishing." She handed over a paper wrapped sausage biscuit. "Want any jelly?"

April took the biscuit. "No, I'm good, thanks. But do give me a water." Taking the offered bottle, she unscrewed the top and took a sip. "Goodness, I'm so sore. I have not danced that much since college. Those boys were nonstop. Between Trip and Baylor, and all those other fellows you know, I don't think I sat out one song from the time we arrived until we left. What time did we get home, by the way?"

"Almost 2 a.m. I'm sore, too, and exhausted. Good exercise, though, so we don't need to work in a power walk later today."

"You're right about that. It was all I could do to make it over the boardwalk to the beach." She took a bite of the biscuit. "Yum. Help me remember to tell Trip thank you for the breakfast."

"Speaking of my older cousin, seems like the two of you have taken a shine to one another." Lovey looked over and waited for a response while April took another bite. Putting the biscuit down, she raised her sunglasses to perch on top of her head and looked over at Lovey. "I'm rather at a loss for words. Not a good thing for a writer, huh? I mean, from the time I first saw him yesterday, there was this instantaneous attraction. I've never felt this way before."

"Well, I can certainly see that the feeling is mutual on his end. It was all he could do not to stare at you throughout dinner. And then when Baylor and I walked out to find you in his arms, well, I have to tell you, it was quite a sight." Lovey teasingly wiggled her eyebrows up and down.

April gave her a serious look. "Let me set the record straight, Louvenia. That was all a coincidence. I had stood up from the rocking chair and caught my sandals on the rug. I stumbled and he caught me. There was nothing more to it than that."

"Right. Absolutely. That explains the breathy "oh my" you purred while you had your hand down his shirt. He does have a hairy chest, doesn't he?" Lovey giggled and gave April an expectant look.

April quickly flipped her Prada shades down over her eyes and sank back onto the recliner. "How embarrassing. Lovey, like I said, I can't explain it. When he caught me, my hand landed right on his chest, and it felt like it was on fire. That 'oh my' came out before I realized I'd opened my mouth. I could hardly look the man in the eye for the rest of the night."

"Don't be embarrassed, sugar. Trip is very attractive and although I tease him about being a bit rigid, he is 100% pure manliness. Broad shoulders, little bitty butt. Plus, he is one of the nicest men you'll ever encounter. I'll be honest with you. I'd hoped that the two of you would hit it off. You both could use the company."

"What frightens me, Lovey, is that I'm so attracted to him. It isn't just a little schoolgirl fascination with the new boy in class. I don't know if I'm ready for a relationship, and he isn't even divorced yet. Being honest on my end, it has me totally rethinking this summer in

Highlands. I don't trust myself to stay away from him, and the last thing I need right now is to fall in love. I'm just not ready."

"Don't be silly, April Anne. If the good Lord sends you a man like Addison Randolph the Third, you better scoop him up and be quick about it. Handsome. Rich. Straight. Carries a sizable package." She gave a sideways, knowing look at her friend.

April sat back up. "What do you mean by sizable package, Lovey?"

Lovey gave a nonchalant shrug. "You know. His package. Down there." To make her point she nodded toward her midsection.

"Oh my God, Lovey. How in the world do you know that your cousin is well endowed? Wait, I might not want to hear it." She put her hand out towards Lovey in a sign for her to stop talking.

"For goodness' sake, I grew up with the man. We've spent forty summers together either up in the mountains or at the beach. I've seen him pee off a boat, and the three of us skinny dipped on more than one occasion when we were kids. Seen his wee-wee several times." She bent her head to the side as in thought. "Actually, more like a like a long dong than a wee-wee."

April had never been comfortable talking about sex; she turned red at the thought of Trip's anatomy. "Can we just change the subject? Please?"

"Yes, Prissy Pants, but let me just add in one thing. You're not getting any younger. You need to take that into consideration, too. The longer in the tooth you get the fewer chances you'll have at hooking a hot man."

"Excuse me, Louvenia. I believe you are actually six months older than I am, thank you very much."

"True, but I'm holding up better. You're too skinny, while my voluptuousness keeps the wrinkles smoothed out." She sighed knowingly and settled back deeper into her chair.

April reached over, grabbed some of Lovey's voluptuousness under her upper arm, and pinched, hard. "OH MY GOD April Anne you're going to bruise me."

"Ha. Good. You don't need to remind me that I'm getting old, that I'm divorced, and that I have crow's feet."

"Temper, temper, Miss South Georgia. Sorry." Lovey looked over and grinned. "But don't you dare back out on me going to Highlands. If you and Trip are meant for each other, great. If not, life will go on. Just because we'll be living in the same spot doesn't mean you have to be around him constantly. The book you're writing will keep you holed up, and Trip spends at least part of each day on the computer. When he isn't working, he's usually out fishing or trudging along some mountain trail."

"What type of career does Trip have? He never said."

"He's the head of the family foundation, the largest in Georgia after the Woodruff's. Plus, he handles all the investments for Randolph Shipping and Marine. He has a tremendous mind for money." She paused for a moment and opened another bottle of water. "So let's get back to sizable packages."

"Lovey, I DO NOT want to discuss Trip's manhood with you. Goodness, you're embarrassing me."

"I'm not talking about Trip's. I'm moving the discussion over onto more interesting areas, which is me and my current love life. I'm referring now about Lachlan's 'thing that has that swing'." Lovey giggled like a schoolgirl. April shook her head in amazement and disbelief. "April, for lord's sake, lighten up. This is just all girls' talk. I've been dying to share this with someone and I'm not about to spill these beans with Trip and Baylor. Trip would spit and sputter, kind of like you're doing, and Baylor would just hold it over me for the next two hundred years."

"OK, fine, let's girl talk. Just keep it clean and without too many intimate details. Let my imagination fill in the blanks. You don't need to say them out loud."

Lovey sighed with impatience. "Swanny to God, you sound like an old spinster aunt who never married." Before April could protest, Lovey breezed along with, "So I was saying. Lachlan and I are very serious, and yes, we finally 'did the deed.' Is that wording appropriate, or should I tone it down even more?"

April squealed, which was a rarity. "What? Oh Lovey, do tell. Wait. Don't tell too much. Oh, whatever, let's just hear it. I'm so excited for you."

Lovey became animated and gushed, "He has been telling me for years that as soon as his eldest son finished high school, he was going to marry me. I thought he was just joking and trying to make me feel good. I mean, I've known the man all my life and had a crush on him since I was a girl. His late wife, Patty, was my second cousin."

April interrupted. "I think everybody in this county is related. So his son is your cousin?"

"Yes, as well as his other two sons. He and Patty had them like doorsteps, and each one of those boys look like Lachlan spit them right out. Line them up and there's four men all about five foot eight, thick, wavy red hair, big blue eyes, and standing around like bow-legged banty roosters."

"What happened to his wife?"

"Such a sad story. Breast cancer. Just like mine, but they didn't catch hers in time. When they found it, it had spread. We Steward women have a history of it. Left him with three boys, and the last one, Prescott, entered the Citadel in Charleston this past fall semester."

"When did you two really start dating? And why did he have to wait until that last one graduated?"

"Prescott took it very hard when Patty died. He became a bit wild, and was almost expelled from Benedictine, that's the local military academy. He's a lovable boy, but was a handful to keep reined in. He kept Lachlan on his toes night and day. Somehow, he managed to graduate, and his dream had been to attend the Citadel, just like his father and the older boys. He seemed to have turned a corner when he got his acceptance letter, and from what I understand has been a model cadet this first year. Lachlan asked me out on our first date the night after he drove Prescott to Charleston back in August."

"Now is Lachlan's family related to your cousin Patrick? What about to Trip and Baylor?"

"To Patrick, yes, but not to the Randolphs. It's too convoluted to explain the family tree in this heat. So anyway, we began seeing one another regularly, and he and the boys even came to my house this past year for both Thanksgiving and Christmas."

"How lovely. It sounds as if the sons all approve of you and their father being together."

"That is another wonderful part of all this. We've always had a warm relationship between our families, even though we didn't spend too much time together over the years. They lived on that big cattle ranch up in the next county, and we'd only see one another on holidays or big special family get togethers. But yes, they love their "Aunt Lovey" as they call me."

"That's just perfect. I'm so happy for you."

"He has been just simply wonderful. He's so attentive, sweet, and patient. We've been on dates for dinner, to local charity balls, and spent several weekends away. It was on the trip to Edinburgh for New Year's when I finally decided I needed to, as the saying goes, 'fish or cut bait'." So I climbed under the sheets of his bed in the Glamis suite at The Balmoral, and let me tell you, I didn't know what I'd been missing. That man is a love machine. I was seeing stars and feeling rockets being launched." Lovey had worked herself into a tizzy and grabbed the magazine from April's chair and furiously fanned herself.

April laughed out loud. "My, my, my, Lovey and The Love Machine. Could be a title of a beach romance novel."

Lovey laughed along with her. "To tell you the truth, that 'machine' seems to be able to run all day and all night, seven days a week. Sometimes I have to just take a break from him. But I'm not complaining. I mean, when I was married to Billy Joe, if we had sex once every year that was a record."

April chuckled again. "What are the plans now, if any?"

Lovey stopped fanning and became serious. "The night before you arrived, we had dinner in one of the private dining rooms at the

Chatham Club, just the two of us overlooking the steeples of downtown. The sun was setting, and it was that magical time at dusk I so love, when the sky is still blue but there's that touch of orange and red that shows in the light. It was such a beautiful setting. Perfect time for someone to pop the marriage question, which he did, with his mother's antique diamond solitaire."

April laughed with delight again, clapped her hands, and thought, *Yep, I'm back home in the South for certain. No one knows how to squeal with happiness like a couple of University of Georgia KDs."*

"Lovey I'm so very happy for you. When's the date? And why in the world did you wait so long to tell me?"

"Well, sugar, he just asked me three nights ago. I was going to announce it at the dinner at Ship Watch, and with all the rigmarole that didn't happen. And after Baylor's story about his heartbreak last night, I figured it'd be best to wait til later to tell the boys." She stopped for a moment and took a deep breath and sip of water. "The date is going to be the second Friday in December. All the Campbell boys will be home for the Christmas break, and I so want a Christmas wedding; you know it is my favorite time of the year, everyone is in such a festive mood. And of course I want you to be my matron of honor."

"Lovey, I'd be honored. Now tell me all the details, and don't leave anything out. I want to hear it all."

And so, for the next two hours the best friends sat, side by side, laughing and crying together, as they made plans for Lovey and Lachlan's December nuptials.

Chapter 13

"Woo-hoo. There you go, baby. "Come to Papa," Trip sang out as he reeled in another spotted sea trout. "I've skunked the hell out of you today, Brother. Eight to four. Means I'm twice the fisherman you are."

"Naw, old man. I've been allowing you 'pity' catches all day. Haven't been trying." Baylor cast his jig to the edge of a nearby oyster bed. The morning water was perfect in the Tybee marshes, the current giving just a gentle swirling.

Trip took the fish off his hook and looked at it. "Another keeper. I say we head home. This is plenty for dinner tonight; I'll fry these if you'll fix a batch of hushpuppies. I'll get Lovey to make some slaw, and we can stop by the produce stand to get some tomatoes to slice."

"We'll need some cheese grits to go with it all; you got any grits at the cottage? I'll make those, too."

"Probably not, we'll grab some at the store just in case." Trip put away the rods and tackle, and Baylor pulled the cord to start the engine. They sat in companionable silence through the ten-minute boat ride back to the marina. Sea gulls and pelicans flew by lazily, and the bright green spartina grass swayed in the coastal breeze. When they arrived, the brothers unloaded the gear and fish into the back of the beach truck, a 1983, two-toned blue and white Ford F150 that had been their father's. As they climbed in, Trip said, "God I love this old wreck. It costs a fortune to keep it going, but every time I drive it, I think of Pops."

"Me, too. Don't know what it is about the two us and Dad's old cars, but I can't part with the Green Lantern either, even though it's constantly in the shop," he answered, referring to the name given to the Jeep Wagoneer he had driven through college and afterwards.

Trip smiled and agreed. "Yep, she's a classic, too." He nervously patted his hands on the steering wheel as he waited for the light to turn green and cleared his throat. "Not to change the subject, Baylor, but I wanted to ask, in private, are you sure all is OK with you? I'm so very sorry about what you went through. I still don't know how I didn't pick up on it."

"Brother, you were a new father with young twins. You had your hands full at home. You were so into being a proud father — as you should have been — nothing would've caught your attention, unless one of us had knocked you upside the head."

Trip nodded in consent. "I suppose you're right. But don't you ever, ever let something get to you like that again and not confide in me. Promise?" He looked over at his younger brother, whom he loved with all his being.

"Promise. And I'm serious about dating again. Though Lord knows how that all will work. If I'm seen out with anyone that even looks like a date, tongues will be wagging across town before the waiter makes it back to the kitchen with our order."

"Hey, look at the scrutiny I'm going through right now," Trip said, giving him a sideways glance as he pulled into traffic. "Sure, eyebrows will be raised for about fifteen minutes and then Savannah, as you know so well, will move right on to the next hot gossip topic."

"That's true. There's always another story coming down the pipeline in this town. Highlands is the same way, you know. Seems like everybody from the coast who can migrates up there in the summer; it's like "Little Savannah." What are you going to do when the cocktail gossip turns to you and April Anne Adams?"

"What?" Trip gave a small laugh that suggested he didn't know what Baylor meant.

"Brother, please. There were some serious sparks flying between the two of you last night. I mean, she had her hand down your shirt rubbing your chest at one point." Baylor snickered, which irritated his brother to no end.

"Look. She tripped; I caught her. She put her hand up to keep from falling over. That's all there was to it."

"That's all there was to it my tight bee-hind. Fess up, old man. There's no shame in what you're feeling. Look at it this way: it's perfect timing. Your marriage is kaput, and your California girl is dreaming back on the west coast. Here walks in a highly successful, interesting, and lovely lady that clearly wants to take a ride on the Tripmobile. I'd say you're pretty damn lucky. I'm still waiting for someone to come around and rock my world like that."

Trip pulled up in front of Davis Produce and parked the truck. "Ok, I guess it is pretty obvious. She's all that you said, lovely and smart and has an incredible literary reputation. It isn't just those things that attracted me to her, though. There's something... I just don't know how to describe it, something seemingly 'whole' and grounded about her. She radiates a sense of genuineness. Does that make sense at all?"

"It absolutely does. I liked her from the get-go. But how are you going to handle being around her all summer long? You going to act on your feelings and actually try and date her?"

Trip took the keys out of the ignition and flopped them back and forth in his hand, thinking. After a moment he said, "Let's just see what happens over the next couple of weeks before we head to the mountains. I don't plan on leaving until Memorial Day weekend. Are we going up at the same time?"

"That's what I had in mind. Come on, let's get those tomatoes, and I'm pretty sure they carry Marsh Hen grits here."

The two brothers got out of the truck, and Baylor put his arm around his older brother's shoulders. "And boiled peanuts. We need at least two bags of boiled peanuts for this fish-fry."

"Man, you are just a bottomless pit, you know that don't you?" Trip shook his head in amazement. Baylor had always had a fierce appetite; even in elementary school the boy could eat half a fried chicken in one sitting,

"Yep, I certainly do know that I'm one big, *damn good-looking*, bottomless pit." He grinned his famous smile, and the two brothers laughed together, a sound that was harmonious to both their ears and their overburdened minds.

Chapter 14

Ten days after Martha's announcement at Ship Watch, Lily received a scheduled phone call that morning from her brother. Ringing promptly at ten a.m., Lily answered, "Good morning, Whitt. How are you? Everything is in order, I take it."

Whittaker cleared his throat, a nervous gesture of his that immediately made Lily suspect. "What's the matter?" she asked in a rush.

"Nothing is the matter, Lily. But our brother Brantley wants to talk with the two of us."

Lily froze. She very much loved her eldest brother, but he both scared and intimidated her, and had since she was a baby. Eleven years older than she and thirteen past Whittaker, he was an imperious jurist who had served as a federal judge for over three decades since his friend the elder George Bush tapped him for the circuit. Even seasoned lawyers who held sway at the most prestigious firms in the South were wary of Brantley Allison Baylor. "What does he want? I don't want to talk to him."

"Right, I know he's anxious to talk to you, too, Sis. He just stepped into my office."

Ice creeped through Lily's veins. If Brantley actually made the trip to Whittaker's midtown office, leaving behind the marble-lined halls of his court, he meant business.

"Lily, are you there? Here, I'm putting us on speaker phone." Whittaker said this slowly, trying to give his sister time to collect herself. "How sweet. Wonderful." She tried to brighten her voice with a little sing-song lilt, which cracked just a bit on the word 'sweet'. "How are you Judge Baylor? And how is your lovely bride? I haven't seen Eloise in over a year now." Quit rambling. Lily admonished herself. Brantley hates small talk. The eldest Baylor sibling's rumbling bass came over the line. "I'm fine, Lily, as is Eloise." He gave a very quick pause. "Let me get right to point. The lawsuit you are planning against Martha Randolph is a waste of time and utterly beneath you. I would strongly advise either dropping it or modifying it so that Martha's sanity is not brought into question."

Lily was stunned. How did Brantley know these details, she wondered? That damn little rascal Whittaker probably ran to him first thing to get his approval. He was constantly trying to brown nose the Judge. "Brantley, dear, I didn't want to bother you about this legal matter. It's a rather small issue and not worth taking up your time."

"Don't 'Brantley, dear' me Elizabeth. You know as well as I what you're doing is no small matter. I've looked at the papers, and Martha Randolph has every right in the world to do what she has put forth. Your legal position is extremely weak. And to call her mental well-being into play? Preposterous. I had lunch with her in London not a month ago. Her mind is like a steel trap."

Though still cowered by her brother, Lily's temper showed in her voice. "I don't care what you say about the legality. I'll do all I can to keep her from snatching away Peyton and Ray's birthright. How dare she make that decision without consulting the rest of the family."

"She dared because she evidently believes she is doing the right thing. The will was done with clear thought, purpose, and skill, and there is only a slim chance you'll be able to break it. My biggest disappointment here is your calling into play her sanity. That ploy is both mean spirited and downright nasty. If you are going to insist on pursuing this suit, at least be gracious about it."

Lily continued to steam. "As always, Brantley, I appreciate your counsel. But this is my concern and not yours."

"Fine. Do as you please. You have always been like a dog with a bone when you set your mind to something; you just will not let go, even if you know that damned bone may well break your teeth. And let me give you fair warning: facing off with such a formidable force as Martha Randolph will have consequences. You'd better be prepared for her wrath." He then turned his ire to the youngest Baylor. "And you, Whittaker, ready at each and every turn for a fight. Your hot-headedness is what is keeping you from a seat on the bench."

He walked purposefully toward the office door but stopped right at the threshold. Turning around, he added more softly, "Elizabeth, little sister. We aren't a large family, and none of us are getting any younger. If you ever decide to come home to Atlanta, we'd be waiting with open arms. Think about that possibility. We miss you here. Savannah has held you long enough." With that invitation, he took his leave.

Brantley rarely showed such sentiment, and it made Lily remember how much she missed her brothers and the family home. She quickly brushed those thoughts aside, though. Regardless of his advice, and tender words at the end, she was determined to move forward. Whittaker was next to speak. "Hey. You're off speaker phone now. Nothing like getting your ass handed to you by a federal judge, especially if it's your brother." He laughed, trying to lighten the moment.

Lily raised her voice an octave. "Why in the world did you tell him? I was hoping we'd get this on course before he found out. Thanks to you, he'll now be watching our every move. Damn."

"Hey, big sis, don't come jumping on me with jets up your arse. I didn't call him, he called me. Eloise was playing bridge yesterday at the Driving Club and every table was talking about the fact that Martha was taking back Ship Watch while you, on the other hand, were telling everyone she had lost her mind. Your conversation with Vincent has made the rounds. So big brother calls me and wants to know if I'm aware of what is going on. No way in hell I'm lying to him. No ma'am, not for you or anyone else."

Lily calmed down a bit. "Well, the cat is out of the bag. I've signed the papers and FedExed them to you this morning. By the way, tell Leigh Anna I'll text her later today with the details on our New York trip."

"What's going on? I don't think she's mentioned anything about it."

"I'm sure she did, but like most men you just hear what you want. Anyway, we're going to fly up for a long weekend to do some shopping and see some shows. We'll pick her up at the Dekalb-Peachtree airport Thursday morning."

"Must be nice having a G650 at your disposal. Living in Savannah as a Randolph does have its merits. Though, seriously, sis, I agree with Brantley. You should think about moving back home. With Add gone, and the twins about to graduate from college, you might enjoy a change of scenery. Just think about it."

"I will," Lily promised vaguely. "In the meantime, I'll send a kiss to you via your wife later this week while we're spending your money on Park Avenue. Love you."

"Love you, too, Lily. You take care." As Whitt turned off his phone, Brantley's words about Martha's wrath played over in his mind. He had a nagging feeling Lily was going to have some regrets over all of this, and not just what might come from the judgment on Ship Watch. Martha Stephens Randolph was, as his brother put it, a formidable force.

Chapter 15

Trip rang Jana right at about the same time Lily, Whittaker, and Brantley were having their phone conversation.

"Good morning, Jana. How are you?"

"I'm fine, Trip, but in hurry. I'm not keen on talking to you right now either so let's make this quick. What is on your mind that the attorneys can't handle?"

He answered in his slow, methodical manner, "Thanks for taking the call. I wanted to speak to you personally about a couple of things, both of which involve the twins."

Despite the difficulties of their marriage, and all of the strain of the divorce proceedings, they did have one mind when it came to the children. "I'm listening. Go ahead."

"First, I wanted to reiterate to you that I knew nothing about Grand Martha's plans regarding Ship Watch. That caught me completely off guard and totally by surprise."

Jana interrupted, ire back in her tone. "I thought you said this conversation was about Peyton and Ray."

"It is, Jana, just give me a moment to get to the point." He cleared his throat and took in a calming breath. "You claim the only reason you are suing for the plantation is to keep the twins' birthright in place. I understand that, though I hate you don't entrust me with that duty."

Jana began to interrupt again, but Trip spoke over her. "Jana, for goodness' sake, allow me to have my say. You'll want to hear it. Please."

"Fine. I'm waiting."

He pressed on, trying to keep his temper in check. "In terms of Ship Watch, I've spoken with Spears at length. What I'd like to propose is that I sign over my rights of ownership, transferring all my claims and title to the twins, *if* you drop the plantation from your suit. That way Ray and Peyton have the property, regardless of what might happen to me in the future, and we can settle in mediation and avoid a court battle."

Jana took a moment to think before answering. Each day seemed to drag on and on with legalities, and though she wanted as much from the settlement as possible, she also very much wished to be free from the Randolph family. If Trip were sincere, this solution would expedite the divorce, as the only contingency they'd not agreed upon was ownership of Ship Watch. "I would be absolutely amenable to those terms, as long as there aren't any loopholes or caveats in place, such as the ones which apparently were in your grandfather's will," she answered. "Our conversation here won't matter at all if the plantation is given over to the Trust. What about the twins' rights then? Are you and your mother planning to challenge that action? My attorneys say I should only get into the fray if you all choose not to dispute the transfer."

On the other end of the call, Trip placed the phone on speaker and rubbed his temples. He had spent over an hour with his mother the day before, and he was not looking forward to what all would be ahead of them. "The Lil is still angrier than I've ever seen her, and I've witnessed some serious hissy fits from her over the years. This tantrum, though, is totally justified. One set of papers have already been filed, and the next should be finalized today or tomorrow. Uncle Whitt advised that Mom take the lead on the suit because the stipulations in the original will listed Daddy as the primary heir."

"Do you mind me asking if Whitt believes if you all have any chance in winning? This whole scenario is unfathomable to me." Jana paced as she talked, her agitation surfacing again at the thought of the property being deeded to the Trust, and not to her two children.

"Honestly, I'm not that optimistic. Uncle Whitt says there's a decent opportunity to quell the provision based on some case history and estate laws. Then again, he just loves to be in the middle of a big court battle." He paused for a moment, hesitating.

Jana knew her husband well enough to realize he was weighing his words. "And?" She waited for his answer.

"He shared we'd have a much better chance of winning if it was proven that the decision was made because of incompetency." He shook his head in disbelief at his words. He still could not come to terms with exactly what such a trial would entail for his family.

Jana stopped pacing; could Trip really be serious? "Am I understanding you to say this suit will claim, in public court, that Grand Martha is not in her right mind?"

"I regret to admit so, but yes, it may well turn out that way." He didn't want to linger any longer on this subject. He changed his tone to a lighter note. "So the other reason I called: tell me how the twins talked you into letting them have M'liss's beach house for the summer? I understand they are bringing some friends along from the University as well. Sounds like a fun time."

"Those boys, they are a pair, aren't they?" Jana smiled despite herself into the phone. "They claimed, since it was their last summer before graduation, I should let them spend it on Sea Island so that they could relax and enjoy themselves before venturing off into adulthood." *Much as the two of us did*, she thought, as did Trip, but neither mentioned those memories. "I'm not going to use the house for the season, and so I agreed. And yes, they are bringing along four of their friends from UVA.

Trip was surprised. "Really? You're going to let six kids romp around your Mom's villa, unsupervised, for two whole months?" He laughed and said teasingly, "You're getting soft in your old age, Jana."

"Haha, Trip. I'm neither soft nor old." She allowed a bit of humor into her voice. "It'll be nice to have them enjoy Mama's house. But let me assure you, there are some serious conditions in place for this stay."

Trip knew his wife was loving and generous with their two children, but strict when it came to material things. They had both agreed early on that, while the twins would never want for anything, they'd never be allowed to show off the family money. Another decision was that they would have to work the during summer breaks. "Let me guess. You made all six of them get jobs?" he asked, knowing the answer was probably 'yes.'

"I certainly did. The twins will be lifeguards at the King & Prince. One of the two girls will be working at a lady's boutique and the other a hostess at Gnat's Landing. The twin's fraternity brothers each have jobs in the pro shop at the Cloister. I want them all to have a memorable summer, but I don't want them to be total sloths, either. The work will do them good."

"I agree. Glad you took care of that. When will they head south? And have you spent any time with the twins since they've been in town? I only catch a glimpse of them coming and going. I took them out for supper the other night, and we had a nice time catching up. Regardless of how our marriage turned out, those boys are solid. Polite, smart, kindhearted, ambitious; we did a good job with them, Jana."

"We did do a very good job at raising the twins. At least we have that to remember in place of these past 22 years." Jana took a deep breath and continued on, wanting to divert any more talk of their failed union. "They all plan on meeting down at Mama's this weekend, and yes, I've seen them a few times since they got home from Charlottesville. As a matter of fact, the three of us had lunch together yesterday at the Yacht Club. They both wanted some fried oysters and put away two double orders. Their appetites never cease to amaze me."

Trip shook his head, smiling. "Yes, they can certainly do some damage when it comes to a restaurant bill. They're like their Uncle Baylor." He hesitated slightly before continuing. "The documents are being drafted now in regard to Ship Watch. Just want to make sure you're OK with what I'm proposing."

"It sounds fine if it is all that you say. Send the paperwork to my attorneys, and we'll be back in touch."

"Jana, before you hang up, I wanted you to know I've not told the twins about the situation with Grand Martha, the plantation, or the countersuit. I didn't want them to worry about it; I figured I'd broach the subject later when things have settled some and we know more about the direction of the case."

Jana shook her head and rolled her eyes. "I think that is a mistake. They are bound to find out from someone; you know how small this town is. But its' your decision. You have always excelled at burying your head in the sand whenever a difficulty arises, and this situation is no different at all." Without saying goodbye, she hit 'end call' and placed the iPhone in her purse.

Trip stared down at the blank screen. "God help me, I never can do anything right in her eyes, no matter how hard I try," he said out loud. He decided to pack and leave for Highlands immediately. Baylor and the rest of the group could come on when they felt like it, he was not going to wait until Memorial Day weekend as they'd discussed. He wanted to be far away from Savannah, and Jana Ray Randolph, as fast as he possibly could.

Chapter 16

At midday, Martha and Auggie enjoyed an al fresco lunch on her veranda overlooking the side garden. Towering camellias that were more than a century old, large mounds of Formosa azaleas, and sweet-scented tea olives bordered an oval shaped pea gravel path. At the center of this subtropical oasis a bronze Triton trickled water into a reflecting pool housing a dozen or so multicolored Koi. Framing this lush scene was a brick wall covered with blooming Confederate jasmine; the star-shaped white flowers were so thick it looked as if there had been a snowfall the night before.

"Your crab salad was excellent, Martha, and those little cheese biscuits, divine. You always were talented in the kitchen." Auggie took a sip of iced tea and smiled across the rim of the glass. "I'm honored that you felt like treating me to a home cooked meal."

"Don't flatter me, Auggie, that was as simple a lunch as one could put together." Martha returned the smile, happy for the compliment. "But let's finish up this business so we can move on to more pleasant topics."

"Go ahead, my dear, I'm listening." Auggie sat back and waited for Martha to continue.

"Tell me about your conversation with Whittaker. He is filing a suit on behalf of Lily, correct? I want to make certain to understand as much as possible before making my next move."

"Yes, I spoke with him, but he gave away little. Very polite and deferential, mind you, but vague. It sounds as if we'll have to wait until the papers are finalized before we learn all the details."

Martha nodded her head. "I see. She is challenging the property transfer, we know that for certain."

"Yes, that seems clear. There is more, Martha, and I don't think you're going to like this at all." Auggie placed his napkin on the table and sat back in his chair.

"Well, don't keep me in suspense. No courtroom dramatics here." She tried to keep her patience, thinking, *Lord, Auggie has always loved to draw out a story.*

"When I could not get anything out of young Whitt, I called Brantley. We've been friends for years; I don't know if you recall but Brantley clerked here for Judge Moore when he was in law school."

"Yes, I do remember. I actually had lunch with him and Eloise a few weeks before I came home; they were in London for a few days. What did he say? Though I'm surprised he'd say anything given that it is his sister and brother bringing about this litigation."

"Brantley owes me a couple of favors from those years ago; I was a bit of a mentor for him when he first started out. But that's another story." Auggie took another sip of tea and continued. "He is absolutely loyal to his siblings, and wouldn't divulge anything of importance. However, he let me know, in a circuitous way, that the suit will call into question your mental stability. From his comments, I surmised he was very disappointed that Lily and Whitt chose to pursue such a tactic." He watched her closely, knowing that this information would be pivotal in terms of how she would want to move forward.

"I see. This certainly takes our situation to an entirely different level. Martha stood and walked to the front end of the veranda and back again, lost in thought. She leaned her back against the banister railing. "You know, I fully expected Lily to take issue with my plans. It would have taken me by complete surprise if she hadn't filed a suit. But to challenge my mental competency in open court?" Pacing in agitation, she went on. "Oh, I realize she's spread the notion that my mind was slipping; I know for a fact she phoned Vincent Judson and point blank told him so. Of course he called and repeated their conversation to · anyone who'd listen." Stopping in front of her chair, she was visibly past the stage of mild irritation. "Lily's ploy with Vinny was simply sophomoric at best. I can handle that silly old queen's silly chatter; no one will pay much attention to him anyway. A legal question in court of my psychological well-being, well, that's an entirely different story."

Auggie waited as Martha closed her eyes for a moment and composed herself. Sitting back down across from him, she regained a bit of her temper. "On to the next steps then, barrister Gamble. I've already taken care of things at Randolph Shipping; just a few minor items meant to poke and irritate Lily. This situation now calls for a more substantial way to get her attention and show who she is dealing with. Draw up those papers we discussed earlier and have them delivered to her and Whitt Friday. That way I will already have left town and won't be able to hear her ranting and raving through the plaster walls." Thinking for a moment, she said with a laugh, "Though I do hate to miss such a sweet scene."

"Leaving town? You aren't going back to England are you, Martha?" Auggie tried to keep the emotion out of his voice, but he hated the thought of her being so far away. He had missed her desperately these past three years.

"With all the issues that will arise this summer, I don't think it wise for me to stay here, at least not while Lily is in residence next door. I'll be moving into the cottage at Sea Island. My good fortune is that the twins will be living at M'liss's place this summer and working with some of their university friends. Hopefully, that arrangement will give me time to spend with them." She paused before she made her next statement. "My hope is that you'll join me."

Auggie sat up a bit straighter in his chair and placed his hands on the table. "Why, Martha, I adore Sea Island, and am thrilled that you'd like my company. But I'm sure at this late date, just before the season starts, there wouldn't be any houses or villas left for me to rent." He shook his head politely. "We'll just have to meet back and forth for whatever paperwork and items that we need to handle in person." *At least she'll only be a short two-hour drive away, instead of across the Atlantic*, he thought.

"Auggie, I didn't mean for you to find a residence there to rent. You can stay with me. I have plenty of room. There is a master suite on each wing of the house; you'd have your own personal area."

Auggie had not been to the Randolph cottage in years, but remembered it was built in a U-shape. The two master bedrooms were located across a formal garden and large lap pool from one another. He hesitated a moment while Martha continued looking at him expectantly. "Martha, the invitation sounds so tempting. Don't you think, though, it would just add more gossip to what is already being said? Two single people living under the same roof?"

Martha laughed again, shaking her head. "No one will care one way or the other if two old geezers share a house together. I mean, we're family." She said the last sentence with a little tilt of her head, almost as if she were teasing him.

Yes, Auggie thought, *second cousins.* Too close for having children, but not too close for a relationship. He quickly put that out of his mind. "Let me think about it. While I love Sea Island, particularly the golfing, there are so many children at the Cloister during the summer. They do so get under foot, especially in the beach cabanas."

"Don't be so tedious. You don't have to go swimming in the kiddy pool. Come on now, make this old biddy happy and keep me company this summer." She looked at him seriously. "It really would mean a great deal to me."

Smiling slightly, he stood up from the table. "Well then, it's decided; I'd be honored to join you for the summer." He went around the table and leaned down to kiss Martha on the cheek. She in turn patted his hand affectionately. "I'll call you later today to work out the details. I'm already packed and ready to leave; Benny will drive me down late this afternoon. I want to be out of the house before the proverbial 'doo-doo hits the fan' next door with Lily. Why don't you plan on joining me Friday? That will give you time to make arrangements and for me to make sure the house is in order before you arrive." Standing up, she reached out and took his hand in hers. "Thank you, Auggie," she said, with meaning. "This makes me very happy."

Auggie's heart raced a bit as he replied, "Then I, too, am very happy." Smiling broadly, and almost with a skip in his step, he took his leave through the garden and out the historic gates onto Bull Street.

Chapter 17

As Benny and Martha crossed the cedar tree lined causeway to Sea Island, Jana sat in Bebe Frank Kahn's penthouse library. Bebe's ancestors were some of the first Jewish settlers of the city in the 1730s, and she was the sixth physician in the Frank family to care for the children of the Georgia coast. She and Jana met through the Junior League as provisional members, and Bebe later came to be Peyton and Ray's pediatrician. Jana's text to her earlier in the day had said that she needed to see her as soon as possible. It was times like these that Bebe was glad she had finally made the move to become a concierge doctor, which assured her of some personal time each week, something rare for most physicians.

Propped across the sleek steel and acrylic coffee table from Jana, with her feet tucked comfortably under her on the sofa, Bebe watched her friend take a large sip of her cocktail. "You usually don't drink anything stronger than a bit of white wine." She pointed her glass of vodka and cranberry juice at Jana's. "I know the divorce must be quite a strain on you, but is there something more going on?"

Jana looked out the large, floor to ceiling window at the spires of St. John's Cathedral and the large gray rainclouds that were closing in on the city. "Very much so. I have to confide in someone; if I don't, I might just have a breakdown of some sort." She sat her now empty glass on the table in front of her and continued. "But you have to promise me what I'm about to share with you is strictly confidential. Swear?" Her voice was almost pleading.

Bebe had never seen Jana anything but cool and uber confident; she realized that whatever was bothering her was critical. "Let's go into doctor patient mode if it will make you feel any better. Consider this an emergency and you are right now in my care. I'm now bound by the laws of confidentiality."

"Thanks, Bebe. The bonds of friendship are enough, but I appreciate the offer." She looked back out the window, too embarrassed to look at her friend as she began to tell her story. "Were you aware of the rumors in town that I'm sleeping with Buck Pearson?"

Bebe had heard whisperings about a supposed affair but brushed them aside. Buck was a fucking asshole in a multitude of ways, and she knew Jana would never lower herself to his level. Or at least she fervently hoped. *Please Lord, don't let her tell me this is all true,* Bebe thought before saying, "Honestly, yes, I heard someone making idle gossip, but of course I didn't believe it for a moment." She paused and then added, "There isn't any truth to it, is there?"

Jana answered immediately with a vehement, "Oh my God, no. I'd never willingly let that man near me, ever." Tears welled in her eyes. The word 'willingly' made Bebe sit up straight on the couch in alarm. "Jana, what has happened? Please tell me. Let me help if I can."

Jana gripped the arms of her chair and closed her eyes as the night of the assault again came back like a vise. With effort, she began.

"It happened at the Brannigan's St. Patrick's Day party at the Isle of Hope. I really didn't want to attend, but thought it might be good to be away from the plantation and get my mind off the divorce and Trip. Well, Buck was there that night, and it seemed wherever I went in the house or out on the dock, he managed to be right next to me. And, each time he came near, he'd lean over and ask me to go out on a date, meet him at a hotel, or to go off on a weekend trip with him. It was disgusting. I finally had enough and left.

I'd arrived a little late to the party and the only parking spots open were way down at the south end by the marina. I walked back in the dark and," she paused to take a deep breath, "apparently Buck followed me. Just as I took the keys out of my purse, he grabbed me from behind, spun me around, and before I could even scream, he had his hand over my mouth. He babbled something along the lines of me 'playing hard to get,' and that 'he knew what I really wanted.' I tried to bite his hand, I kicked, and did my best to get away, but he had me in such a grip I couldn't move." Her voice trembled badly, but she braved on, "He bent me over the hood of my car, reached up under my skirt, and grabbed me, there, hard. I knew what was coming next when he shoved me again, but this time he did it so hard, and with such force, the alarm on the car started blaring, thank God. He jumped back and tripped over something, maybe one of those big oak tree roots. I was parked under a tree. Anyway, the keys were still somehow miraculously in my hand; I clicked the lock, jumped in, and was screeching away just as he stood up, and put his," she hesitated a bit, as she rarely used vulgar terms, "dick into his pants. He never entered me, but he sure as hell almost did. Still, my privates where he yanked at me hurt for weeks, the muscles in my shoulder strained, and the bruises across my chest from being thrown onto the car have still not all gone away." She stopped and opened her eyes. *There. I finally got it out*, she thought as she turned back to face her friend.

Bebe sat stock still for a moment, pale and visibly shaking. "I cannot tell you how sorry I'm for what you've been through. What you described was pure hell. And God how I admire your courage for being able to tell someone." She stood up and walked over to the window; the thunder was getting closer, and the rain would start any minute. "I've never been able to do so myself."

Jana wasn't sure if she heard correctly. "What was that, Bebe? What do you mean?"

"Let me just say that you are not the first woman Buck Pearson has assaulted or raped. I know of two others who have gone through the agony you suffered at his hands. One of them was a former patient of mine, someone you'd know."

"Who was the other woman, Bebe? Can you say?" Jana stood and placed her arm around the other woman's shoulder. Bebe nodded her head. Looking out at the downpour that was covering the city, she answered simply, "Yes. It was me."

"Basically, this monster is a serial rapist." Jana's head was reeling with a thousand different thoughts. It was just too much to fathom. "I can't believe I'm saying this, but I need another cocktail."

"Me too, Jana, me too. Sit down, and I'll pour us one." Stepping to the bar, she tinkled in a couple scoops of ice, poured in equal parts Grey Goose vodka and organic cranberry juice, and topped the glasses off with a splash of soda and wedge of lime. She handed one to Jana and sat back on the couch.

Jana hated asking; she knew how hard it was to verbalize this torment but felt she needed to reach out. "Do you want to tell me about it? Would that help? You let me pour my story out to you. Please, if you want to, need to, I'm all ears."

Bebe thought for a moment before answering. "I won't go into all the details, there's no need to relive those moments aloud. But it happened in a similar way with you; he found me alone, caught me off guard, and" she closed her eyes for a second, "the bastard finished what he started." Taking a big sip of her drink, she continued, "You know he was an Olympic wrestler? He even won the bronze medal one year."

Jana was puzzled. "No, I never heard anything about him at the Olympics. Is that where he assaulted the other woman you were speaking of?"

Bebe shook her head and waived her hand back and forth in front of her. "No, no that's not it. What I'm saying is the reason he can hold and pin someone down so easily is that the man has the training to do so."

"That explains it then. He grabbed me and with just one arm had my whole body in a knot. I couldn't move a muscle." Jana shuddered remembering the incident. She had never in her life felt so vulnerable. "And I'm guessing, like me, you knew there wasn't any reason to go to the police."

Bebe's voice carried with it two years of exasperation. "There was no way in hell I could go to the police. Most of the time the victim is on trial more so than the pervert. And oh Lord God in heaven, if A. J. Kahn found out, he'd hunt Buck down and kill him himself. You know what a temper that man has. He'd be in jail right now for murder."

"Speaking of A. J., where is he tonight? Will he be home soon, and do I need to leave? The last thing he probably wants to see is two women sitting here getting hammered and raving about the male pigs of the world." Jana could only imagine Bebe's intense husband walking into the scene in the library.

"Oh, no, he's in New Orleans at a convention; Merrill Lynch has them set up at the Ritz for a few days and he won't be home til the weekend." Getting up and reaching out to motion Jana to stand, she continued. "Since he's out of town, and it is raining so hard, plan on staying here tonight with me. We'll order in Thai delivery, you can borrow some of my jammies, and we'll spill our guts and talk smack." She hugged Jana for a quick moment and stood back. "What do you say?"

"Actually, I'd love to. The thought of driving back to that mausoleum of a house in this storm, and being by myself, isn't appealing at all."

"C'mon then; I'll grab you some clothes and get you settled." The pair walked down the hall to the master bedroom where Bebe retrieved a comfortable cotton nightgown and a pair of slippers. She then escorted Jana to the guest suite, turned down the comforter and sheets on the bed, and showed her where the towels and toiletries were kept. At the door she said, "Make yourself at home. There are some wonderful Italian sea salts by the tub if you want to do a hot bath, and Siri on the table there has a dozen classical and jazz stations you can play."

"I'm all good, thank you, Bebe. I'll be out before too long."

"No rush at all take your time." She turned to go, thought for a moment, and turned back around. "Jana?"

"Yes?"

"I've done nothing but plot and plan over these past couple of years on how to get back at the SOB. I've been consumed by it almost."

"Trust me, I'd like nothing better than to shear his balls off. I swore to myself the other night, after another exhausting crying episode, that I would somehow make him pay. I just honestly don't know how without going to jail," she answered, shrugging her shoulders.

"Well, I think I have a way, and it shouldn't involve any jail time. I've thought this scenario through a thousand times, and if you can help me, we can make Buck Pearson wish he'd never touched either one of us, or for that matter, any other woman in Chatham County."

Jana placed the pajamas she was holding back on the bed. "I'm all ears. Of course I'll help you. What do you have in mind?" Her head raced at the idea of hurting the man who had caused her so much physical and emotional grief.

"There's not enough time to explain right now; let me run take a shower first. I feel nasty just talking about Buck. And I need to make a phone call that will take a while. Meet me back in the library in an hour. Then I'll tell you what's up my sleeve over dinner and some vino. Hopefully you won't think I'm crazy."

"Bebe, my friend, we're both a little bit crazy. Who wouldn't be after such an ordeal?"

"I know, right? Anyway, get comfortable, and I'll see you in a bit."

Jana went into the spacious bathroom, turned on a station with Michael Bublé crooning a sweet song, and ran a hot, steamy bath in the oversized spa tub. She was able to relax for the first time in recent memory. Unburdening her ordeal to Bebe had been a relief. Too, knowing that there might be a way to pay that monster back was exhilarating. She could hardly wait to hear what Bebe had to say, and what she thought they might be able to do to carry out their own sense of justice.

Chapter 18

While Savannah was being deluged with a massive thunderstorm, the night skies in Highlands were crystal clear. The Milky Way shone like a large blanket of white glitter, and the moon was so bright Trip could easily make his way around the yard without the aid of a flashlight. He built a roaring fire in the fieldstone pit and settled into a wooden Adirondack chair with George sitting by his side. The air was a brisk 50 degrees, not unusual in May at this high 4,000+ foot altitude. Trip loved the cool as well as the smell of the oak logs burning and the clean scent of the pine forest that surrounded the Motel 6. This peace and solitude were a balm to his overburdened mind, and he was glad he'd made the journey up before his brother and the rest of the group. Some time alone would do him good. He slowly rubbed the dog's head, sipped on his cocktail, and relished the taste of his Macanudo El Gordo. "George, I believe it was Mark Twain who said, "If I can't drink bourbon or smoke cigars in heaven, I shall not go." George replied with a few thumps of his tail; he was resting well after eating the fat ribeye steak Trip had cooked for him for supper.

On the five-hour drive up that day, Trip had vowed to stop worrying about the divorce and move on with his life. Hopefully this last concession of signing over ownership rights to Ship Watch to Peyton and Ray would satisfy Jana; with no courtroom battles maybe an end date could be set sometime soon. He was also determined to stay out of the fray between The Lil and Grand Martha. After his first reaction of anger at his grandmother's behind-the-scenes maneuvering, he came to realize that he really didn't care if the plantation stayed in the family or was turned into a museum; there were merits to both outcomes. For too long he'd did his best to make other people in his life happy, namely his parents and Jana. His children would soon graduate, and each had promising careers in front of them. It was time to focus on Trip.

He definitely wanted to continue as head of the family foundation. He enjoyed making the financial decisions that assured continued expansion of the corpus of the organization, and took great satisfaction in distributing that wealth to worthy causes. This work, however, only took up a small part of his time, and he was anxious to do something else besides fish and play golf. Two of his good friends in Atlanta had started their own small, private wealth investment firm which handled well-heeled and upwardly mobile clients. The two men had approached him twice about joining as a principal at Haddock & Mason, and Trip thought it was time he took them up on their offer.

Also in the forefront of his mind was April Anne Adams. The young lady intrigued him like no others he had met, not even Jana with her extraordinary beauty. He had such an immediate and intense attraction to her that at first it almost felt disturbing. Trip intuitively knew, too, that the feeling was mutual. If Baylor and Lovey had not walked in when they did that night at the beach, he was almost certain he and April Anne would have kissed right there on the porch when she slipped into his arms. Yes, he told himself, he believed she might well be that special one.

A fourth vow was then made by the eldest Randolph son that day, one that followed his promises to put the divorce out of his mind, avoid the confrontation between his mother and grandmother, and to join in with his two friends in an expanded career. Instead of avoiding a new relationship, he was going to meet it head on and try his hand again at happiness.

Chapter 19

April Anne had spent the majority of the day on her laptop making final edits to her latest novel. She was well within her deadline, and happy with how the book was coming together, although she'd been going nonstop on a social schedule with Lovey since she'd arrived in Savannah. Her agent had called earlier in the week with the news that the network had starting casting for the upcoming movie based on April's famous Amy Allyn Swann character. With sixteen novels under her belt, there was a lot of Amy to go around, and if the movie was a hit, there was a possibility of a series as well. People loved the larger-than-life, big city crime reporter who originally hailed from the tiny hamlet of Claxton, Georgia. Inevitably, while recording her stories on felonies and moral corruption, this Rubenesque, wise-cracking, and outspoken character also solved murder mysteries. Male readers liked her because of her salty language and love of fishing and duck hunting. Women read from cover to cover because they empathized with the big-hearted woman who, while successful at the office, failed miserably at love. Like Amy, there were scores of girls who often turned to a carton of Haagen Daz, a pack of Marlboro Lights, and a house full of cats for solace after suffering through yet another disappointing breakup. This literary favorite, though, never gave up hope in any of her stories, and it was with dogged determination that she kept looking for love from one novel to the next.

April had fingers crossed for the success of the television venture, and believed the new book, *A Grave Mistake,* would likely hit the bestseller's list. After this, however, she'd only do one more Amy Allyn, one that would end the series. She wanted to try her hand at another genre, something more tied to her roots and the people back home. She had not shared this news with her agent, who would probably implode on the spot upon hearing her plans. However, over the course of long, extended talks with her friends Janis Owens and Michael Morris, two of the most well-regarded writers from her neck of the woods in the Deep South, she knew she was ready to make a change.

Looking at the clock she found it was already 8:30, and she was starved. Lunch had been a cup of yogurt and a banana many hours ago. She headed down to the MacGregor kitchen to fix herself one of her guilty pleasures: a grilled cheese sandwich and bowl of Campbell's tomato soup. As she flipped on the lights, Babette, Lovey's very vocal Siamese cat, padded into the room, rubbing against April's legs, and singing out a greeting.

After digging some kitty treats from the pantry for Babette, April prepared her supper and sat down to enjoy the meal and the solitude. Lovey and Lachlan had gone out dinner and had asked her to join them. April had politely declined the offer. She'd been thrilled to meet Lachlan at last, and what a dear man he seemed to be. It was obvious that he was totally smitten with his 'wee lass.' From what she'd seen in their bit of time together over a short cocktail, the pair were meant for each other. The thought of their happiness made April smile.

But while her affection for Lovey was immense, and she was genuinely pleased for her best friend's newfound love, Lovey's constant chatter sometimes exhausted her. Truth be told, April was also finding it hard to fit comfortably within the whirl of all that was Savannah society. It was a nonstop beehive of activity: brunches, lunches, rounds of bridge, almost nightly cocktail soirees, and dinner parties that lasted past midnight. And even though the people in Lovey's circles all welcomed April with open arms, and were charming and interesting people, there was still a sense of class distinction that only someone from a blue-collar small town could detect.

While April was herself a millionaire several times over now, her father had worked as a broiler repairman in the local Budweiser plant for three decades, and her Mom had retired as the manager of the lunchroom at the sole elementary school back in Quitman. Her parents had played poker, not bridge, and a special dinner out for the family was the 'all-you-can-eat fried catfish' at Creekside Diner.

The irony wasn't lost on April that twenty years ago she would've been overjoyed in the midst of these sophisticated coastal ladies and their Rolex wearing husbands, sharing conversations regarding the latest fashions, and listening intently about hunting trips to places such as Argentina and Wales. Interesting how life was bringing her full circle, she mused, slowly stirring the tomato soup in her bowl. She was now at the point where she thought she always wanted to be, but found instead longing for the comfort of her Maw-Maw's screened-in porch back home, shelling peas in the quiet of a summer twilight, with just the soft, musical sounds of crickets and cicadas singing in the background.

Back in those sweet and fragrant pine woods of her South Georgia youth, she wanted nothing more but to trade her peaceful life for the bright lights and urbane society of Atlanta and New York. She'd vowed to herself when wiping off the red clay dust from her high heels at high school graduation to never look back. But that was all she had been doing since her divorce, looking back, and realizing what she'd left behind.

As she contemplated this slow revelation evolving in her mind about where life might take her next, she thought again about Lovey's eldest cousin. April had a hundred butterflies in her stomach whenever Trip Randolph popped into her head, and each time the image of their embrace at the beach came back, when her hand landed in the middle of his chest, she unconsciously blushed. It wasn't just the physical attraction that held April's attention; it was also the fact that she found Trip fascinating and immensely interesting. He was a bit the odd man out within the tight-knit circle of three cousins, April observed as she came to know them all in better measure. While she would never consider either Lovey or Baylor pretentious, they moved with more ease in the converging circles of high society than did Trip. The few times she had been in social settings with him, he seemed to sit on the edge of the conversations rather than putting himself in the middle of the party. He drove a 1999 Chevy Suburban, one that had over 250,000 miles on its second motor, and his wardrobe apparently consisted mostly of well-worn but well-starched Bill's khakis, penny loafers with no socks, and white button-down shirts. The only indulgences April noticed were the expensive cigars he smoked and the fine bourbon he poured. She guessed, though, that if you drove an old car with faded leather seats, you could rightly indulge in a couple of extravagances. Compared to Baylor's hundred plus grand convertible and Lovey's vintage Bentley, Trip's auto was absolutely low key.

What really amazed her was how very comfortable she was in Trip's company. Their conversations had been relaxed and easy, with a good bit of talk about the things they both loved, including family, good books, and being outdoors. The big question on her mind now was how the summer would unfold with the two of them living next door to each other in Highlands. The prospect both scared and excited her.

Throughout the whole divorce ordeal and for months afterward, she was certain she'd never again fall in love again. That assertion drastically changed, though, since meeting Trip Randolph.

The only thing to do, she decided, would be take it all one day at a time. She promised herself to accept any gifts that came her way, and to never ignore her instincts. She also decided, and blushed doing so due to her deep-water Baptist upbringing, that she would refill her birth control prescription as well as buy some condoms. No need in denying there was a strong physical and emotional spark between them, and she could not predict what might happen under the twinkling stars of the North Carolina mountain sky.

Chapter 20

At exactly 8:00 pm Lily's doorbell rang, and a packet slipped through the mail slot of the townhouse's massive oak front door. Lily placed the book she had been reading in the library on a side table and walked down the entrance hall, wondering who would be calling on her at this hour on a Monday. Finding the large envelope embossed with the Randolph Shipping logo on the floor, she picked it up and undid the seal. In it was a memo which was addressed directly to Lily from Martha Stephens Randolph, Chairman of the Board, and Thomas Trotter, President & CEO of the company. It read:

> As of today, no persons, except on the authorized listing below, may use or utilize any Randolph Shipping, Incorporated, assets. These assets include both of the company's jets as well as the fleet of automobiles.
>
> Thus, the scheduled itinerary you have planned for this Thursday (roundtrip to New York with a stopover in Atlanta) is hereby cancelled.
>
> In addition, please have the Lincoln Navigator in your possession, Georgia license plate KEP 2975 and registered in the name of Randolph Shipping, Inc., available for pickup by company personnel as of close of business tomorrow. It will be returned to Randolph Shipping, Inc.
>
> Any questions may be directed to corporate counsel.

A yellow post-it note was attached to the bottom of the letter next to the listing of names that didn't include Lily Randolph. In Martha's well-trained, finishing school handwriting, were the words *"Sweet dreams, Lily. Hope you have a restful night. Fondly, Martha."*

The courier, who had stopped on the sidewalk in front of the house to read a text, could distinctly hear, even at 100 feet away behind brick and stone walls, the breaking of the crystal vase Lily had thrown against the door as well as her long tirade of expletives. "News must've not been good," he said out loud as he mounted his bike and rode away into the dusk that was settling over the city.

Chapter 21

Over basil rolls and Pad Thai, Bebe laid out her plans for Buck. Jana listened intently to what was to happen, how it would be implemented, and the results, which should be exacting and permanent. There was some risk involved, but with caution and care it could be minimized. Bebe finished explaining just as Jana was taking the last bite of the noodles she had rolled onto her spoon. Wiping her mouth with her napkin, she sat back in her chair and spoke for the first time in the last five minutes.

"Bebe, you're brilliant. I'm blown away with how much thought you've put into this; down to the last detail you've got it covered. That bastard deserves to pay. Count me in." She placed her napkin on her plate and continued. "But I have some questions. First of all, why can't you be the 'bait'? Why does it have to be me?"

Bebe gave a short laugh. "Well, the last time I ran into that mother trucker I told him, in no uncertain terms, if he ever came near me again, I'd cut his dick off with a scalpel. Then, I took out my can of mace from my purse and sprayed him right in the middle of the Publix parking lot at Twelve Oaks. Left the bastard hollering and crying as I drove off. I don't think he'd believe a change of heart ever came my way."

Jana nodded. "Understood. I'd rather not play the part, but I will. Next question: why in the world would your cousin Bernie want to help us in such a way? If we were caught, he'd be in as much or more trouble than we would. I just don't get it."

"It's rather a long story, and more than a little sad. Let me try and give you the Cliff Notes version." She poured herself a second glass of pinot grigio, took a sip, and continued. "Mary Nan, Buck's widow, and Bernie grew up together; their families lived across the park from one another on Madison Square. They were inseparable all the way through high school. Nothing romantic, mind you, just the very best of friends. Even through college, while Mary Nan was up at Sweet Briar and Bernie at Emory, they kept in touch and visited back and forth throughout until they were about to graduate. Well, their senior year Miss Mary Nan Bishop met the SOB, Buckner Pearson, at a sorority social. Apparently, his father owned some big construction company in Charlotte and was making boatloads of money in the building surge they were having there at the time. Four years older, an Olympian athlete, and driving a flashy new Porsche, he swept our innocent little Mary Nan off her feet."

Bebe paused for more wine and to catch her breath. "Well, Mary Nan invited Buck down to Savannah for a long weekend that spring and when Bernie and Buck met at a party, it was immediate mutual loathing. First thing out of Buck's mouth when introduced was "well, at last I get to meet Mary Nan's little Jew-boy I've been hearing about." Bernie cold-cocked him on the spot, breaking Buck's nose — he and AJ share the same temper — and a huge fight ensued. Buck then got Bernie in some wrestling hold and almost choked him to death until a group of fellows pulled them apart.

Things were never the same after that between Bernie and Mary Nan; Bernie could not understand or accept the fact that his dearest friend would marry someone so prejudiced and bigoted. Mary Nan repeatedly begged for Bernie's forgiveness, but she wasn't willing to give up the man she'd fallen in love with. The whole situation almost put an end to their life-long friendship.

After that weekend, they didn't speak for years, not until after Mary Nan and Buck's first child was born. By that time, people were whispering about Buck's philandering, and he would be gone for weeks at a time on business. It was during those long absences that Bernie and Mary Nan began communicating again, and some of the old wounds healed. After the second baby came, Mary Nan was suffering from ongoing depression. She was always an extremely shy, pensive person, and no doubt her marriage to Buck put a terrible strain on her mentally. At this point, everyone in town knew about his fooling around; he didn't even try and hide it.

On one of those nightly chats Mary Nan confided in Bernie that she just didn't know how to go on living. Bernie was beside himself and begged her to leave Buck. A devout Catholic, she refused, even though she knew of Buck's ongoing adultery. Not knowing what else to do, Bernie made it a point to start calling her every night at 10 to check in with her; it was their unofficial appointed time. Well, one night Mary Nan didn't pick up the phone. Bernie panicked and called Savannah EMS. When they arrived at the house, the au pair was upstairs asleep, as were the kids; Mary Nan was in her bed, too, but dead with an empty bottle of Percocet by her bedside."

Bebe wiped away a tear and finished her glass of wine in one gulp. Jana became emotional as well and dabbed her eyes to keep from crying. "I don't remember too much of the matter. Mary Nan and I met socially on a few occasions right after I moved here, and then I had the twins, and my life was centered around them until they were toddlers. She died soon afterwards. But didn't they rule her death an accidental overdose?"

Bebe leaned forward and nodded. "Yes, that was what the coroner said, and friends repeated in polite society. And I believe it, too. Think about it. If Mary Nan were so committed to her religion that she would not divorce, she certainly wouldn't purposefully kill herself, either." She paused for just a second then went on. "Mary Nan was taking the Percocet for a badly herniated disc in her back, plus her doctor had prescribed a muscle relaxer as well." Bebe held up two fingers for emphasizing the medications, and then raised two more as she said, "Plus she was on not one, but two anti-depressants. All four of those prescriptions were in strong dosages, and I'm sure they kept her spaced out, for lack of a better nonmedical term. It probably happened like this: she takes her anti-depressants as scheduled, then pops a muscle relaxer and swallows down a Percocet with a glass of wine or two because of the pain. After that point, she is so out of it, she doesn't remember if she had taken her medicine, so she takes another muscle relaxer and yet another pain pill. She passes out. Wakes up, reaches for the bottle, and not knowing what she is doing, empties the last six Percocets into her system. And that is how she died. I've seen it happen more times than I care to count; someone that is overmedicated and in a drugged state of mind takes too many pills in succession."

"I guess that is easier to do than people realize," Jana said. "I know a simple Benadryl makes me so sleepy I can stay in bed half the next day after taking one."

"Exactly, and Mary Nan was maybe 105 pounds soaking wet, and taking 20 to 30 milligrams of something like Percocet can just...." Bebe trailed off, again getting teary eyed. "My cousin puts the blame right smack dab on Buck; he says if that ass hadn't treated Mary Nan so badly, she'd never have been on all those meds to begin with." Bebe wiped her eyes and cleared her throat. "So yes, Bernie is in 100% and said he'd make all the arrangements. We just need to come up with the money and guarantee a private time with Buck."

"I know we need to discuss the money part, but I just have to ask — and I don't mean to be so downright nosy, but exactly how and why did Bernard Lischer get into *porn*? I thought he was a photojournalist and filmed wildlife documentaries. It hasn't been that long ago I saw one of his shows about the Everglades on PBS."

"He is absolutely legit, and his heart is totally in those nature productions. He has another one coming out this fall about the loss of the oyster habitats in the Florida Gulf coast. But" Bebe shook her head and raised her eyebrows "he declared bankruptcy back when the economy took a nosedive in 2008. Three of his biggest corporate investors went belly-up, and most of the contributing charitable trusts closed their purse strings. He lost it all except for his house which was in his Mom's, my Aunt Ruth's, name. He was desperate for work, and even though the stock market went to hell in a handbasket, there was still, as Bernie puts it very tongue in cheek, 'a very hard, raging, demand' for porn. And according to him, Miami is the porn video capital of the country. Knowing he was in dire straits, one of his friends in the industry gave him a job filming a movie. Seems Bernie did so well, finishing the project ahead of schedule and with some incredible shots that were at angles not yet used, other projects came along to him in a succession. Soon, he was in hot demand, and making twenty times what he had made before. He eventually bought out his friend and now owns the entire studio. And good ol' Bernie, he is nondiscriminatory; he says the gay porn often pays better than straight scenes, so he produces both, and has outlets all over the US, Europe, and the Far East. That's how he has that penthouse in Miami as well as a limo and a driver. And those fuck films, excuse the expression, are now bankrolling the nature films."

Jana's eyes widened and her jaw hung just a bit in disbelief. "Wow. Who would ever have thought? What do your Mom and Aunt Ruth have to say about having an adult movie producer in the family? I can only imagine what the conversations would be like at family dinners."

Bebe giggled and said "Yep, it now usually goes something like *"Esther, this matzo ball soup is to die for. So dee-lish. Hey, speaking of balls, did you see the set on that guy in Bernie's new movie? They're HUGE."*

Both women burst out laughing at the thought. Bebe went on to add, "Seriously, no one, I mean *no one*, in the family knows about this except me and AJ. If Aunt Ruth found out, she'd personally rope and tie Bernie and dump him in Biscayne Bay. She's liberal when it comes to world affairs, but anything that hits close to home better be something you can talk about at synagogue."

"I understand, and trust me, I won't let on to anyone about how Bernie makes his money. But speaking of money, what price was quoted to you to do the job?"

"Fifty grand, all in advance."

"Done. Just let me know where and when to get my half. It's well worth it; hell, I'd pay double that if we had to. I want that bastard to be hurt, humiliated, and gone."

"I totally agree, sister. Worth every dime and thank God we can come up with that kind of cash. Only small thing that is irritating here is the wait. The fellow Bernie has lined up to do the deed is in the middle of working on a film right now and won't be back available until at least the middle of July."

Jana was curious about the man who would be taking their money. "What all did Bernie say about this guy? I mean, is this sort of arrangement typical in those adult film circles, men who are willing, and able, to do this sort of thing for hire?"

"He didn't say much, except that he's a big, muscular Brazilian who knows his moves and is accustomed to 'side gigs' as Bernie called them. He assured me that the fellow would be able to do the job without fail."

Jana clapped her hands and smiled. "Bravo. Since Buck is such as racist it'll be icing on the cake that someone he'd call a 'wet-back' will dispense the justice. Splendid. Just imagine the thoughts going through that worm's mind when realizes what's about to happen to him."

Bebe gave a short, sarcastic laugh. "Rapists and bullies are all the same when it comes down to the nitty gritty. They are weak and afraid. He'll probably piss his pants and cry, and maybe if he's able, beg for mercy."

Jana smiled broadly and poured a little more wine in each of their glasses, raising hers across the table. Clinking the crystal together, she said "Here's to you and to the humiliation, and demise, of Buckner effing Pearson."

Chapter 22

It was almost midnight, and Baylor had hovered over the "accept terms and conditions" box on the website for almost an hour. Struggling through the process, he was certain he had overthought, and over analyzed, each and every part. The whole ordeal seemed like a complicated personality profile, something to be completed if applying to be an executive in a start-up tech company. Then again, he guessed, when it all boils down, you rather are looking for a sort of job, and at the same time, hiring for one, on these dating apps. He hadn't been on a date since his relationship with Adam ended all those years ago. He didn't even know how to begin, or really how these matchups worked.

It wouldn't be a problem getting someone to go out with him, not with his looks and money, but he didn't want to waste his time, or anyone else's, for that matter. So, at the advice of one of his few gay friends, he was going to bite the bullet and use the internet.

The site, "Men of Substance," touted itself as featuring only professional gay men who were looking for love. There were dozens and dozens of reviews, all showing couples of well-groomed fellows testifying to the effectiveness of the service; all claimed that MOS targeted the very best fit for each participant. The personality piece had taken a while; it dwelled mostly on how Baylor viewed himself and then how he felt others perceived him. That took a good bit of soul searching and honesty. The rest of the 32-page questionnaire was somewhat easier because he had firm beliefs in what he liked in a person, and what he didn't. While not a prude, religion was important to him; he didn't care if his future companion was Christian or Jewish, but he needed to be one or the other and active within the church or synagogue. Politically, he fell in line with the rest of his family, all who were fiscally conservative but socially progressive. The Randolphs were some of the few wealthy holdouts of the Democratic party in the Deep

South. He was extremely wary of gay men who called themselves "Log Cabin Republicans."

In his 'must haves' for his companion, there was a need of a career. He didn't mind if it were working for an hourly wage earned at a factory, but the fellow had to be gainfully employed; Baylor wasn't looking to be anyone's sugar daddy, or baby, for that matter. Age wasn't a deal, either, but after considerable thought, he provided as being open to all from "25 to 60."

Another very important part of his considerations was the activity level of the man. Baylor lived for tennis and golf and loved to fish and hunt. He was OK dating a bookworm, but only if the fellow could put down the literature long enough for nine holes, or a day out on the boat.

Luckily, the site allowed for more than one physical location; since it catered to business professionals, and men who were financially successful, many had more than one home and traveled frequently. Baylor plugged in both Savannah and Highlands; he also added Asheville since it was the closest major city to the mountain house. Finally, after three hours and three glasses of Knob Creek, he followed Grand Martha's sage advice, "nothing ventured, sugar, nothing gained."

The last box was checked. He hit 'enter,' and sat back to wonder what would be sitting in his email file the next morning.

Chapter 23

Instead of shopping on Fifth Avenue as planned, Lily found herself in Whittaker's midtown law office. She had arrived early and was sitting by herself, looking over the green beauty of Piedmont Park and the shimmering water of Lake Clara Mead. In all of her sixty-plus years, life had never been so out of control and frustrating. And Lily hated not being in control. As maddening and spiteful as they were, Lily easily handled the predicaments of the plane and auto presented by Martha. While Lily loved the convenience and luxury of the Gulfstream jets, she could comfortably afford to travel first class wherever she wanted to go, and if push came to shove, she could always hire a private plane; they were easily attained these days. With the car, she simply called the local Mercedes dealership and spoke with the owner. She had recently ridden with his wife, Lila, up to Charleston for a bridal shower, and thought the big S-Class her friend drove was the most stylish and comfortable car she'd seen. Four hours later, there was an exact replica of the same make and model waiting outside her front door. All she had to do was sign that she'd taken delivery.

This new wrinkle in her life, another courtesy of Martha Stephens Randolph, was a much bigger hurdle to clear. Since she and Add had moved into the Gamble townhouse on Forsyth Park, it was understood Lily could make that her home indefinitely. Baylor enjoyed living in the commodious carriage house in back, and Lily figured he would eventually move into Martha's side of the building when the old bag finally kicked the bucket. But Martha had not kicked the bucket. She had instead kicked Lily out of her home.

The eviction notice had arrived the previous morning, right as Lily was finishing breakfast; a copy had been delivered at almost the exact same time to Whittaker. It was, as the memo had stated on Tuesday, short and to the point. Basically, Lily had ninety days from time of receipt to vacate, in its entirety, the home she'd lived in for almost twenty years. She didn't break a vase nor throw another spectacular hissy fit as she had when she received the news about the plane and car. She actually rather expected this move on behalf of Martha. It was just a matter of time, so she was more mentally prepared. Ninety days, though, was a short turn-around. Where would she go and what would she do? She of course had the means to purchase any available upscale property in the entire state; the problem was rather having the time to find something to accommodate her furnishings, particularly her expansive wardrobe. The abode would have to be in a suitable location, and one fitting to her exacting tastes. Too, there was the social question. How would she handle this embarrassing situation: being thrown out of her beautiful and historically significant home, one that had been on numerous tours and featured in several national magazines?

The only possible way to save face was to make it known, as soon as possible, that she had decided to downsize and simplify her life. Add had been gone several years now, and the twins would graduate UVA this next term. Lily already spent half her time in Highlands, arriving in May and staying through Thanksgiving. The explanation would be perfectly plausible, and she doubted anyone would bat an eye. But again, where would she go on such short notice?

As she pondered this question for the hundredth time that morning, Whitt came into the room, dutifully kissed her on the cheek, and sat behind his desk. Looking across at Lily, who even in the middle of a crisis look perfectly turned out, he commented with a bemused expression "Well, good morning, Miss Mary Sunshine."

"Hush. I'm not in the mood for your humor. Baylor has inherited your sarcasm, and frankly it gets quite stale after a while from the both of you." Lily narrowed her eyes at him with impatience.

"Lord, sister dear, you are so incredibly thin skinned. Lighten up some. You knew from the start something like this might happen. 'If you can't run with the big dogs, you gotta stay on the porch, or maybe better, 'if you can't stand the heat, then you need to get outta the kitchen'." Whitt laughed and reached for his bottle of water next to his computer.

"I swear on Mama's grave, Whittaker, if you throw one more insufferable saying my way, I will find another attorney to represent this case."

"Ah, sis, you're just no fun anymore," he said, ignoring her threat and taking a long drink of water. "OK, let's talk about this morning. I know you and Leigh Anna are disappointed about canceling the New York trip, but you needed to be here anyway, so it all worked out for the best. This morning was the only time I could set up a meeting with Dr. Lockwood; otherwise, we'd have to wait another three weeks. He should be here any minute now." Looking at his watch, he saw it was just one minute until nine, the set appointment hour.

Lily knew of the doctor's credentials. He was a renowned psychiatrist, and his works had been published in some of the world's most distinguished medical journals. Also, an impressive orator, Dr. Lockwood lectured around the globe in his areas of expertise, mental stability and cognizant reasoning. His extensive knowledge, and talent at the podium, placed him in high demand for giving expert testimony in both civil and criminal cases. A few seconds later a knock on the door announced Whitt's secretary, and with her was the renowned Dr. Lockwood. Lily saw instantly he would cut a striking figure on the witness stand; while Jackson Lockwood was in his mid-sixties, he looked a good decade younger, with tanned features framed by a thick head of dark hair graying elegantly at the temples. The way he wore his expensive and conservatively cut suit Lily could tell he was also very physically fit. He looked like a Southern Gregory Peck at the height of his career.

In his rich but quiet baritone voice, the one that gilded Lockwood's presentations, he spoke first to Lily. "It is an honor and pleasure to meet you, Mrs. Randolph." Turning to Whitt, he extended his hand and followed with, "Good morning, counselor. Thank you for thinking of me in this matter."

Whitt pointed to the chair and motioned for the doctor to sit down. "Well, Jackson, Lily and I certainly appreciate you seeing us on such short notice. I know what a busy schedule you keep."

Giving a warm smile, the doctor answered. "No worries at all, glad it worked out. But I do fly out to London for an extended trip later this week, so let's get started. Too, at a thousand dollars an hour, I'm sure that while you want me to be thorough, you also want me to be aware of the time." Turning to Lily, he continued. "Mrs. Randolph, Whitt has filled me in on the contents of the suit and what you are asking me to do. The first thing I need is to read and analyze the letters from Martha to you. Do you have them in your possession?"

Returning the doctor's steady gaze, she said, "Please, call me Lily." Then turning to her brother, she continued, "Whittaker has the original letters."

Her brother nodded and picked up a large manila envelope and handed it to him across the table. "Here are copies of the eight letters, all in Martha's handwriting, plus two Lily received from Martha's cousin in England."

Jackson untied the string and pulled out the contents of the package. Glancing over the twenty-some pages, he remarked, almost to himself, "What extraordinary handwriting."

Lily nodded in agreement. "Yes, Martha's cursive is almost like calligraphy. She claimed it was ingrained when she attended Ashley Hall," she said, referring to the exclusive girls' school in Charleston. "Does her handwriting have anything to say about her state of mind?"

"No, no, sorry, just marveling at what is a lost art these days." Looking up from the photocopies, he continued, "Of course the contents, especially the wording and sequencing, will provide tremendous insight. Do you mind giving me, in your own words, what these letters say?"

Lily gave a short cough to clear her throat and answer. "As my brother has probably told you, Martha had a very, very difficult time after her husband passed away. His death followed the loss of my husband, her only child. While we all expected the grief to be painful for her, we never expected it in such intensity."

Dr. Lockwood held up his hand. "Sorry to interrupt, but why did you all find the degree of grief so surprising?"

Lily thought for a moment. "Let me restate. We were rather surprised at how the grieving had such a profound effect on Martha. She has always been known for her astoundingly strong opinions and matter-of-fact way of dealing with life. My other brother, who is the model of a stern and impassive federal judge," she turned for a second and gave Whitt a knowing look, "remarked just the other day that Martha was a "formidable" woman. Her grandchildren and great-grandchildren even call her "Grand Martha." She always had nerves of steel. But then, after Addison Senior's death, she seemed to close in and retreat into herself. She said little, just went through the motions for the extensive visitation and then the funeral itself. She commented to me and my two sons afterwards that she 'thought she was losing her mind' and could not bear to be in Savannah a moment longer. She then moved to England to live with a cousin without consulting any of the immediate family. Martha stayed with him for more than three years with no return visits home until earlier this month."

Jackson nodded. "It may not seem to make sense, but oftentimes traumatic experiences involving the loss of loved ones will bear down harder on persons with strong, precise personalities more than those who aren't quite as unbending. Now back to the letters." He gave a nod of toward Lily.

"Yes, the letters. Martha is still old school and often chooses paper and pen rather than emails or phone calls. As does her British cousin, Anthony, whom she lived with during this period in London and Chipping Camden. The first two letters received came from Anthony and were brief but friendly. Both basically shared Martha had settled in comfortably, and while her state of mind was still rather withdrawn, he believed she'd be back to her old self soon enough. Then the first letter from Martha came about a month after she moved to England. She states she was still in the midst of great despair over the loss of Addison, her husband, and Add, her son. A few letters later she wrote she was seeking the counsel of a local curate, one who apparently was known for his guidance during grief, and that she was making progress. All in all, the letters to me from Martha relate that she was overwhelmed and doing her best to reconcile herself with the situation."

"While she was in England, was this the only correspondence you had with Martha Randolph? Were there phone calls, or other letters, perhaps?"

"The first year the letters were my only contact with her, along with the ones written back in return. I have to confess that I, too, still like to converse in the written form. Anyway, all of the letters you have here came within a twelve-month period, roughly. I did receive a few phone calls from my mother-in-law last year, just routine chats. One was to wish me a happy birthday, another was on the anniversary of my husband's death, and the last she asked about the wedding arrangements for a family friend. There were two additional letters, all from the second year she was abroad, but neither made any mention of her mental health or how she was feeling."

The psychiatrist held out the stack of papers in his hand slightly toward Lily. "Are those two letters copied here?"

"No, since they didn't indicate anything was wrong, I didn't include them. Should I have?"

"I would like to see them, yes." Turning to Whitt, he said, "Please have them scanned and emailed to me." He then continued on to Lily, explaining, "Even though they might not definitively state what was going through her mind at the time, the contents could still help me with the overall assessment."

Whitt spoke up at this point and directed his question toward Dr. Lockwood. "So, doc, I know this is premature, but given what you know at this point, what kind of case do you think we have? Is it worth pursuing, in your professional opinion?"

Jackson tapped the stack of letters against his leg a couple of times and smiled at Lily and Whitt, both who had expectant looks on their faces. "You know the law much better than I, counselor, but we just have to put doubt into the minds of the judge and jury, correct?"

The attorney answered in the affirmative. "Yep, we'd need to convince the court that Martha didn't have the capacity to fully understand what she was doing when she made the decision we're contesting. If they doubt her stability, we can almost certainly have the transfer of the property to the Trust declared null and void."

"Well, then, I'd say you have an extremely strong opportunity to save Ship Watch. The letters here are the same as having Martha on the stand admitting to the jury that she was not of sound mind. Too, when I depose her, I'm certain that you will be pleased with the results." Looking back and forth at the two sitting across from him, Jackson gave a small shrug and added, "Not to sound conceited, but I know how to make even the most confident of persons come to doubt themselves. It's my job."

With that, Dr. Lockwood stood to shake Whitt's hand. "I'll reach back out to you after analyzing the letters. Give me a week and you'll receive an email with preliminary findings." Then, looking at Lily, he gave a slight bow. "Lily, I'll be in touch after returning from my trip. I will have a number of questions to ask you to fill in with more background. Maybe we can do so over lunch, or perhaps maybe dinner?" He gave her a confident smile that had won over many a juror.

A bit of color rose into Lily's cheeks, and her right eyebrow raised in an arch that seemed to her brother it would soon meet her hairline. He restrained a short laugh and said, "Jackson, Lily's schedule has her all over the South this summer from Savannah to Atlanta to Highlands. I'll work with you to set up the next meeting with the two of us."

Undeterred, Jackson continued to look at the very attractive woman. "Highlands for the season, I see. I'll be summering at Lake Toxaway; maybe we can make arrangements to meet while in the cool of the mountains?"

Smiling, Whittaker came around from his desk, put a hand on the doctor's forearm, and guided him toward the door. "Safe travels,

Jackson, and we'll look forward to hearing from you in about a week. Enjoy your time in Europe."

Dr. Lockwood gave a last look over his shoulder as he exited the room to give Lily an almost undiscernible wink. Lily returned his flirting look with a bored stare. Whitt closed the door and turned to his sister. He was grinning ear to ear. "Wipe that smirk off your face, Whittaker, and sit down. What a cheeky man. He certainly is full of himself." Lily flushed, and crossed and re-crossed her legs in a bit of frustration.

"Oh, come on. Take a compliment with some grace, sis dear. He's handsome, rich, and single. Straight, too. You don't find that too often in Atlanta. At least not in that combination."

Lily rolled her eyes. "I don't care if he is the Prince of Wales, I'm not accustomed to someone being so forward the first time I meet them. And no, I'm not meeting him for lunch or dinner, regardless of how talented he is."

Whitt leaned back on the wide, mahogany desk that had been his father's. "Let's be serious here, on a personal note. Add has been gone now for how many years? Five? Six? You're an incredibly attractive and interesting woman. You might as well face the fact that you're going to have men chasing after you. And what would hurt to have some nice company? Nobody said you had to get married." As much as he teased his older sister, he loved her dearly. "And besides," he added with a devilish look, "you certainly don't look sixty-nine."

Lily took her right foot and kicked her brother squarely in the shin with a highly polished Ferragamo. "Ow, damn, now that hurt, Lil." Whit reached down to rub his leg and gave his sister an exasperated look.

"You know full and well I'm not sixty-nine. I'm just barely on the other side of my sixth decade." She laughed and swiped at her brother again with her foot; Whitt hopped quickly out of the way and took safety on the other side of his desk, sitting down. Both started laughing at the same time, enjoying the moment. Lily thought again how much her youngest son had taken after his uncle; they both were handsome devils with the same features and coloring, as well as sense of humor. Baylor was just larger and more squarely built, having inherited at least a few of the Randolph genes. Being in Whitt's company always made Lily feel loved, even if he did aggravate the stew out of her at times. But that is what baby brothers did, didn't they?

"So, Mr. Baylor, tell me. Based on what Dr. Charming had to say, what do you think?" Lily felt confident but wanted some reassurance from her brother. Shrugging nonchalantly, he answered, "Honestly, I always have doubts in any case. It's what keeps me working and seeking until the bitter end. However, I cannot imagine a judge or jury not finding in our favor, based on those letters you have from Martha. Like the doctor said, she admits it herself: she was not in her right mind. In my humble opinion, it should be a slam dunk."

Lily considered Whitt's summation. "Then it all is worth it: losing my house, my car, my rights at the company. If we can save Ship Watch for the twins, I'm a happy woman." Standing, she walked over and kissed her brother on the top of his head. "I'll see you tonight for dinner. I'm so looking forward to being with you all."

With that, Lily made her way through the hall to the elevators and down to the garage. As she sat down in her new automobile, she thought, *This Mercedes is so much nicer than that big, bulky SUV.* She also wondered how the Navigator would smell by now. The morning after she had received the memo, she took the car out of the garage and parked it on the open street in front of the house. She then emptied an entire can of tuna fish into the spare tire compartment. It was still sitting there this morning according to Benny, baking two days under the hot, semi-tropical Savannah sunshine. It made her smile.

Chapter 24

Lovey, April Anne, Baylor, and Patrick had left Savannah that morning just as Lily and Whitt were meeting with Dr. Lockwood. The three-car caravan made quite a sight, and turned a number of heads, as they passed through sleepy small towns on the backroads leading to Highlands. Patrick drove the vintage two-toned Bentley with Lovey in tow, while her cousin drove his sleek BMW. April followed behind in a black 2005 Cadillac Sedan de Ville. The old car was in immaculate condition with only a little over 40,000 miles on the odometer. According to Lovey, it has been her late father's last car, and "she just could not bear to part with it" for sentimental reasons. It drove like a boat. April didn't own an auto, having lived in NYC for so long, so Lovey lent her the sedan to use while staying in Highlands. When they stopped in tiny Sparta, Georgia, for gas, the station attendant asked if Lovey and Baylor were movie stars. Lovey laughed and said no, but she wished they were. When the big lady, who was a cross between Nell Carter and Della Reese, complimented Lovey on her over-sized leopard skin and zebra print bangle bracelets, Lovey took them off and insisted the cashier keep them. "Honey, I got dozens of those babies. And they will look so good on you." In turn, all four of them got a huge hug from the astounded woman. As they drove away from the station, Miss Maxine stood outside and waved goodbye, her new jewelry circling each of her wrists.

A few hours later, the entourage enjoyed a fine, family style lunch at the famous Dillard House in Rabun County, just inside the state line from North Carolina. April thought the spread looked like a Sunday pot-luck dinner at a Baptist church. There were platters of fried chicken, glazed ham, and sliced roast beef along with bowls of creamed corn, stewed squash, pole beans, cole slaw, pickled beets, and baked apples, all set out on their table along with biscuits, cornbread, and a thick, rich banana pudding. As the lunch progressed, Baylor mentioned to the group, in an aside, that he had joined an online dating service. That was all it took to get Lovey in high gear; she had a thousand questions and was effusive as only she could be in telling her cousin how happy she was for him. It was strange, though, April mused, that the more Lovey talked, and Baylor elaborated, the more Patrick withdrew from the conversation. The young man actually stopped eating, and just sat and stared out the windows overlooking the valley and farmland in the distance. After several minutes into the mostly one topic conversation, Lovey looked over at Patrick and asked, "Hey there. Earth to Patrick. Aren't you just so, so happy for Baylor? He may be on his way to finding himself Mr. Right after all these years." Patrick didn't even glance at Lovey; he simply got up, put his napkin in his chair, and left the room.

All three were stunned as they watched Patrick retreat through a side door and walk out into the restaurant gardens. Baylor shook his head and looked over at Lovey. "Hey, what's with Patrick? Was he this way the whole drive up here this morning?"

"No, no," she said, shaking her head. "He was his usual jolly self. But you know, every once in a while, he can jump from one mood to another. He's been like that since he came home this last time." Lovey noticed the puzzled look on April's face. "Oh, hon. I haven't told you, sorry. Patrick was in Special Ops and did two tours in Afghanistan, and though he won't come out and tell us, I think he has PTSD. He was highly decorated, and loved, loved, loved his job. But when he returned this last time, he said he wasn't going back." She had the start of tears in her eyes as she looked out at her cousin, who stood alone and forlorn on the front lawn of the Inn.

April joined the other two as they gazed out the window. Thinking about what Lovey just told her, it all did seem to make sense. While Patrick had a wonderful sense of humor, the young man carried a seriousness about him that bespoke a military background. He was certainly built for Special Ops, or at least in April's mind: he had a solid, square frame with a presence that was alert and flexible. She had also wondered about his age when she first learned he only had one semester left in graduate school. While he had boyish good looks with deep dimples and bright blue eyes, all set off with a thick head of shortly trimmed red and gold hair, he appeared older than someone in graduate school. Adding the numbers together, with five years of school and five or six in the military, she figured he was somewhere near thirty.

"He doesn't seem to get like this until he is in a group of people. When it is just the two of us, he rarely has one of these swings, if ever," Lovey said, shaking her head. "I just don't understand it."

"Well, I can't say the same. Even before he left for college, he was always so quiet around me, almost tongue-tied. It seems to have gotten worse since he's been home." Baylor fiddled with his tea glass, rattling the ice. "Do you think it's because I'm gay and that makes him uncomfortable? My dating life is all we talked about for the last half hour."

Lovey thought for a moment before answering. "You know, he does rather clam up when you're around. When he does talk during those times, he's just this side of being timid. It's like he's scared to say anything." Shaking her head again, she continued, "But to answer your question, no, I don't believe it has anything to do with you, or your lifestyle. I've never, ever heard Patrick say one thing even slightly homophobic, or racist, for that matter."

"OK, if you say so." Baylor was not overly convinced. He stood and pulled out the chairs for Lovey and April. "Let's get on the road and to the house in time to unpack all of our stuff and get settled before dinner. Brother said he was going to grill some steaks tonight, and we've got to stop and get some wine along the way." He shook his head and chuckled. "Lord, we just finished this huge meal, and my mind is now set directly on what's next to eat."

Lovey patted him on the cheek. "I know, Handsome. We Southerners do live from one meal to the next. Ooh, and speaking of food, let's don't forget to buy some jars of that Dillard House apple butter at the check-out. It is divine on a hot, buttered biscuit."

As the three made their way back to the cars, Patrick sat behind the wheel of the Bentley, a wet handkerchief wadded in his right hand. *Lord, please give me the strength to make it through this summer,* he prayed silently, watching Baylor stride over to his BMW. He then sighed, turned on the radio, and eased his neck onto the head rest to wait for his cousin, who had stopped to talk to a couple of tourists who had crossed her garrulous path.

Chapter 25

As Lily walked through the front doors, she marveled as she did each time she came into the venerable Piedmont Driving Club, taking in the ornate and elaborate plaster crown moldings, coffered ceilings, and gilt finished crystal chandeliers. Memories flashed back of all the happy days spent there as a youngster and later as a debutante, and the crowning moment: the dinner and dancing on her wedding night. Her parents had hired the Lester Lanin Orchestra to play, and she and Add, Jr. had laughed and danced well past midnight with the more than two hundred guests in the club's elegant ballroom.

Lily basked in these warm reminisces as the host walked her back to the slate veranda where her elder sister-in-law, Eloise, sat waiting for her. Eloise was a Calhoun of South Carolina, and her mother one of the heralded Pinckneys from that state. She was a distinguished woman who carried her wealth and privilege in quiet reserve, the perfect match for Lily's serious minded and cerebral brother. Eloise had long been friends with Barbara Bush, who babysat a young Eloise when the former first lady was a student at the exclusive Ashley Hall in Charleston. It was through Eloise's ties with Barbara that her brother became friends with George H. W., leading him to become undersecretary of the treasury and later a federal judge. Eloise stood up from her wicker chair and gave Lily a warm hug and a light kiss on each cheek. "Lily, you look beautiful as always; here, take a seat, my dear," she said, placing a hand on the chair next to her. "I took the liberty of ordering your cocktail. I trust you still prefer Campari and soda." A tall glass filled with tiny bubbles and a bright green slice of lime sat waiting atop one of the Club's monogrammed napkins.

Sitting down, she answered, "Thank you, Eloise, I do need something cool and refreshing. It is a hot spring this year, don't you think?" She took a refreshing sip and continued, "Oh, yes, that is just what the doctor ordered." Looking at her sister-in-law, she smiled and said, "You look beautiful as well. Envy is not a nice emotion, but every time I see you, I wish my hair was still its natural color." One of Eloise's most noticeable features was her coal black hair, which even at 76, she had never had to color. "Love your Barbara pearls, too, by the way. Is that the strand she gave you?"

Eloise sat her glass of white wine down and touched the triple-strand of faux jewelry that her friend had gifted her several years ago and with a small laugh, said, "Yes, they are, and I've bought myself a few more like them with different clasps. I've found that they hide very well this droopy, wrinkled old neck of mine, and are a whole lot less expensive than a seeing a plastic surgeon."

"Seriously, you look stunning." She admired the woman sitting across from her, someone who had been like a surrogate mother since Lily'd lost her own more than thirty years ago. With Eloise's lush hair, enormous and expressive brown eyes, and sculpted cheekbones, she was considered one of Atlanta's most lovely, and gracious, ladies. "Thank you, too, for orchestrating the dinner tonight. It will do my soul good to be in y'alls company."

"Darling, no need for thanks. We are just dying to see you and spend some time together. I don't think we've had you all to ourselves since you came to visit at Easter. That was two years ago, or three?"

"I can't recall; time has just flown by these last few years." Glancing down at her Tiffany watch to check the time, she asked, "When will my two brothers and Leigh Anna arrive? I know Brantley doesn't like to eat late."

"Whitt and Leigh Anna should pick up Brant right about now, so they'll be here about twenty minutes or so. Our dinner reservation is at 7:00, so we have a few minutes to chat alone." Taking another short sip of wine, she placed the glass back on the table and sat back in her chair. Her expression turned thoughtful as she continued. "I really want to have a serious discussion with you, Lily, and ask that you consider carefully what I say, and know that I do so out of love. You've been not only like a loving sister to me all these years, but almost like a daughter." Eloise reached over to squeeze Lily's arm with what she hoped would convey warm affection.

Lily took in a short breath and tried not to let herself go rigid. She knew she had the tendency to become defensive, and the last thing she wanted was to offend Eloise. She was so very tired, though, of heavy topics and just wanted a night of laughter and congenial companionship. Keeping her emotions in check, she simply said, "I'm listening. Please, go on."

"This whole situation with your lawsuit against Martha will have some very real implications for you. I don't know that you really considered how bringing into question her mental stability, in such a public way, will change things for you.

Lily started to speak, but Eloise held up her hand in a motion for her to stop. "Let me finish, Lily. I'll hear you out, but please listen to what I have to say." Pressing on, she continued. "I realize your social standing in Savannah is at the very pinnacle of the top circle, but that will soon change. While you married into the Randolph family, you are not, or ever will be, a native Savannahian, as is Martha Randolph. I don't care how many boards you've chaired or balls you've underwritten. The old guard there will close ranks on you and probably have already begun to do so. Oh, you'll be invited to the big events and parties, but the asks to the small gatherings, the special dinners, and intimate get togethers will cease. The 'newbies' in town," and the 'climbers,'" Eloise gestured making quotation marks with each hand, "will want to keep up with you, but my dear sister, you have effectively shut yourself out of the group of friends you've had since you moved to the coast."

A thousand thoughts raced through Lily's mind as she struggled for words. Her first reaction was *No. You are wrong. What a ridiculous thing to say.*

Yet as Eloise looked on at her with a patient stare, Lily came to realize her sister-in-law was right. She had seen it happen before to a number of women and men over the years. Savannah was a welcoming city, and hospitality there could not be warmer or more cordial, but if you stepped out of the established boundaries of polite society, and particularly if you offended someone of the inner circle, the doors would be firmly shut.

Lily closed her eyes and sighed. "Eloise, I have been so caught up with the sheer shock of Ship Watch being given away, and what it would mean to the twins, that I've just not considered anything else." She reached for her drink and added, "Well I suppose I can now stop shaving my legs and can start wearing Birkenstocks to Mass; no one will care."

Eloise could not help herself and laughed out loud, choking a bit on her wine. "Oh, Lily, darling, I know this is all so serious, but just the thought of you in a pair of hippy sandals and hairy legs is priceless." She reached over and again squeezed her sister-in-law's arm. "I'm glad you aren't upset with me about bringing this up. I just," she paused for a moment and nodded once, "want you to consider what Brant mentioned the other day."

Seeing the puzzled look on Lily's face, she went on, "That you should move back to Atlanta, my dear. While your family didn't settle Savannah, you *are* an Atlanta Baylor, and this city wouldn't be what it is today without both sides of your family. You'll always have prominent standing here, and I can promise you'll be welcomed back with open arms. As a matter of fact, I know for certain that there is a board seat waiting for you both at the High Museum *and* at The Atlanta History Center." She smiled and gave an encouraging look. "What do you think?"

"I can't promise anything, but I'll think about it. To be honest, when walking into the Club earlier I thought to myself how wonderful it was to be back. So many beautiful memories here." She stopped talking and took a moment to take in the view of the park, and the stunning skyline of midtown over the treetops. After all she had been through in Savannah — the death of her husband, the public divorce of Trip and Jana, and now this horrible battle over Ship Watch — maybe it was time for a change. She smiled, titled her head, and looked fondly at her sister-in-law. "Well, if I do return to Atlanta, you've got to help me find a suitable place to live. I can't bear the awful traffic here, so I want something nearby, or back in the old neighborhood off West Paces."

"I've already thought of that and have taken the liberty of arranging brunch with William Dozier in the morning back here at the Club. He is the absolute best realtor in this city and always has a cachet of 'secret' properties that aren't yet on the market." Eloise looked on excitedly at Lily as she spoke, happy to see that Lily was indeed thinking about coming home to Atlanta.

"*William* Dozier?" Lily asked. "Is that Lovey's ex-husband you're talking about? I heard he was in real estate here, but the last time I saw him he was called Billy Joe. What happened there, pray tell?"

"Yes, the one and only. Apparently, the sound of "William Joseph" has more upscale appeal, and he has done quite well for himself here in this market."

Lily laughed again. The last time she'd seen Billy Joe, or William Joseph, he was outside the MacGregor mansion, wearing cutoff jeans and a Lynyrd Skynyrd T-shirt, supervising a crew of men moving his furniture and boxes into two large U-Haul trailers. "That sounds fine, Eloise. I'm happy for his success, and Lovey seems to have forgiven him completely. Did you hear why she divorced him, and what she caught him doing?" she asked with a conspiratorial look.

"Noooo, do tell. I'm all ears." Glancing at her watch, she added, "but tell me on the way to the ladies' room; it is just a few minutes before seven now." The two women picked up their clutches and headed for the door. Both needed to freshen their lipstick, and neither would ever dream of doing so in public. "Well, sister dear, according to Baylor, who just recently told me, it happened on a Caribbean cruise to St. Barts, and apparently it involved a hot tub *and* a Bulgarian butler," Lily dramatically stage whispered into Eloise's ear as they stepped back inside, arm in arm.

Chapter 26

The next evening Martha sat propped up in bed; she had started re-reading Eugenia Price's St. Simon's trilogy, a series she had always loved as it so romantically describes the beautiful Golden Isles of Georgia. She could not keep her mind on the pages, though, and sleep eluded her as well. Her first Saturday back on Sea Island had gone perfectly, and she kept reliving it from start to finish. Although the twins were at M'liss's house just a few blocks over, she had promised herself not to interfere with them this summer. She figured the last thing they wanted was a doddering old granny snooping into their business. Yet it was the twins who reached out first and invited themselves over for an afternoon swim.

They arrived with their four friends in tow, and what charming young people they were. Polite, deferential, and all politically savvy, they each were easy to engage in conversation, and seemed to genuinely enjoy hers and Auggie's company. Augustus could always hold an audience in sway, though; he was an expert in the courtroom, and people gravitated to his eloquence and soft patrician accent which sounded a bit British. Peyton and Ray had hovered over their great-grandmother all afternoon, and she'd reveled in the attention. While they were identical, she could easily tell them apart: it was the way they carried themselves, even as toddlers. Peyton was seriously determined; even reaching for a bottle was a deliberate movement. Ray, on the other hand, seemed to be all over the room at one time, jumping, running, and playing with abandon. Their characteristics as children carried through as young adults and had dictated their professional careers; Ray was following in his uncle Baylor's footsteps and would be competing on the pro-golf circuit, and after graduation Peyton would pursue his master's in international business. He hoped to attend Wharton, and Martha had no doubt that he'd be accepted. Martha thought contentedly more than once that day that the two young men, with their Nordic good looks inherited from both their mother and Lily's Stephens' side of the family, were a golden pair.

By the end of the afternoon, Martha offered to feed them supper, and instead of getting dressed and going to the Cloister for dinner as she offered, the group asked to stay on around the pool and order in barbeque. Apparently, *the* place for ribs and Brunswick stew was a place called Southern Soul on the adjacent island of St. Simons, and the twins drove over, along with Martha's platinum Amex card, and brought back platters of smoked meat, cole slaw, stew, fried okra, and two key lime pies. Auggie called the Club and had a case of wine and another of beer delivered, and the group sat outside, eating, talking, and drinking, until way past dark. The students finally walked home, full and content, just past ten o'clock.

Martha had not brought up any talk about the lawsuit, and neither had the twins. While she was pretty certain they knew about it, no one spoiled the evening with family drama. Auggie did his part by steering the conversation toward golf, travel, the best places to eat in New York's theater district, and a variety of other light and entertaining subjects.

The thought of Auggie also kept her mind whirling. Being back home, and alone with him, had brought back many memories, most of which were buried away long ago. Thinking of those halcyon days just after WWII, Martha placed her copy of *Lighthouse* on the bedside table, placed her feet in her slippers, and walked over to the window. She peered through a small crack in the sheers and saw a light was on in the other master suite across the garden; apparently Auggie was still awake.

How long had it been since she'd allowed herself to visit back on that time of life? Both sets of their parents had built large, rambling cottages at Tybee on the ocean side of Butler Avenue. Their fathers were first cousins, each an only son and close like two brothers. Martha was a rising sophomore at the Pape School, and Augustus a senior at Benedictine Academy. While there were a number of other young people their age on the island that summer, Martha and Auggie were most often in each other's company because of the close relationship of their parents. Their days were spent splashing in the surf, and the evenings sitting on one of their screened porches, while indoors their parents' played records, drank martinis, and smoked cigarettes, enjoying life after those horrendous years of the Second World War. They paid little attention to the two youngsters, who, with each passing day, were drawn closer and closer together. Soon the teens were inseparable, and all came to a head one late July afternoon. While playing touch football, Martha and Auggie fell down atop one another.

When they stopped giggling and laughing, they found themselves in a very hot, long embrace, and a lasting kiss. Martha's mother had stepped onto the porch just as the kiss was in full bloom. She'd ordered her daughter immediately into the house and sent Auggie home with a piercing look. After a chilly dressing down, one that not only shamed her for kissing her cousin but also for doing so like 'a commoner' in public for all the world to see, Martha spent two days crying and refused to come out of her room. When she finally emerged, she learned that Auggie had been shipped off to Phillips Academy in New Hampshire for his senior year. He stayed in the Northeast for college and finished law school at Harvard. Afterwards he spent several years in England at Oxford, rarely ever coming home during all those years.

When he did move back to Savannah, with a hint of a British accent, Martha was by then married to Addison and pregnant with their son. They never spoke of that summer, and it took years for them to find a comfortable peace in each other's company. Augustus had remained a bachelor his entire life, and Martha knew, in her heart, that it was because of her. She had found the letters he had written to her while at Phillips, professing his undying love, in the bottom of her mother's Chippendale wardrobe after she had died. Her marriage to Addison had been strong, and she had loved him dearly. But she admitted to herself, now almost seven decades later, that she had always, and would always, love Augustus Gamble Stephens, regardless of their kinship.

And what, pray tell, am I going to do about it? she thought, taking another discrete glance out of the window. *I'm always offering the advice to others 'nothing ventured, nothing gained' and here I stand pining away like a schoolgirl.* She stepped back and into the bathroom. *Auggie is too much of a gentleman to make the first move; if left up to him we'll keep doing this arms-length dance to the grave.* The memory of her Mother and the sharp admonishing words about inappropriate relations between cousins flashed through her mind, but Martha pushed it quickly aside. *Please. We're both in our eighties. No chance of any two-headed babies at this point.*

She brushed her thick white hair with a few thoughtful strokes, dabbed a bit of Chanel No. 5 behind her ears and put on a bathrobe. Giving herself a quick glance in the beveled mirror, Martha walked into the hallway and determinedly made her way toward the opposite wing of her house to the room where a light was still burning after all these years.

Part II

July

Chapter 27

April sat outside at the Randolphs' Highlands estate; since her arrival she'd spent hours at a time looking out on the beautiful and expansive view of the Blue Ridge Mountains. From the high elevation, both South Carolina and Georgia were visible in the distance as the ancient hills rolled south and east. Dusk was settling in, and the sky was a magical rosemary blue tinged with blush and rose. Stars were beginning to twinkle, and a perfectly shaped crescent moon hung over the next mountain. The air was cool and crisp and smelled of the clean scents of fir trees and pines.

"It certainly has been an incredible place to spend a summer," she said aloud to Tammy and George, who sat on either side of her rocking chair. Not only was the location right out of a storybook, but the accommodation was five-star as well. The 'Motel 6' was handsomely and comfortably appointed with classic American Arts & Crafts furnishings and fabrics, and her kitchenette stocked with compact, yet top grade, appliances. She spent most of her days writing in the company of the two Labradors. She looked over at 'the pool' Lovey and Baylor had first told her about. There wasn't an inch of concrete or an ounce of chlorine to be found. Rather, the swimming area was a clear, pebble-lined pond surrounded by laurels, evergreens, and flowering rhododendrons, complete with a small, cascading waterfall. Tammy and George spent hours each day in the icy water, frolicking and playing while April would sit on the rock outcroppings and dangle her feet into the 'hotel pool.'

The main house sat to the side and behind the terrace. It was a traditional Highlands style, two and a half-storied cottage boasting a pair of impressive native stone chimneys and sided with dark, bottle green cedar shingles. The frames of the multi paned windows were painted white and graced with matching flower boxes, each showcasing a profusion of bright red geraniums. A massive, wooden front door, weathered to a perfect shade of gray and accented with wrought iron hardware, centered the front of the cottage.

April was nervously looking forward to the evening ahead. While she and Trip had spent a great deal of time together during the past couple of months, it was always in the company of others. Tonight, though, Baylor was in Asheville with a fellow he had met through the dating service, and Lovey was attending a party in nearby Cashiers with Lachlan, with Patrick serving as chauffeur. When Trip learned that everyone would be otherwise occupied, he asked April if she would go to dinner with him that evening in town. She made the quick decision not to play coy and asked him directly if the invitation was meant as a date. He answered with a very warm smile and said, "That would be my intention, yes, ma'am."

So promptly at 7 p. m. Addison the Third walked out of his Motel 6 accommodations and strolled over to April Anne as she rocked. The dogs thumped their tails in unison as he reached out his hand for her to rise out of the chair. Her heart thumped, too, along with the dogs' tails, and she worried it might be beating loud enough for him to actually hear. There was something so very strong and comforting about this man that attracted her like no other fellow she'd ever met. As he pulled her up from the rocker, she got just a faint whiff of his aftershave and had the so 'unlike April Anne' thought that he smelled good enough to eat. Grinning slightly, Trip gave her an inquisitive look as she stood before him. "Are you OK? You seem a bit flushed."

"Oh, I'm fine, I'm just going over in my mind a scene for my next chapter and I'm a bit vexed trying to figure out the right move for one of the characters." *Yeah, that move would be me burying my head in your thick, hairy chest and deep breathing in Old Spice.*

To try and get her mind off the fact that her libido was going into overdrive, she looked down at the two Labs and said, "I'm really looking forward to dinner, but hate leaving these fur babies behind. I certainly have gotten attached to them." Both dogs were looking up adoringly at April as she spoke

Trip chuckled and reached down to rub each pup between the ears. "They seem to have fallen in love with you, too. No worries, though, they're coming with us. Hope you don't mind. I reserved a table on the outdoor patio, and the owner is very dog friendly. He'll even have two bowls of water and some Beggin' Strips ready for them when we eat."

Jingling keys in his hands made the dogs race to the Suburban, and all twelve legs piled in and headed to Adolpho's, a lakeside eatery that had been in business since the 60s. Their table sat alongside a trickling stream looking into the woods of Appalachia. The food was fabulous: dinner was a shared Caesar salad tossed table side, and two orders of pan-roasted, thinly sliced duck breast served with a peach and shallot reduction. Conversation throughout the meal had been constant, yet at the same time quiet, unrushed, and so easy neither noticed that it was after nine o'clock when their desserts arrived. As they polished off a crème Brulé, one topped with local blackberries, Trip brought up the subject of his mother. "I spoke with my Mom today; she is anxious to meet you and said to send her best regards."

"How nice. I'm looking forward to meeting her as well," April Anne replied looking at Trip over the candlelit table. "When do you think she'll arrive here in Highlands?"

"Originally, she planned to be here for the Fourth of July celebrations, but there were some issues on the availability for her new place. Seems she is still in the middle of the move to Atlanta but said she should arrive in the next week or so."

April caught a bit of angst in Trip's tone. Not wanting to pry, but being concerned, she asked, "So how are you feeling about her leaving Savannah and moving to Atlanta? That must be a big adjustment for all of you."

Trip placed his forearms on the table and clasped his hands together. "I honestly don't know. It's not that she's moving, it's more of why. She is telling everyone that she's ready to downsize and make a change since the twins are graduating, and with Dad gone." He shook his head. "And those might be a couple of good reasons, but I'm not buying it. Not to get into too much family theatrics with you, but I actually found out that Grand Martha evicted The Lil from the townhouse."

April's eyes grew a bit wide; she thought that the whole situation was unfolding like a Southern gothic soap opera. Even the most gifted scriptwriters would have a hard time matching this storyline. "I'm happy to listen if you want to talk about it."

Trip pulled her hand to his lips, and kissed it softly before letting it go. "You do know, don't you, that you really are special to me?" April blushed from both the warm touch of his lips as well as the intimate way Trip had whispered his words.

April answered, looking him in the eyes "Yes, I do. I feel absolutely the same about you. And I'm here if it would help to air out what you're thinking. Sometimes it's good just to say the words aloud."

"There is just so much happening at one time with my family. The divorce, the twins graduating, finding out about Brother's troubles, and topping it all off with this lawsuit between the two women who raised me, well, there's just a lot to adjust to."

"I can understand; that is an enormous amount of drama going on at one time. It has to be hard on all of you. I'm so sorry for what you and your family are going through."

Trip chuckled softly, trying to lighten the conversation a bit. "Yes, if we were being filmed it'd make a pretty darn interesting reality show for television. It could be called something like Southern Discomfort.

April laughed along with Trip as he signaled the waiter for their check. "What an appropriate title. Do you mind telling me why Martha is asking your Mom to vacate? That seems pretty drastic. She's lived there for how long did you say? Almost twenty years? Everyone has heard or read about that famous dressing room she has. Lovey said it was like something off of a Hollywood movie set."

Trip raised his eyebrows and shoulders with a look that was half comedic and the other sarcastic. "Well, in the lawsuit The Lil contends Grand Martha is mentally unstable and does not have the capacity to fully execute a legal document, therefore making the transfer of Ship Watch to the National Trust null and void." Then he exhaled a long breath of air paired with another shoulder shrug. "And Martha Stephens Randolph, the most imposing woman I've ever met, even more so than my steel magnolia of a mama, does *not* take lightly to being called a nutcase in Savannah society."

April Anne literally didn't know what to make of such a situation. "Well, I don't suppose I'd like to be referred to as unstable, either."

"And in public at that. The lawsuit is all open records, so there isn't a soul in Savannah society or up and down the east coast from the Hamptons to Palm Beach that isn't talking about our family. Now Grand Martha is firing back with a full arsenal of ammo. So far, she has taken away Mom's company-owned SUV, her rights to book flights on the corporate jets, and evicted her from the Gamble townhome."

"I don't mean to be nosy, but will your Mom be OK financially? Those are some big hits to take."

Trip answered while reaching into a pocket to retrieve his money clip. "Mom is loaded, no worries there. She was rich when she married Daddy. Coca-Cola and banking money, plus she and my two uncles' own tons of property in Buckhead and all over the north side of Atlanta; they've made three fortunes on all that awful expansion up in Alpharetta and Roswell." Placing his card on the bill tray and handing it to their waiter, he laughed softly. "It's funny, too. She's telling everyone she is downsizing. Yet she's moving into a 4,000 square foot penthouse in Buckhead overlooking a park and the downtown skyline."

"Well, how big was the townhouse in Savannah?" April was mesmerized by this aristocratic family's dynamics.

"Four floors, and 6,000 square feet." Tri sounded embarrassed that this whole discussion seemed pretentious, particularly in front of April Anne, who he knew grew up in a small town in South Georgia. "Well, she did downsize. By almost a third," April answered, "though my apartment in New York was only 1,000 square feet, it sold for just under two million. The prices in that city are unreal."

Trip had to remind himself that although the lovely lady sitting across from him was very unassuming, and from rural Georgia, she was quite successful in her own right, both as a writer and attorney. "Wow.

The listing Mom bought was right at three point five. Quite a difference in square foot costs between the two cities." He paused for a moment. "Are you going to return to New York to live? What are your plans if you don't mind my asking."

April shook her head. "No, I don't ever plan on living in New York again. 'Been there, done that,' as the saying goes." She twisted the stem of her wineglass, saying out loud what had been on her mind for quite some time. "As a teen my dream was to live in the big city. I could hardly wait to get out of Quitman, Georgia. I thought if I never saw another pine tree or drove down another dirt road, it would suit me just fine. Things change, though, and I've changed, particularly after this divorce. Now I'm ready to move back home to the South."

Trip took in what she said before answering. "Well, have you thought about staying in Savannah? I don't want to sound too forward, but I very much would enjoy having you there when the summer is over."

"I can't say right now, Trip, but in all honesty, the answer probably would be no. I so love your company and know what we have seems to be moving along nicely, but I need to go home, back to my family. At least for a while. While our Adamses tribulations aren't quite as high stakes as the Randolphs' in terms of money and property, I need to feel grounded, and whole, if that makes any sense. Plus, there are some fences to mend."

As April finished speaking, the waiter stopped by the table to drop off Trip's card and receipt, leaving a gap of a minute or so in conversation. April then asked, "What about you? What are your plans? Will you stay on the coast?"

"I'm not sure, although I do plan on joining a couple of my friends in their boutique investment firm. They've asked me in as a partner, and I'm pretty excited. The foundation work only takes up a fraction of my time. As far as other plans go, I just don't know. It seems that most of the family is leaving Savannah. Mom to Atlanta, Peyton is bound for Wharton for two years and Ray is moving to Pinehurst; he'll be one of the assistant golf pros there at the Club, and who knows if Grand

Martha will stay or head back to England. Brother seems pretty wrapped up in searching for a boyfriend right now, and I expect any minute he'll be off somewhere with a new love. Lovey will probably spend most of her time up at Lachlan's cattle ranch; his place is a good two-hour drive from Tybee. So, to answer your question, I really don't know right now." Placing his napkin on the table, he stood and went to pull her chair out for April.

As she turned to face him, he continued, "One thing I do know, however, is that I very much enjoyed tonight. I'm sorry it's come to an end." He then gave her a brief, but thoughtful kiss.

April's blood rushed to her cheeks as she took in the masculine smell of aftershave and the heat of the touch of his lips. She leaned up on her toes and kissed him back, her hands planted firmly on his broad shoulders. "Who says the night is over? It's pretty darn cold here in this mountain air. Let's go back to our 'motel' — she paused and grinned — and build a fire."

Trip's reaction had blood running both to his cheeks and to the area contained in his Fruit of the Looms, which showed immediately. Blushing, he used one hand to shield the bulge in his trousers as they walked the short distance to his car.

April could not help but notice and she tried to contain a giggle. Embarrassed, Trip cut his eyes over to her as he climbed in behind the wheel. "I'm sorry, but why are you laughing?"

His date waved her hand in a dismissive way. "Oh, it's nothing at all. I was just thinking about Lovey and something she said the other day."

Trip looked relieved and started the engine, backing out of the parking spot. April Anne smiled and blushed in the dark car and thought, *Yes ma'am, you were right, Lovey Mac. I can see that the eldest Randolph son does indeed have quite a sizable package.*

Chapter 28

As April Anne and Trip were having their dinner, Bebe, Jana, and cousin Bernie had enjoyed a meal at the 1790 Inn and Restaurant. The bar at the historic hotel boasted flagstone floors, brick walls, and beamed ceilings; it had been a favorite watering hole of Bernie's when he lived in Savannah. The three conspirators huddled in a far corner away from the tourist crowd and sipped on Irish coffees. Jana had enjoyed the evening, although she was still nervous about what they were about to do. Yet Bernie, who she found very friendly, but a bit shy, was fully confident the plan would come off without any hitches. She spoke after taking the first sip of her drink. "You're sure he won't be able to taste the drug, Bebe? How can something so strong be tasteless?"

Bebe had her back to the crowd and leaned forward to whisper. "There is some taste to it, but from what we know about Buck and his drinking habits, he takes his bourbon or scotch straight up. He won't be able tell it is in there, no. And anyway, it is only going take one good swig, and he'll be out."

Bernie, whose seat allowed him to look into the room, interrupted. In an even tone, he said, "You don't have to whisper, Bebe. No one is close by; if anyone comes near enough to hear, I'll let you know."

Bebe glanced over her shoulder as Bernie spoke, and carried on in more of a normal voice. "Like I said, it is the strongest 'date rape' drug known; doesn't take much, not at all." She smiled and added, "Very fitting dose of medication for him, don't you think?"

"Absolutely fitting. I just hope no one finds out you have some in your possession. Even if you are a doctor." Jana was concerned her friend could get in trouble with the authorities. There were numerous stories on the news about people in the medical profession being arrested for misuse of medications. Bebe waived her hand. "I mixed this tiny batch myself; it's made of three compounds that are all easy to acquire. You just need to know the ratios." She winked at Jana. "So don't worry."

Bernie took a sip of his coffee. "I really don't think there is anything to worry about in terms of what we planned. With his fingers, he counted off, "One: the drug is not traceable. Two: Buck lives down that long dirt road out on Wilmington Island; you can't see his house unless you are on a boat in the river or on his dock. Three: My guy Fernando is a pro. He's experienced and knows what he is doing; I totally trust him. He comes in after you drug Buck and takes care of the matter." For emphasis Bernie lightly slapped his hand on the table, and adds, "Boom. Done." He glanced at Jana, who he tried not to look at any more than necessary because when he did, he felt he was blatantly staring. She was the prettiest woman he had ever gazed upon in his 45 years. "My only real worry is if Buck tries something on you before he drinks his special cocktail."

Jana shrugged. "It's a risk worth taking. But I read out the script you gave me, and he seems to have bought it. Totally. He was audibly panting on the phone when we hung up." She then blushed three shades of red, which was noticeable to the other two even in the dim lighting of the bar. What she had said to Buck, and promised to do, sounded straight out of one of Bernie's movies. She had never, ever, uttered anything even remotely close to those graphic and sexual words. Bebe and Bernie tried to hold it in, but finally both covered their mouths with their hands, trying to suppress the laughter. "Oh my God, Jana, I know it isn't funny, but if I could have heard you — you of all people, Jana Ray Chandler Randolph, Ice Princess — talking smut on the phone."

Jana gave a fake 'ha-ha', wadded up her cocktail napkin, and threw it at her friend, hitting her right on the forehead. "You know good and well, Bebe Frank, that I don't have a sense of humor." She then laughed herself, joining in with the other two. Bernie stood up after their laughter had subsided. "Let me go pay the bill. I'm guessing you all are about ready to head out." He had taken a room for the week at the Inn, staying there the entire time he needed to be in town. Bebe looked up at her tall, stylishly dressed cousin, and playfully pointed at his wrist. "When did you start wearing gold bracelets, Bernard? And do you have a gold chain under that silk shirt? My goodness, you have become so very Miami." She laughed and went on, "No, I'm not ready to go home. I don't have to work tomorrow, and AJ is out with clients on Hilton Head. What about you, Miss Priss?" She looked at Jana, who shook her head slightly and said, "It's only 9 o'clock. I heard that the bar here doesn't start jumping until late. I'm game for another round if you all are. My driver doesn't have a set time to get me back to the Ship Watch."

"OK ladies, then what can I get you? Another Irish coffee?"

Bebe was full of nervous energy and was ready for something stronger. "Nope, Bern, get me something with more of a kick. I want a vodka stinger. Straight up." They both then looked at Jana. "Let me have a Bailey's on the rocks, Bernie. Thank you." When Bernie walked over to the bar to find their waitress, Jana looked at Bebe.

"I don't think Bernie wants to stay out any longer. He may be tired. Let's head out after we finish this round."

"Honey, he isn't tired. He is just nervous as a cat around you. He thinks you're gorgeous and is doing all he can not to ask you out on a date. I know him too well."

Jana thought for a moment and looked over at him now standing next to the antique oak bar. Bernie was handsome, tall, and solidly built. But more importantly he had wonderful manners, even if he did produce porn films, and she found that she enjoyed being with him in the little time they had spent together. Looking back at Bebe she smiled and said, "Well, maybe when this is all over, I might take him up on an offer if he extended one. You never know."

Chapter 29

The next morning Lovey walked out of her suite at the Motel 6 into the courtyard and headed toward April Anne's unit to say goodbye before leaving town. On her way out the door, she ran into Trip, who was just coming off his porch. He tipped his Masters golf cap at his cousin, and said, in a chipper voice, "Top of the morning to you, Lovey. Beautiful day, isn't it?"

Lovey gave him a kiss on the cheek. "Good morning, cousin. You sure seem in a good mood. Where are you headed?"

Trip picked up his bag of golf clubs sitting by the screened door and said, "Off to play golf with Brother. He had two morning cancellations so is free enough for us to get in nine holes." Looking up at the sky, he said, "And a perfect day for it." He noticed Lovey's luggage sitting on the stoop and asked, "You're on your way to Atlanta to see Mom? When will you be back?"

"Patrick and I will be leaving right on the hour. I'll be there two nights; Lily and I are going to spend time at the Mart and at the design studios over in Buckhead."

Lightly tweaking her chin, he smiled. "Give her a hug for me and y'all have fun. See you in a couple of days." And with that he turned, whistling "I'm Going to Jackson" all the way to his truck. Lovey stared for a moment. *I haven't seen him in this happy of a humor in ages,* she thought as she tapped on April Anne's door. She waited a moment, and tapped again, a bit harder. "Yoo hoo, April Anne, get away from the computer and let me in."

Her friend finally opened the door and stepped outside wearing her bathrobe. She had obviously just gotten out of bed; Lovey noticed April's disheveled hair, which was tied up in a scrunchie, and her face and neck which were a blotchy shade of red. "Morning, Lovey."

Lovey's radar went 'BEEP BEEP BEEP.' Something was amiss here. "Well morning to you, too. And thanks for asking me inside, Miss Manners." She put her hands on her hips and stared inquisitively at her friend.

"I'm sorry, Lovey, I'm just getting myself together. I haven't been out of bed for too long." April pointed toward the Bentley with Lovey's cousin behind the wheel. "I don't have any coffee made, and it looks as if Patrick is waiting for you in the car."

She's trying to get rid of me. Something definitely is up, Lovey thought as she waved over to Patrick and gave him three fingers, meaning she'd be there in a few. Patrick saw the gesture and muttered aloud, "More like thirty minutes the way she talks."

Lovey turned her attention back to April. "Well, well. You're usually the first one up around here, pecking away at the computer. Early bird gets the worm is usually your mantra." Then it finally dawned on her. "Oh my God. It looks like the early bird DID get the worm." Leaning in toward April, who had taken a step back, Lovey wiggled her eyebrows up and down. "And it IS a big worm, isn't it, April Anne Adams?" Lovey shrieked with laughter. "No wonder Trip was in such high humor this morning and looking so happy. Y'all did the deed last night."

April wished a big hole would open up and swallow her right then and there. She was totally caught and so embarrassed. Trying to keep her dignity, she cinched the belt around her robe tightly. "Lovey, for once in your sweet life, mind your own business."

Lovey laughed again. "Oh, darling, I will, I will," she said jingling the bangles on her wrists as her hands flew through the air with excitement. "But only for right now. When I get back from Atlanta, I want to hear all about it." She reached out and gave her best friend a hug before walking to the limo. Halfway to the car, Lovey turned around and added, "And by the way, if you go out in public today, you need to go heavy on the foundation and powder. Your little cheeks and neck show all the signs of some serious beard burn. Tah-tah."

Chapter 30

Lovey texted Baylor about April and Trip's encounter immediately upon getting into the Bentley. *So that is why his lights weren't on when I got home last night.* With that knowledge, the younger Randolph brother was leaning with one arm on a new T-series Iron he was going to try out, while the other was cocked on his side swinging idly back and forth as Trip approached him on the green, still whistling. Trip handed his bag over to one of the caddies and looked at Baylor. "Morning, Brother." Baylor didn't say anything, just kept his stance and smiled broadly. "What are you looking so smug about? I don't care if you are the pro, you know I can still kick your butt in nine holes."

"Yeah, right, in your dreams." Baylor twirled the golf club in his hand and walked over to his brother so the caddies couldn't hear him. "So. Tell me about last night. I came back from Asheville at midnight, and not nary a light was on in your suite, not the porch light nor your bath night light."

Trip squinted his eyes and pulled out his sunglasses. Putting them on, he answered, "I had a little too much to drink last night and forgot to turn them on. So what? And I should be the one asking about last night. How did the date go?"

"Nice guy, but he failed to mention on his profile that he was recently divorced and has two kids in high school. Quoting Miss Kimberly "Sweet Brown" Wilkins, 'ain't nobody got time for that.'" He paused before he pressed on, smiling like the Cheshire Cat. "And don't change the subject. What exactly *were* you up to last night after your date with April Anne? Hmm?"

Trip froze for a moment. His brother was drilling him because he knew something. While Baylor wasn't dim, he wasn't Sherlock Holmes, either, and would never by himself have put two and two together based on a whether the porch light was on or not. He then recalled Lovey walking toward April's room as he was leaving the compound. "I gather you've spoken with Miss Louvenia MacGregor this morning. Whatever she said to you, it is none of her business, nor yours, Brother boy." He motioned over to the caddy and looked back at Baylor. "Let's tee up."

Baylor put his hand up in a 'halt' motion, and said, "Jimmy, hold on fellow. We're not quite ready yet." The caddy stopped and waited. Turning back to Trip he said, "Oh, come on. Talk to your baby brother. I swear I won't tease, or pry too hard." He put his hand on Trip's shoulder and squeezed. "I just want you to be happy."

Trip thought for a quick moment, then reached up and put his arm on Baylor's. He said, "Well, to be honest, Brother, I think that" and he paused to grin timidly, "I'm actually, maybe, in love."

Chapter 31

Lovey walked around Lily's apartment, taking measurements of windows, placing furniture in her decorator's eye, and giving the space an overall estimation. The living room and dining room both had expansive windows facing the elegant Midtown skyline and the wooded parks of Buckhead; the downtown skyscrapers were in the distance. *I can't wait to see this at nighttime,* thought Lovey. *What a spectacular view.* Her mind then took her back to the scene from this morning, which had been racing back and forth over what might happen in the future for Trip and April. She believed them perfectly fit for one another, and would like nothing more than to add her best friend to the family.

Then her imagination, which twirled like a kaleidoscope sometimes, was on Baylor and Patrick. She and Patrick had chatted back and forth, enjoying one another's company on the traffic-packed drive down I-85 into Atlanta, until she brought up the subject of Baylor's date the night before. Just like that, with the image of fingers snapping in her head, he stopped talking. Pressing him for several minutes, and with no answers, Lovey was tired of mincing words. She finally asked what she, Trip, and Baylor had all been wanting to know. "Patrick, tell me this: do you have a problem with homosexuals? Are you homophobic?" She wasn't entirely happy with his ambiguous answer. "Lovey, I don't have a 'problem' as you say with Baylor. I've known him all my life. I just don't want to hear about all these dates he goes on with men. I don't even want to think about it."

Sadly, the scene led Lovey to believe Patrick was one of those people, and there were many that she knew of, who would tolerate someone being gay, and might even have them as a superficial friend. But they absolutely didn't want to hear about, discuss, nor be privy to anything personal about a same sex relationship. She really hated to learn this was the way Patrick felt. It would change the whole dynamic of their group. The thought brought tears to her eyes. Then there was the lawsuit which still had Savannah talking. What would happen to Ship Watch? If it stayed in the family, who would live there and manage it? How would that affect Trip and April? And if the transfer did go through, and the National Trust took it over, how would the family cope with such an enormous change in their lives? The homestead had been in the Randolph family for generations. And here she was, about to be married and embark on a new life. She so hoped all of these matters would be cleared up before then. Getting all worked up and emotional, as she often did, she said out loud to herself, "It is just too much for words."

Right at that moment Lily walked into the room. Amused, she asked, "Dear, are you talking to yourself again?"

Lovey swung around, surprised. "Oh, Lily, hi. I didn't hear you come back in." She didn't want to start off today's conversation about the woes of the Randolph family, so she said instead, "I was exclaiming that this penthouse is simply too much for words. I mean, Lily, honestly, what a view this is during the daytime, but at night it must be simply magical."

Lily came to stand next to her and took in the vista. "Yes, at night it is magical. I actually can't wait to have my first cocktail party and show it off."

"It is the perfect space for entertaining. That enormous patio looks like it could hold 50 people, easily."

"Now that I've got a home secured and in place, I'm not in a hurry to move in, so don't rush on my account. I plan on heading to Highlands next week and staying there while all the work is completed here. I'll just pop down with you when needed and make sure all is going as it should."

Lovey nodded her head. "I understand. The biggest part was finding a spot that suited you." Cocking her head to one side, she continued. "I hear you hired my ex, that run-about, Billy Joe, as your realtor."

Lily smiled awkwardly. "Well, Lovey, darling, I was told that he was the best agent in Atlanta. Eloise said he always has a hidden stash of properties that no one else would know about. This fabulous place was one of them. It wasn't even on the market."

Lovey continued with her narrowed look for just slight moment, and then laughed. "Oh Lily, I don't mind that you used Billy Joe. I'm tickled pink for him and his success. You do know he's getting married, and at about the same time as I am, right? It all worked out for the best. I mean, we've invited each other to both of our weddings."

Whew, thought Lily. She had purposefully not mentioned Lovey's ex and had hoped word hadn't gotten to her. "All good then. By the way, you know he now goes by William Joseph. He seemed to have left the 'Billy Joe' back in South Georgia."

"Good for him. He just simply found himself once his parents died." Changing the subject, she went on. "I sent Patrick over to the St. Regis to check us in and park the car. I don't like riding around Atlanta in the Bentley, and I don't trust the valets in this city. If you don't mind, we'll just use UberSelect while I'm here."

"No worries. I'm the same way about my new Mercedes. Seems those cars are just ding magnets in this city. What will Patrick do while he's in town? He is welcome to come with us, but I can't imagine he'd enjoy looking at fabrics and furniture."

"Oh, he's going out with some of his military buddies to an Irish sports bar and watch rugby tournaments. They're on tomorrow, too, so he'll pal around with them while we're busy."

Lily reached into her purse and pulled out her smartphone. "Here, I've emailed you a few more pictures of the items coming in later today, and then most of my wardrobe should arrive tomorrow."

"That sounds fine. Perfect. I have our list of what all you want, and what needs recovering and replacing. With all of your wonderful things from Savannah, this won't take too long, just getting the wallpaper up, drapes and cornice boards done, a few other items. It is going to be stunning. Hope you don't mind, but I've already contacted my friends at *Town & Country.* They'd love to do a photo spread and story on your new showplace once it's all put together."

Lily smiled. "How wonderful. I'd be flattered."

Lovey then remembered to ask about Lily's wardrobe. "By the way, you didn't say what you were actually going to do for a dressing room here. Was there a space that worked?"

Lily nodded. "Actually, it worked out perfectly. The prior owners had purchased the smaller unit next door for their live-in butler and housekeeper, a married couple. I bought it along with this condo and am going to use it solely for my new wardrobe rooms. There is already an internal entry right outside my bedroom door."

Lovey clapped her hands. "Sweet. Take me there first so I can see where we need to start. Lead the way." She mused thoughtfully to herself as she followed down the wide, parquet hallway, *Lily might not have chosen to leave Savannah on her own, but she seems very happy, and she sure has landed nicely.* There was no doubt in the decorator's mind that all of Atlanta would soon be clamoring to be in the midst of Lily Baylor Randolph's company.

Chapter 32

Martha's nerves had been on edge for the last few days since viewing Dr. Lockwood's deposition of Anthony Darlington-Smythe. While her cousin was completely devoted to Martha, his testimony came across as nothing short of unfavorable. His honest answers, prompted by the very talented and shrewd doctor, gave affirmation to Martha's extreme depression and morose state of mind while in England. Auggie reminded her over and over again, though, depression didn't mean lack of capacity, and they would solidly prove that fact with their own expert. Those reassurances had not been a balm to her anxiety, at least not until later in the afternoon. Her spirits had been much lifted, and she was looking forward to dinner out that night with the President and CEO of Randolph Shipping, Thomas Trotter, and his leadership team from the company.

The group had met with Martha at the Cloister for the majority of the day setting the agenda for the upcoming annual board meeting. It was during this planning pow wow that Auggie made an observation giving solid proof the Randolph matriarch did indeed have a sound mind and was perfectly capable of making major business decisions. Reading over a very complicated and lucrative contract renewal with the New York Ports Authority, Martha made several keen suggestions in the interest of the company. One of the points was so significant Thomas made the comment "Folks, you see why we do not ever make a major decision without this lady's consultation or approval."

Auggie held up his hand and spoke. "Martha, during the time you were abroad, did you stay active in your role as chair of the board?"

Peering over her halfmoon shaped reading glasses, she said, "Yes, of course. Why do you ask?"

Then turning to Thomas, Auggie asked, "Tell me, Thomas, during those years, were there any large, or what you would consider consequential, contracts in which Martha played a role in negotiating?"

Thomas didn't hesitate. "Absolutely. She had an active role in several that I can think of. And had to sign the contracts."

Auggie stood up at that point. "Thomas and Martha, if you don't mind, let's table the rest of the items until tomorrow morning. The remainder contain only a few minor details."

Martha and Thomas looked at each other and nodded in agreement. Martha stood as well and spoke to the group. "It's been a very productive day. Thank you all for being here. I'll see you at The Lodge at 7 this evening for cocktails, and our dinner reservation is at 8. Come thirsty and come hungry."

The group gathered their laptops and departed, all thanking Martha for her hospitality. Auggie asked Thomas and Martha to stay behind for a few more minutes. Sitting back down, they looked at him expectantly. "Thomas, you're well aware of the situation with Ship Watch and the lawsuit that Lily has filed. We've tried to keep you abreast of the important issues since it could impact Randolph Shipping, at least in terms of publicity."

Thomas nodded. "Yes, I'm aware." Martha and Addison had been his mentors for over two decades, and he not only admired, but also loved the company's matriarch like a second mother. "I'm so sorry Lily is putting you through this, Martha. Not that it surprises me, though." He tilted his head slightly before adding, "As you know, she and I do not share a mutual admiration society."

Martha looked on warmly at the young man who had long been Addison's and Add Jr. 's second in command, and who had stepped into the role of CEO with great confidence and ability when her husband passed away. Lily had always resented Thomas, feeling Trip should have held his seat and title, though Trip was not interested in running the company, being content at the helm of the Foundation. Lily unjustly felt Thomas Trotter had taken the job from her son. "Well, fortunately you don't have to deal with her directly anymore."

Looking at Auggie, she said, "All right, Augustus, don't keep us waiting. What is on your mind?"

"We now have concrete, verifiable evidence to shut down this absurd lawsuit. Turning to Thomas, he said, "I take it there are notes and records of the past board meetings and executive planning sessions like today, ones that would show Martha as a part of the proceedings."

Thomas nodded, following exactly the older gentleman's line of thinking. "Yes, absolutely. Lisa tapes each planning session and then distributes confidential minutes to the leadership team; plus, all board meetings are videotaped and archived. The couple of meetings where Martha could not attend in person she skyped in, and we have those recordings, too." Grinning broadly, he winked at Martha. "And in all of these documented recordings, with multiple witnesses present, Mrs. Randolph was front and center in all contract discussions and negotiations."

Auggie put his hands outwards, palms up in a 'there you have it' gesture. "I assume all of these contracts, such as the sales and purchases, realignments, etc., were considered successful for the company?"

Martha was now smiling broadly and nodding along with the two men. "Each has added to a record three years of growth and profitability at Randolph Shipping, counselor."

In his trained courtroom voice, Auggie grandly summarized with good humor, "So Thomas, in your professional capacity as President & CEO of said company, would it be in your learned opinion that, since starting in the position as Chairman of the board, that Martha Stephens Randolph has faithfully, and with sound and solid judgement, fulfilled her role?"

Thomas stood, and as if on the witness stand, held his right hand over his heart and his left in the air, and said solemnly, "It is indeed, your honor."

With that, Martha laughed with happiness and gave Thomas a warm hug and a kiss on each cheek. She then walked over to Auggie and grabbed his hands in hers. Auggie peered down at the woman he had loved for decades and said, "How do you feel, my dear?"

"I'm absolutely ecstatic. Let's go get ready for dinner. I may have *two* martinis tonight to celebrate."

She happily replayed that scene several times over in her head as Auggie maneuvered the golf cart down the oak and palm lined streets back to the cottage. As they pulled into her driveway, she gave him a sweet smile of contentment. She would never dream of confiding with the proper and dignified barrister the most unladylike thought gleefully going through her mind at the time, which was *Lily Baylor Randolph can now take those letters and shove them right up her uptight and pretentious Atlanta ass.*

Chapter 33

The first part of the evening was easier than Jana had imagined. Buck never suspected anything afoul; she supposed it was because he thought mostly with his dick and not his mind. The only thing he had heard was the promise she made of exquisite sex. No notice was taken that she asked to meet at his house after dark. Nor had he batted an eye when she showed up dressed all in black, with her shoulder length hair, which she always kept loose and casual, slicked back and tied into a French knot. Fortunately, Jana looked as good without makeup as she did with it on; there shouldn't be any trace of her presence in his house after all was finished and done.

Knowing Buck was a whiskey snob and loved his drink, Jana brought a prized bottle of bottle of single malt she nabbed from Trip's private collection. She suggested to Buck that they have a drink to loosen everything up; he gladly took the large shot Jana poured and drank it down in one gulp. She offered another round, and aware of the five-hundred-dollar price tag that came with the bottle, Buck accepted. What he didn't realize was that in each glass Jana had slipped a heaping dose of the date rape drug prepared by Bebe. By the time Buck had finished the second round, he was almost comatose. Jana had no problem at all leading him into the master suite and pushing him onto the king-sized bed.

She then texted Bebe a friendly note, a code that all was clear. Bebe in turn sent a message to Bernie, who was in AJ's twin-engine Rabolo fishing boat with Fernando. When Bebe's go-ahead came across his phone, Bernie made his way downriver from the Savannah Yacht Club, a quick half mile journey. He eased the boat alongside Buck's dock. After tying the "Reel Magic" to a piling, the two men moved quietly along the two-hundred-yard wooden walkway to the back porch of the house. The skies were overcast and the moon at only a quarter; the night was almost as dark as the outfits the two men wore.

Jana opened the door and let them in, leading the way into the great room. She pointed toward the ground floor bedroom where Buck lay half naked, moaning occasionally. "He's in there."

Bernie took a good look around the room and sat the small canvas bag on the floor. "How'd it go?"

Jana answered in an even tone, though she was still extremely nervous. "Without a hitch so far. The bastard was so engrossed rubbing his pecker through his pants that he never noticed what I put in his glass, or that fact that I had on gloves." She held up two fingers encased in expensive black leather, indicating the number of drinks he had. "And he got seconds."

"No wonder he was out so quickly. I didn't expect to get a call for another half hour or so." Looking over toward Jana's oversized Louis Vuitton purse on the bar counter, he then asked, "Did you clean everything up? Nothing out of place?"

Jana nodded. "I washed both our glasses, dried them with the paper towels, and put the towels in my purse. The glasses are back on the rack where I found them. I also did three rounds looking in all the spots I'd walked, from the front door, in the bar, and back to his bedroom, and didn't find any stray hairs. This gel and knot have held everything in place." She patted the back of her head absently, as she was not accustomed to having her hair pinned up. She then took full notice of Fernando. He had removed his hooded shirt and folded it neatly to sit by Bernie's bag. The South American was solidly built and well-muscled at about six feet tall. His body was partially covered in tattoos from his shaved head down to his calves, including the brightly colored flag of Brazil across his meaty right forearm. Standing in his sweatpants, he nodded to Jana and gave her a glowing smile, sporting a prominent gold tooth. Nodding back, she then turned to Bernie with a worried expression. "We've gone to all this trouble to hide our tracks. But don't you think Fernando is easily recognizable? He'd be immediately picked out of a lineup with those tattoos and," she turned

185

to look at the actor, "excuse me, I don't mean to be rude, Fernando," and went on to Bernie, "his golden incisor."

Bernie and Fernando exchanged knowing glances, and the actor spoke for the first time upon entering the house. His speech contained no accent; there was no hint of any of the romantic languages. "Mrs. Randolph, whenever I do a job like this, I come in a different disguise."

Jana was stunned. "But you are from Brazil, aren't you?" Looking at Bernie, she said, "I don't understand."

Fernando continued patiently. "Yes, I'm from Brazil, and my mother is Portuguese. But my father was British, and I inherited some of his fairer features. For tonight, I have a dark, spray-on tan, my eyes brown from contacts lenses, the tatts are temporary, and the gold tooth a removable cap. I also shaved my head." Gesturing toward his privates, he added, "I actually shaved everywhere." Jana's jaw drop slightly. "But the muscles, all of them, are real."

"I see. Well, thanks for explaining, and thank you for doing this. I appreciate it."

Fernando laughed. "You Southerners are all so polite. Here you are thanking me for what I'm about to do. Mrs. Randolph, you don't need to thank me. The $ 50,000 is ample appreciation."

Jana didn't like being laughed at, particularly in a situation like this. Before she could give a tart response, Bernie said to Fernando, "There is a lot at stake here and let's not lose focus. Go on in the bedroom and finish getting him undressed." The actor shrugged, nodded his head to Jana to say goodbye, and turned to make his way toward the bed. Bernie then added as the man walked away, "I want to use Buck's head for the first shot; get him in a position so it can be done clearly and quickly."

He then took Jana by her arm, led her to the bar, and picked up her purse to hand her. Looking intently at her for a quick moment he said, "You know, you really are brave. Buck could have hurt you. Again. It took a whole lot of guts to do what you did tonight."

Jana was accustomed to men ogling her because of her looks, but it was rare that one gave her a real compliment. She blushed a bit and spoke. "I admit to being scared witless. But if I can stop that monster from doing to someone else what he did to me, and to Bebe, well, then, the fear and the cost is worth it."

Bernie nodded in agreement and opened the front door to let Jana outside. "Can you make your way down the drive without using the headlights?"

Jana had left her keys in the ignition and the doors unlocked of her car in case of the need for a fast getaway. As she got into the SUV she said, "Yes, no worries, though no one would notice them on, anyway. The Harrison's from the property to the left are in Highlands for the summer with most of the rest of Savannah. The old Wimberly property on the other side is tied up in an estate. No one has lived there for years now."

"Bit of good fortune for us," Bernie said as he closed the car door for Jana. When she let down her window, he added, "This should only take about twenty to thirty minutes, from start to finish. When we get back to the Yacht Club, and docked, I'll be in touch with Bebe."

Jana reached through the window and placed her hand warmly on his cheek. While she was not a demonstrative person physically, she was extremely grateful to all that Bernie had planned, implemented, and was about to carry out. "Take care, Bernie. Be careful."

Bernie nodded solemnly in return. Bringing her arm back into the car, she clicked the window button, started her car, and eased her SUV through the dark along the packed dirt driveway to make her way back toward town.

Part III

October

Chapter 34

Lily had spent most of the months of August and September in Highlands while the penthouse was being refurbished and decorated; she was back in Atlanta now for a week to attend a series of events at the Botanical Gardens. She had enjoyed the time with Baylor and Trip and found herself completely charmed by Trip's new girlfriend. Lily approved of the young lady's low key but colorful style; she looked like she had stepped off the pages of a Kate Spade magazine spread. Her South Georgia upbringing shown through in her manners and conversation; she was warm and polite and a pleasure to be around, welcome traits after two decades of dealing with Jana. It was evident to everyone around that April Anne and Trip were crazy about each other, and maybe even in love.

She was also happy to know that Baylor was finally allowing himself to date and look for companionship, though she hoped he wouldn't rush into any relationship just yet. That sweet boy had been through enough and could be easily misled. She would have to keep an eye on that situation. As Lily stepped into her kitchen to get a cup of coffee, her phone's ringtone told her she had a text. Walking over to the charger port, she picked up the phone and found, to her surprise, she actually had over 20 new texts and a dozen voice mail messages. "Oh Lord what in the world has happened," she wondered aloud as she pressed Trip's voice message first. "Mom, hi. I wanted to get you before you left for church. I hate to tell you, but the news about the lawsuit has broken in a very public way. All three stations in Savannah are carrying a story about it. I just emailed you the link from WGSV; you'll want to take a look at it. Call me when you can. Love you."

Lily sat down at the kitchen island and logged onto her computer. She clicked on the link that Trip sent, which pulled up the two evening news anchors at WGSV sitting at their desks. The screen read "Historic Savannah Custody Battle."

"Good evening, everyone. Tonight on WGSV we have the most astounding news that might prove to be one of the toughest, and most unusual, custody battles ever witnessed here in Savannah. And the most unique part of this unfolding story is that this courtroom drama isn't about a child, but rather over one of Georgia's most historic and notable homes, Ship Watch, located right here in Chatham County."

A photo of Ship Watch flashed onto the screen.

"That's right, Dawn," answered the other anchor. "Today attorneys for Elizabeth Baylor Randolph filed papers in Chatham Superior Court to stop the transfer of Ship Watch to the National Trust for Historic Preservation, an action that had been set in motion by the matriarch of the Randolph family, Martha Stephens Randolph. These two women are prominently known not just here, but in high society social circles across the country."

Two side-by-side photos were then broadcast of Lily and Martha. Dawn took another turn to speak.

"You know, Mike, I've met both Mrs. Randolphs, and they are such lovely ladies, and have done so much for the community. That is Elizabeth on the left of the screen, though her friends call her 'Lily,' when she was President of Savannah's Junior League. The photo of Martha Randolph, Lily's mother-in-law, shows her when she held the impressive position as President of the Colonial Dames of America. Here to tell you more about this fascinating story is our investigative reporter, Alyson Takei. Alyson is standing by at the Randolph family's historic Monterey Square townhomes. Alyson?"

The camera cut to the young reporter, who was in front of the wrought iron gates leading to Eurelia's and Eulalie's original structures.

"Thank you, Dawn and Mike. I could not gain access to Ship Watch; the house and grounds are behind locked gates and the security guard would not let me in." The young reporter shook her head in disbelief as she made the statement.

Lily thought, *Well of course not, silly girl. You just don't ring the bell like the Avon Lady,* as she hit the pause button for a moment to get a cup of coffee. Sitting back down, she started the news clip again.

"I'm standing in front of the townhomes of the two Randolph ladies who are pivotal to this story. No one at either house would answer the doorbells, and the family has not returned our phone calls inquiring into the matter. However, we do have a close relative of the Randolph's with us tonight, their cousin, Mrs. Eileen Roland."

Into view came a plump, heavily made up, middle-aged woman wearing a wide, flamingo pink silk head scarf and matching quilted caftan.

Lily paused the computer again and shook her head. *Jesus wept. How in the world did they find Bitsy? That's all we need. Having Savannah's very own Little Edie Beale front and center with the press.* She hit play again, worried sick about what would come out of the eccentric's mouth.

"That's 'Miss,' please, Miss Eileen Hubbard Roland. My friends call me Bitsy, though, and you all can, too." She batted her eyes directly into the camera."

Alyson brought the mike back from Bitsy and said:

"Well, Miss Bitsy. I understand you are a part of the extended Randolph family; thank you for agreeing to see us tonight. Do you mind telling us what you know? From our understanding, Martha Randolph, who owns the two townhomes behind us, signed a contract that gives ownership of the family plantation, Ship Watch, to the National Trust."

Alyson placed the microphone close to Bitsy to answer. The older woman, who now clutched her oversized, multi-strand of pearls with one hand, quickly snatched the mike from the unsuspecting reporter with the other, who tried to retrieve it to no avail. The camera continued rolling as Bitsy started:

"Oh, Alyson, this story is just the miniscule tip of an enormous iceberg of intrigue. We could film a whole mini-series about the foils and deeds of the Randolphs and the Stephens."

Bitsy raised an overly long, penciled-on eyebrow, giving a look meant to convey great suspense. By this time, the television crew had found another microphone, which now was held by the news reporter. The screen cut to Alyson.

"That sounds very dramatic, Miss Bitsy, and I'm sure our listeners would love to hear the whole story at some point. But for our limited time tonight, can you just give us the highlights, as you know them, of the fate of Ship Watch?"

Bitsy moved in closer to stand next to Alyson, and said:

"Yes, it is very dramatic. And, as you know, I'm sure, I'm a dramatic actress. I graduated with honors from the New York School of Theater and worked for many years on Broadway."

Lily said aloud to the screen, "For God's sake, woman, you never landed a part on Broadway. You spent 20 years in New York and ran through every penny of your inheritance." Bitsy now lived in one of the family's rowhouses downtown and lived off a small trust which was tightly controlled by Martha. Alyson looked a bit questioningly at the aging, curiously dressed woman standing beside her, but continued on:

"Yes, of course. But tell us, please, about how this lawsuit came about, if you can, and what you think the results will be in court."

Bitsy waved her free hand in a large circle, framing the townhouses behind her.

"The tradition in the Randolph family is that when the heir has children, he moves into Ship Watch, and the older generations move here, into these two glorious homes on Monterey Square, which were built by my ancestor. Why in the world my dear cousin Martha would try and stop this tradition is a mystery to the entire family. But it doesn't surprise me at all, no, not at all."

She stopped and gazed expectantly at the reporter, prompting the question.

"And why does this not surprise you? Most people think it very strange that someone would just simply give away such a historic and valuable property."

Bitsy looked at the camera knowing she had just landed a much better part than any she had ever played on stage and was determined to make the best of it.

"Because my cousin is a very controlling and selfish woman. She enjoys pulling the strings on the family puppets, and I'm one of them. The very grand and imperious Martha Stephens Randolph controls my meager inheritance, doling out pennies here and there, and sequestering me in a tiny, one-bedroom house while she jets around in a Gulfstream plane and lives in mansions."

By now large tears were running down Bitsy's cheeks, and a crewmember off camera handed her a tissue. Lily was listening in earnest, wondering where else this might go. While Bitsy was telling the truth, she had always held a very strong resentment and jealous streak in regard to Martha. Lily begrudgingly gave Martha credit of character in that her mother-in-law took Bitsy under her wing and set up a trust for her when she returned home penniless from New York. And Bitsy also didn't tell the reporter that her 'tiny one-bedroom house' was in one of the trendiest spots on the eastside and worth upwards of half a million dollars. Or that Martha had paid for the four trips Bitsy had to take to Charter by the Sea with nervous breakdowns.

"I'm so sorry for your predicament, Miss Bitsy, as I'm sure our listeners are. Before we say goodbye, why do you think Lily Randolph sued to keep Ship Watch? The lawsuit was filed on her behalf."

Bitsy was now dry eyed and ready to sling a few more shovels of mud. While she resented her cousin Martha, she absolutely loathed the smug and haughty Elizabeth Baylor Randolph, who she felt was a social upstart. Too, she could not disappoint her new fans, even if they were of television and not real patrons of the arts that appreciated the stage.

"Oh, Lily Randolph has always been a climber of the first order; you know she is from Atlanta new money. She would rather die a thousand deaths than allow that plantation to slip through her grasping fingers."

Bitsy smiled like a cat and looked right at the camera. Lily slammed her computer screen closed. *That crazy bitch called me nouveau riche on television. My family has had money, real money, for generations. I will kill her with my bare hands when I see her next.*

With clinched fists and nostrils flared, she stormed down the hallway to the bathroom to find a Xanax to calm her nerves. She'd just have to take an Uber to Mass; she couldn't drive in this agitated state of mind.

Chapter 35

As Lily was driven to Mass, Trip was sitting a plate filled with a cheese omelet, some locally made sausage, and a toasted leftover biscuit in front of April Anne. They had spent another wonderful night together snuggled under a homemade quilt at the Motel 6. April Anne smiled up at him as he hummed "Ode to Joy" and kissed her lightly on the cheek. He could not get enough of this wonderful woman, and she had given the affection back just as freely. Trip had never been this happy in his entire life; he hoped it would last forever as he sat down at the table across from her. "You've outdone yourself. I can't tell you how much I love toasted biscuits. You've fixed it just as I like, split in half, and pan fried in butter." April Anne scooped a spoonful of blackberry jam atop a golden circle.

"I'm here to make you happy and if that's as simple as a toasted biscuit, I'll fix you one each and every day," he beamed across the table, now whistling the Beethoven melody.

"You certainly seem chipper this morning," April commented as she took a bite of omelet. "And these eggs are just perfect. What type of cheese did you use?"

"I am chipper; I woke up next to the lady I love," he said as he winked across the table. He then pointed to the omelet with his fork. "And it's Cabot extra sharp cheddar."

"And I get a morning symphony, too. "Ode to Joy" is my favorite hymn. Joyful, joyful, we adore thee, God of glory, Lord of love," she sang brightly.

"Hearts unfold like flowers before thee, opening to the Sun above." Trip sang back. "It's on the 10 o'clock mass schedule, we'll get to sing the entire song later this morning. It's one of my favorites, too." He slid two pieces of sausage to Tammy and George and then dug into his own eggs. April looked thoughtfully across the table as Trip ate contentedly.

They had admitted to the "L" word just a few weeks back. It was scary at first; both were reticent to verbalize what they felt because things had moved so rapidly, and each had certainly been burned badly in failed marriages. They were so much alike in temperament and thought, though, that the two lovers realized almost at the same time life had given them a special gift: a second chance. However, the pull April Anne felt to move back to her childhood home was just as strong as the love she now held for Trip. She dreaded telling him she planned to head home to Quitman the following week. "I hate to bring this up now. But you know how I've talked about wanting to make a home for myself back in South Georgia. Well, the builder I'm using to move Granny's house and construct the new wing had a project cancel. He can meet me next week to get started."

Trip looked up from his half-finished breakfast, then carefully set his knife and fork on the table. With so much uncertainty in his life, the steadiness of having April with him was a blessing. Though she had described her longing to return to South Georgia, he didn't understand the depth of her feelings. In his mind, by now April, seeing how much in love they were, would have dismissed her intentions of any such move. Why she'd rather live out in the middle of nowhere, instead of Savannah with him, was beyond his comprehension. A definite chill permeated the room.

"Well, I can't say I'm happy you're leaving. You have been an anchor for me these last few months, and things look like they'll just be getting even more complicated over this lawsuit."

April thought he looked like a scolded puppy and her heart ached. "Well, the separation won't be forever," she said gently. "And admit it, a break might be good. Things between us have been intense. We don't want to end up like that Conway and Loretta song. What is it again? 'There's nothing as cold as ashes once the fire is gone,'" she teased with a light laugh, knowing that Trip dearly loved classic country music as his Dad before him.

Trip didn't trust himself to speak so he continued looking at her for a long moment. Choosing to at least try and seem supportive, he finally asked, "So tell me about the house plans. I know you're so excited about the prospect. Did you and the architect finally nail everything down?"

April's eyes lit up as she reached for her iPad. "Yes, we've got it worked out perfectly. Granny's house sits next door to Mama and Daddy's, and while I do want a place back home, I don't want to live right up underneath the two of them. The property I bought is just under 20 acres and two miles from my parents' place. The house will be moved and sit on a ridge where the pasture meets the woods, and right by a 5-acre pond rimmed in cypress trees." She got up from her chair and circled around the table in front of Trip to show the photos of the pastoral setting. Trip glanced at the pictures and admitted to himself that it was a beautiful landscape. Looking up at April, he said, "It's really lovely. Are there any fish in that pond?"

"Yes, Sport, it is spring-fed and has bass, bream, and catfish. On the other side of the woods, I have about 100 feet of land on both sides of Ochloknee Creek, and it's full of fish, too. Which is wonderful because when you come down you can spend as much time wetting a hook as you'd like."

Trip didn't want to entertain thoughts of having to make a six-hour drive, one way, each time he wanted to see the woman he loved. Instead of answering that annoying concept, he asked instead if there were renderings of the house renovation and addition. "Any pictures of the house and floor plan?"

"Oh, yes, here, swipe to the right." Up popped a photo of a modest white clapboard house featuring a pitched tin roof and wide, covered front porch with a floor painted dark, forest green. "This is the original house; my grandfather built it in the 1920s. It's only about twelve hundred square feet. I'm going to refinish the hardwood floors and have the bead-board stripped and painted. The wall between the two bedrooms will be removed, making that space one large room to use as my study. The front room here," she pointed to the window on the right side of the porch, "which was the old living room, will now be my bedroom, and I'm having the kitchen removed and will combine it with the old bathroom to make one large master suite."

She then reached over and clicked the link to a PDF showing the planned addition. "Here is the new wing which will be connected to the old structure by what was called a 'dog trot' in old Southern houses. The biggest area includes a great room with built-in bookshelves and a fireplace made of old stone. There's also a connected dining room and kitchen, and two bedrooms and two baths as well. My favorite part is the screened-in front porch running the length of the house overlooking the pond." April was beaming with happiness. She hoped her enthusiasm would spill over to Trip. But she could tell he was not warming to her plans.

April Anne thought about the past summer, and how she had often opened up to Trip about the importance of her spending time with her family, and mending fences that had not really been broken, but certainly had fallen into disrepair. She had tried to make him understand, but this morning it didn't appear that he'd been listening. She took the iPad and sat back in her chair and glanced at the clock on the stove; Mass didn't start for another fifty minutes. She didn't want to argue but she knew that they needed to find a solution to the situation. "Trip, you know I've told you, even before we became romantically involved, of my plans to move home to Quitman. This shouldn't come as a surprise to you. I need that time with my family, and I need that grounding to write this next set of books." She made the statement gently, and imploringly.

Trip looked back at April and shook his head. "I'm sorry, April Anne. I simply don't get it. Things are different now. We've fallen in love, and I want us to always be together. Hell, when this divorce is over, I want you to be my wife." He got up from the table and walked to look out the window over the valley and mountains beyond.

April was doing her best not to get upset, but she was disappointed at Trip's reaction. In their time together, she'd felt that their bond was stronger than what was showing through this morning. "Trip, please look at me. I don't want to talk to your back, and I don't want us to be angry with one another."

Trip turned around and leaned against the sink, crossing his large arms across his chest. "Why can't you live with me in Savannah? I already have the cottage at Tybee. We can move in there to start, and then find a house downtown, or move into Ardsley Park near Lovey. You can build your house near your parents and just visit when you need to." He then gave a loud, frustrated sigh and sat back down. Continuing, he added, "And you've written an entire novel here this summer. Why do you have to move back to the sticks to do another? Why can't it be done in Savannah?"

April Anne counted to five before answering. While Trip wasn't a snob at heart, he was still from what was referred to by the rest of Georgia as 'the Great State of Chatham.' And it just pissed her off to have anyone, including the fellow she loved, refer to her hometown as 'being in the sticks.' "First of all, *Mr. Randolph*, while Quitman is located in rural Georgia, we do wear shoes there, even in the summer, and everyone in my family still has their own teeth. We are not something you'd find out of *Deliverance* with dueling banjos being played across the trailer parks." She noisily slapped her napkin into her plate, rattling the silverware.

Trip realized he had hit a nerve. "Look, I'm sorry I said that. I'm just trying to digest what you're telling me."

April Anne took a sip of coffee, which was now cold, and looked intently across the table. "I'm going to let that comment pass about the sticks; let's pretend you didn't even say it. As for the books, it's not easy to explain. You'd have to be a writer to understand. Yes, I wrote an entire novel this summer, and while it wasn't exactly easy, it was a remake of the other Amy Swann books I've written. I have a formula down pat for that series; many writers have the same sort of suit. We create a captivating protagonist who people like and connect with, retool interesting plot lines, and rewrite them over and over. Luckily, people keep buying them; it's like watching a good television series through the years. I'm fortunate, too, that Amy's character and the storylines are so much in my mind I just need peace and quiet to chug one out."

She scooted her chair around the table to sit next to Trip. Taking his hand in hers she said, "But what I want to do after this last Amy book is vastly different than my previous works. The stories I want to write now are ones that are real, and about people who no one would ever know of unless they lived in the same, small world. A world like Quitman, or any of the other small towns that are dots on the map and connected by two lane county roads in South Georgia."

She was trying to contain her emotions; the combination of his harsh words and her feelings of homesickness were bringing tears to her eyes. Trip took a starched handkerchief from his blazer pocket and handed it to April. "Honey, please don't cry. I'm listening, and I promise I'm trying to understand. Don't be upset." He wiped a tear away as it rolled down her cheek.

"Much of what I want to write is about my family and the people who raised me. I want a record of who they were and what they did in their extraordinarily ordinary lives if that even makes sense to you. Like my Grandmother Pauline, who was born in 1908. She never moved away from the family farm, but she was the wisest and most caring woman I've ever met. Think about how she saw the world evolve around her. She traveled in a horse-drawn carriage when she was a child, and then had a Prius parked in her driveway when she died." She paused to blow her nose and take a deep breath. "Or my Uncle Ken and Aunt Jane, each of whom suffered from cerebral palsy. There was no such thing as physical therapy when they grew up; they learned to walk on their own with canes an old African American gentleman carved for them as kids. Their speech was hard to understand, and life was an obstacle each and every day. But the folks in our little hometown, out in the sticks as you called it, embraced the two of them and made sure that they felt like any other child who grew up during the Depression. When they were born no one expected them to make it out of infancy, but they lived well into their sixties. God, how I love and miss them all." By then tears were freely flowing. She stood and blew her nose, then took a couple of deep breaths to regain her composure. She then looked directly at Trip, and without raising her voice, she simply said, "And for me to write about their lives I have to go home. To live. Not just visit now and again."

Trip stood as well and pulled her into his arms, kissing the top of her head. "Don't worry, honey. We'll work through this. We have to." Though his words were meant to be reassuring, he felt anything but. April Anne had made it clear she was not going to live with him in Savannah, and she had yet to invite him to move in with her in the new home she was putting together. Not that he knew how he would answer such a request if it even came up. He didn't know a soul in Quitman, not that there were too many people there to begin with. Too, he had such a love of the coast, the salt water and the marshes and the beach, he didn't know if he would be happy so far away from the ocean. Pushing those thoughts aside, he stepped back from April and held her at arms' length. "I just need some time to digest all this change. I don't want to think about being without you for any length of time. An uncertain future scares me."

"It scares me, too. But we love each other, and we'll figure it out." April glanced again at the clock. "Before we leave this morning, there's two other things I want to talk to you about."

Trip exhaled slowly. "Whew. OK. Shoot. But I hope what you've got to say isn't as heavy a topic like the one we've just been discussing."

April sat back next to him and gave a smile. "Well, I hope what I say will actually make you happy." She kissed her forefinger and pressed it quickly to his lips. "First off, did you happen to take a peek at the financials and my investment portfolio I emailed to you?"

Trip had agreed to share his thoughts on how her finances were structured and invested since her divorce. "Yes, I gave them a good gleaning over, and your portfolio appears incredibly well balanced and strongly positioned. Was there anything in particular you were concerned about?"

April shook her head. "No, no concerns. I simply want you to take over the management of my money. I want to be your first client when you start off with Haddock & Mason." She smiled and sat back waiting for his reaction. Trip looked a little surprised but pleased. "Seriously? Well, of course, I'd be flattered to be your advisor. And Chad and Collier would be tickled that we could list you as one of our clients." April's net worth in stocks, bonds, and other financial investments was upwards of ten million dollars; she also held a few million in real estate holdings.

"Wonderful. Next item, I'm taking my parents along with my sister and her husband on a week-long cruise in the Caribbean over Thanksgiving." As she reached to take a sip of water, Trip's face fell from being pleased to one of hurt.

Before she could add anything further, he said, "You mean we won't spend the holiday together? You're moving away and our first big holiday you'll be gone, too?" He asked, sitting back in his chair.

"Trip, if you'd let me finish, please," she answered, trying to be patient. "I was about to tell you that I wanted you to go with us. It is about time you met my family. I've booked a small suite for the two of us, and two other balcony staterooms for the family. They're all anxious to meet you and it'll be the perfect way to spend some time together on neutral ground." She was praying that he'd say yes.

Trip was relieved. "That might actually be a nice way to spend the holiday."

April leaned in and kissed him on the cheek. "Oh, it will be fun. I've only been on one years ago for Dad's 55th birthday, and it was so relaxing and carefree." She pulled open her iPad again and went to another saved link. "Here, look, we're sailing on the Celebrity Equinox, and here is a visual of our stateroom and balcony."

Trip looked at the sleek ship and thought, *What the hell? The twins are going with Jana to New York to see the Macy's Thanksgiving parade, and who knows what Lily will want to do with the mood she is in.* "I'd love to go, sugar. And I can't wait to meet your Mom and Dad." He knew her father was a big fisherman, and also had a hankering for good bourbon and cigars. And her Mom sounded like an older version of April Anne; her picture showed a petite lady with sparkling eyes and a warm smile. "What about Brother, though? I don't want to leave him home by himself. Mom will probably spend the holiday in Atlanta with Uncle Whitt and Uncle Brantley and my cousins, although I'm sure they'll ask him to join in."

April patted his hand. "I'd love for him to come. We can ask him at church later this morning. There's still plenty of staterooms left on the ship. I checked last night just in case."

"One last thing. Your Mom and Dad sound great, but you've not painted a pretty picture of your sister and her husband. How will it be to travel with them for a week? You said y'all's relationship had been strained for some time." Trip had dealt with enough family angst lately and didn't want to step into another family drama.

April's older sister Jenny Lynnette was a nurse at the hospital in nearby Thomasville, and her brother-in-law the assistant principal and head football coach at Brooks County High. She adored them growing up, but as April drifted away from the family and her career took off in New York, they seldom saw one another. The distance had turned to resentment on the part of her sister, and she often made comments to the effect that April Anne tried to buy her parent's favoritism with money and material things. Not that Jenny Lynnette ever turned down the many expensive and thoughtful gifts April had given to her and her husband over the years. "Don't worry about them. They'll warm up to you immediately and you'll get along splendidly. They're both Georgia Bulldog fans. Just keep up the talk with them about football and you'll be a hit."

She very much hoped her relationship with Trip would help pave a way back into the lives of her folks back in Quitman. Her ex had driven a wedge in her family that was even deeper than what April had carved out on her own. "OK, I'll trust you on that. Give me a kiss and let's get going." The couple gave each other a quick peck on their way out the door. Both felt they were on better ground than earlier in the morning but worry and concern still crouched in the corners of their minds. April Anne was willing to love Trip with all her heart, but she was also determined to fulfill her promise about rediscovering herself, her family, and her writing. Trip continued wondering why, if April loved him as much as she claimed, she would not consider splitting her time between Savannah and Quitman. It was evident they were at a crossroads, and each knew much would be at stake as the next few months unfolded.

Chapter 36

Lily stood in the parish hall with Eloise and Whit chatting during coffee hour. The Judge had slipped out of the Cathedral to play golf as soon as the final blessing was given, and Leigh Anna was home with a nasty cold. They were discussing plans for Thanksgiving when Eloise caught Jackson Lockwood in her line of vision. "Lily, darling, don't look now, but your handsome doctor friend is walking our way."

Jackson and his late wife had joined the parish when they first moved to Atlanta from Nashville a few decades back. Anytime he spied Lily, he always made it a point to come over and exchange Sunday pleasantries. And to flirt

The last time she had seen him here was three Sundays ago. She had been in the middle of a conversation with a group of friends, talking about an upcoming wedding they were all to attend, and he casually approached the group, his smile at full wattage. The six women standing with Lily parted like the Red Sea to let the striking doctor into their circle. They 'oohed' and 'aahed' and batted their eyes at him, each one thinking that Lily Randolph was a fool to not have snatched him up already. It was obvious to everyone that he was smitten.

So far Lily had been coolly polite and evasive with Jackson since their first meeting in Whittaker's office months back. However, today was going to be a different story. She had undergone a clarifying moment during the homily. Maybe it was because of the influence of Xanax that allowed her to see things with a bit more ease and clarity. During the service, Bishop Shipps had worked the Gospel into his sermon and received a chuckle from the progressive congregation. It was from 1 Peter, and relates "Husbands, in the same way be considerate as you live with your wives, and treat them with respect as the weaker partner." The image of her late husband popped into her mind. Oh, Addison had always treated Lily with the utmost respect, and she had never suspected that he had strayed from his marital vows. Since he had passed, she'd used her marriage to her late husband as a shield to keep at arm's length any man that might show even the slightest interest in her. She finally admitted to herself, though, as the high churchman droned on, that Addison Randolph, Jr. would have remarried within the year if she had been the one to die first. Add was the type of man who needed a wife, someone to look after him and make him feel important. Women can sense those things in a man, and Lily joked in her mind that a dozen women dressed to the nines, and all carrying casseroles, would have been on the front steps waiting for Add when he returned home from her funeral. She decided it was time to move on with life. Along with her new home, it might be nice to have a new man on her arm. As he walked toward her this morning, instead of the usual detached look she gave, Lily smiled warmly and extended her hand. "Hello, Doctor. How are you today?"

The handsome psychiatrist took the outstretched hand into both of his and smiled back. "I'm doing very well, Lily. It's good to see you back home in Atlanta. And as always, you look lovely."

At this point both Whitt and Eloise placed their coffee cups on their respective saucers and looked on expectantly. "Thank you, Jackson." Lily smiled again and withdrew her hand from his to sit her cup of Earl Gray on the table beside her. "I'm in town through Friday, and then heading back to the mountains to make sure I see all the fall color. It is supposed to be a glorious autumn. Will you perhaps be back at Lake Toxaway anytime soon?"

Whitt was not believing his ears nor his eyes. What had gotten into his big sister? She was actually being nice to Jackson. At the same time, Eloise was musing that Lily had been awfully calm all morning, which surprised her. After seeing those news clips of Bitsy, she didn't think her sister-in-law would even make it to Mass, let alone return niceties to a fellow who, until just recently, she had ignored with indifference.

The good doctor paused for a moment, experiencing similar thoughts to those running through the heads of the other two guests in their small circle. While he admittedly was one of the nation's top authorities in his profession, the mind of a woman never ceased to amaze him. "I'm actually going up tomorrow and staying until the Monday before Thanksgiving," he answered with another smile. "Maybe on this trip up you'll finally allow me to take you to dinner one evening? A fellow can always hope."

Lily gave an easy laugh. Besides being incredibly handsome, Jackson Lockwood was also incredibly persistent. "You know, Jackson, I'd like that. Why don't you call me in a couple of days, and we'll make plans."

"I certainly will and look forward to it. Be thinking about where you'd like to go," he answered, thrilled about the prospect of a date, and the fact that Elizabeth Baylor Randolph had finally warmed to him. Changing tones at this point, he turned to Whitt. "I do have some business to discuss with you and Lily. Maybe we can step over to a quiet corner. It won't take long, and this way I won't have to make a trip to your office, Whitt, before I head out of town." He looked apologetically at Eloise. "Mrs. Baylor, I'm sorry, I know this is rude of me, but it won't take long, and they can join you back in just a moment."

Eloise shook her head and gave her hand out to Dr. Lockwood's to shake. "No worries at all, Doctor. I need to run anyway; I'm hosting some friends for lunch and need to get to the Club." She turned and gave Whitt a kiss on the cheek and did the same with Lily.

As Eloise left the room, Jackson led his clients to one of the far corners of the large fellowship hall. In a quiet voice, he said, "I watched the deposition of Thomas Trotter and listened to the tapings from the board meetings. And yes, it is evident that Martha was closely involved in making some important financial and other business decisions while she was in England. She actually is a very shrewd woman when it comes to running Randolph Shipping."

Whitt and Lily both had looks of disappointment on their faces as he finished speaking. Seeing this, he pressed on. "Hear what I said: 'she is a very shrewd woman when it comes to running Randolph Shipping.' I didn't mention anything about her capacity in the area of her personal life, did I?"

Whitt and Lily both answered simultaneously, "What do you mean?"

"Just because a person can be perfectly lucid in one area of life does not mean they are functioning in another. Someone can be at the top of their game mentally for business, but at the same time lack capacity to fully negotiate their way through personal aspects. This happens more often than people realize, particularly with people in high stress jobs who also experience excessive anxiety within their personal lives. They simply cannot deal with both."

Lily and Whitt exchanged glances, and Lily spoke. "So what does this mean for our case? Do you think Martha still has a chance of having the suit dismissed?" Worry lines creased her forehead, and Whitt tapped his foot anxiously to hear the reply. "Don't worry about having it dismissed; the letters from Martha, along with the Darlington-Smythe deposition, make your stance extremely viable. And, as I indicated, I can argue with solid proof that mental clarity in one area does not rule out the inability to function properly in another."

"But?" Whitt ask, hearing a slight hesitation in Jackson's voice.

"The 'but' here is that juries find it hard to conceive this concept of varied capacity. It is a much harder sell, and although documented precedents have been set in court law around its legitimacy, it may be tough to get those 12 people sitting in the box at court to buy into it. In other words, what I thought would be an easy win, I'd now only give a fifty-fifty chance. I wish there were better odds, but this new evidence changes the game."

Whitt let out a low whistle. He looked at Lily. "What do you think, Sis? There is a lot at stake here. I mean, you were just blasted on TV by cousin Bitsy. There will be more publicity to come; that *New York Times* reporter has called my office three times this past week wanting a comment. Who knows where she'll go next." By this point, Whitt actually was hoping Lily would drop the suit. It was not going to be fun moving forward.

Lily thought for a mere two seconds. "We're pushing ahead. I will not have Martha signing away the twins' lawful rights to their family home. Publicity be damned. There isn't any real dirt in this family to report; let the press try and parody us into a soap opera if they want." She patted her brother on the cheek and gave him a quick kiss. "I'll see you in in Highlands next weekend." Turning to Jackson, she smiled and said as she walked away, "And I'll look forward to hearing from you soon."

Chapter 37

Peyton and Ray sat at a small table at one of Charlottesville's many downtown pubs, enjoying a sampling of locally made craft beer and a couple of fat cheeseburgers and a pizza. They were resting after a chilly afternoon of biking the twisting turns of Walnut Creek Trail. Like their dad and uncle, both loved being active outdoors, and each other's company. They were in many ways like Trip and Baylor in temperament and personality, and the similarities even showed through in how they spoke to one another. The twins had picked up the older siblings' habit of referring to one another as 'Brother' from the time they were young boys in pre-school.

For the most part, their conversations were always lighthearted and at ease. Growing up, they had been able to shrug off the underlying tenseness of their parents' relationship, and childhood and the teen years had been one of comfort at home and of acceptance at school. Today's exchange had been much more serious than usual, though. While no one in their family had spoken to them about the situation with Ship Watch and between their grandmother and great-grandmother, the twins were aware of what was going on. Then, after months of trying to stay on the sidelines, two situations arose over the weekend, making them realize it was time to get involved. First, each had been contacted by news reporters. One was from *People* magazine, and the other from *The New York Times.* The second incident involved a fraternity brother from Atlanta, who had joked at a keg party over the weekend about the possibility of the two affluent Randolph twins becoming 'homeless.'

As Peyton drained his pint and reached over to grab the last slice of pizza from the serving platter, he asked his twin, "So we're in agreement about what we want to do? You don't have any second thoughts?"

Ray deftly grabbed a hunk of sausage mid-air from the piece of pie in Peyton's hand and popped it in his mouth before his brother could get it onto his plate. "Yep. I'm good." He then reached over to help himself to a couple of his brother's French fries. "It just astounds me that no one, not a single soul, from Mama to Daddy to anybody else in this entire family, has said a word to us about this lawsuit. Do they think we're just totally oblivious?"

Picking up his fork, and pointing it toward Ray, Peyton answered, "Brother, if you touch any of my food again, I will stab you. That is a solemn promise."

"Well, there's nothing left now, so don't worry." Catching the waitress's eye, he pointed to his pint mug and held up two fingers. Looking back at his brother, he continued on, more seriously. "Yes, I'm in agreement. First, we will not speak to any reporters. Nor will we mention this conversation or our plans to anyone else. And finally, I will call Grand Martha and invite ourselves down to Sea Island for the weekend."

"Great. If anyone in the family will give us some straight answers, it'll be Grand Martha. We might or might not agree with her, but we know she'll tell the truth."

Ray shook his head with a slightly puzzled look on his face. "I know. That is part of what confuses me. Of all the relatives, I would have thought she and Auggie would've taken us aside and told us what was going on. It's not like there wasn't ample opportunity; I mean, we were at the cottage two or three times a week this whole summer."

Peyton thought a moment and reached over the table to slap his brother affectionately on the shoulder. "She was just trying to protect us. Just like Mama and Daddy have done all these years, never verbally letting on about their marital problems, always trying to hide it from me and you, trying to save us from any hurt."

Ray nodded slightly. "You're right. The intentions were good. But I do agree, we need to move on this. Here, I'll go ahead and get in touch with Grand Martha now." He picked up his phone and walked outside to the quiet of the sidewalk to make the call. If he knew his great-grandmother like he thought he did, she probably would be wondering why it had taken so long for him and Brother to come asking for explanations.

Chapter 38

The Savannah Golf Club Challenge is held each year over Columbus Day weekend and is the biggest charitable sport tournament in the city. The area's most serious players, at least the ones willing to donate ten grand a foursome, are on the course that day. Jana and Bebe had waited patiently for this outing; it would prove to be the perfect time to 'drop the bomb.'

Buck Pearson's company was always one of the tournament's largest sponsors, and he usually looked forward to this day on the links. Being a sponsor gave him center stage, and he loved the spotlight. But since that night when Jana was at his house, his mind was totally preoccupied with what exactly had happened; he could not remember anything at all. He recalled Jana's walking through his door, bag in hand, but from that moment forward, nothing. He had woken up just after 3 p.m. the following afternoon, naked in his bed. After he had showered and taken four Advil, chased down with a beer, he searched the house but could not find a trace of anything from the night before. He started to call Jana several times, but always stopped short. He didn't want to hear that he had passed out from too much to drink and couldn't perform. And she certainly had not contacted him.

These thoughts were rolling around in his head as he made his way into the club's bar for the pre-tournament lunch. The place was already crowded, and as he came through the doorway, and folks noticed he was there, the room became quiet. The four dozen or so men, whether they were standing in groups or sitting down at tables, all stopped to stare at him for a moment. Several snickered into their drinks, while others put their heads together and whispered. *What the fuck is going on here*, Buck wondered as he made his way to the bar and ordered a double scotch from Andrew, a bartender who had worked at the club for almost three decades.

The two men he stood between, neither of whom he liked, turned their backs as Andrew silently passed the Johnny Walker Blue Label across the polished wood to Buck. This whole situation was almost surreal. Looking to his left, he tapped the man on his shoulder, determined to make someone speak. "Marty, how's it going, fella?" he said, trying to be as casual as possible. Before the man could answer, Buck barked across the table, "Hey, Andrew, hurry up and slide me a bowl of those nuts over here." He then added in a voice loud enough for a few people to hear, "Lazy ass."

Buck's condescending command got the attention of Marty, and several of the golfers in the vicinity of the bar. Marty Clifton was one of the town's most "hail-fellow-well-met" sort of men and possessed a wicked sense of humor. He now turned around, put up his hand toward the bartender, and said in a loud voice that carried across the room, "Hey, Andrew, my friend. Make sure that bowl of has plenty of Brazil nuts in it for Mr. Pearson. I hear he *really* likes to," and he paused for effect, "eat Brazil nuts."

Buck stood there with a puzzled look on his face as people around the room broke out into laughter. Again, he wondered just what the fuck was happening here. After the snickering died down a few seconds later, another Savannah golf fixture, and one of Marty's buddies since childhood, chimed in from down the bar with a shout. "Hey, Buck. They're grilling foot-long hot dogs today for lunch. We understand they're your favorite thing to gnaw on."

Again, the group burst into laughter. Marty, who was a renowned cook and knew his food, added in, "Yeah, hopefully the chef has some of those exotic hot dogs on hand like ol' Buck likes. Some of those spicy ones like a big, fat chorizo."

Andrew timed it perfectly; while the men were laughing, he slid a plain, 6 x 9-inch manila envelope onto the bar right in front of Buck. It was just like the other twenty he had placed in the men's locker room that morning before the club had opened. Since starting work at the club in 1980, he had not encountered a more unpleasant and distasteful man than Buck Pearson within the walls of the establishment. Behind the bar, he overheard private conversations and often was taken into confidence by many of the members. He knew that the old guard at the club merely tolerated the man because of his well-beloved late wife and her family. The newer members, those who weren't natives to the area, limited their company with him, but took advantage of his need to show off how much he could spend on a chit. Buck bought companionship with steaks and expensive scotch and bourbon.

And while Buck was his most disliked of patrons, Jana Randolph had been one of his favorites. She and her brother-in-law, Baylor, often played tennis together and would then sit and visit at the bar after a set. Sometimes she would come in alone as well and take a seat out on the veranda to read a book and wait for her sons while they played golf or tennis, or swam in the pool. She always engaged Andrew in pleasantries, asked about his family, and was a genuinely nice person. He felt she was a bit out of place amongst the other members; while she was a Randolph, she just didn't seem to be interested in all the trappings of local society. When she approached him with a favor, he'd readily accepted. Too, she had slipped him fifty, one-hundred-dollar bills in the chit presenter. That five thousand dollars was taking his family of six to Disney World over Christmas.

Buck, clearly agitated and his brow tensed up in knots, slung back his drink, banged it down on the polished wood, and said impatiently to Andrew, "Another." He then saw the envelope. When he picked it up and opened the flap, photos spilled out onto the bar. He stared down at ten, full color, glossy pictures of two men who were apparently having sex. "What the hell is this?"

At this point, the entire bar became silent. Andrew leaned against the back counter, towel folded under one arm, a blank look on his face. Buck glanced around the room and saw that all eyes were on him. He then looked back down at the photos. The camera had captured two naked men in bed, and in positions fit for a porn shoot. Buck quickly recognized his bedroom but had no idea of who the tanned and muscled man with the Brazilian flag tattoo was. Then horror and cold shock set in when he realized that *he* was the second person in the trashy clips. He started having flashbacks, one after the other, none particularly clear, but enough to remember Jana, and then two men in the house, and a heavy body straddling him in his bed. Then nothing else. His head was swimming, and he thought he would pass out right there at the bar. He looked up as people were continuing to stare at him. "This is all some sort of sick joke." He said aloud in disbelief. Buck then turned in the direction of Marty, who just stared at him in bored disgust. "This is NOT me. I'm NOT gay. I only have sex with women." What he failed to add, of course, was that a large percentage of those women were not given a choice in the matter.

One of Marty's golf partners, and a cousin of Mary Nan, stepped up to the bar. He had long waited for a moment like this. No one in the family liked Buck, and all blamed him for his wife's death. They had kept quiet these many years, but here was the chance when no one would care what was said. "Buck, there isn't anyone in this room who knows or cares if you are straight or gay; that doesn't matter. What does matter, though, is that you are low-life scum who tries to fit in with your money and by marrying into my family." Before he turned his back, he finished with, "Why don't you take your bigoted, racist ass and get the hell out of here?"

Buck realized no one was looking at him now; he was being completely shunned. Always the bully, even he knew what an idiot he seemed to these men: time and time again he had made both racial and sexual slurs about Latinos, gays and lesbians, and here he was pictured, in graphic detail, in bed with a dark-skinned man. *This was all Jana's doings. She must've drugged me and set me up. I'll kill that bitch.* He stormed out of the room, photos in hand, the embarrassment unbearable.

He half ran across the parking lot and flung himself into his Porsche 911 coupe; opening the glove compartment, he pulled out his pistol and checked to see that it was fully loaded. Satisfied, he tossed it into the passenger seat. He floored the gas and swung onto the magnolia lined road leading from the historic club grounds. *That whore!*

screamed over and over in his mind. How he had taken advantage of, and hurt, dozens of women over the years never entered his self-centered, narcissistic thoughts. Buck raced through the brick and wrought iron entrance gates with barely a glance into the four lanes of traffic that comprised President Street. He never heard the blasting horn of the massive ProService dump truck that was hauling a load of construction waste. The driver of the truck swerved, but still clipped the back end of the coupe. The force of the multi-ton truck, which was traveling at a steady 45 miles an hour, and the speed of Buck's sports car, sent the Porsche spiraling into the air. It flipped over onto itself half a dozen times and landed with a solid thud into a wooded lot across the road. Before the truck driver could come to a stop and climb down from his vehicle, the Porsche burst into flames, the fire roaring up into a column that engulfed the surrounding pine trees. Passersby stopped to get out of their cars and see the spectacle. Many prayed for whoever the poor soul was in the burning vehicle. Everyone watching knew that no one could possibly come out of that inferno alive.

Chapter 39

The following Friday night, Trip, April Anne, Lovey, and Baylor gathered in the main house for a going away dinner. April Anne would head to Quitman the next morning, and the foursome would not all be together again until Lovey's wedding two months away. They were in good spirits, but the meal was still tinged with sadness. Both Baylor and Lovey were happy for April Anne's recent successes; the novel she had written over the summer was finished and sent to her publisher, and filming of the Amy Allyn Swann detective movie had begun. April had been excited the award-winning actress Laura Dern was cast as the leading role, though she believed Ms. Dern would need to gain thirty pounds to play the part. The two cousins were going to miss having her in Highlands, and they knew that Trip was going to have a rough go of it; he was head over heels in love with the author. The group lingered over a delicious entrée of fresh mountain trout that Lovey had sautéed in a rich butter and lemon sauce. She'd prepared a pilaf to go along with it, made with aromatic Satilla River rice, and served a dish of fresh creamed spinach alongside. "Lovey, you outdid yourself again. Lachlan is going to be fatter than one of his bulls with all this good cooking." Baylor laughed and swatted Lovey as she placed a homemade apple cobbler on the table.

Lovey swatted back with a light cuff to his blonde head. "Pour the champagne, you big lug. It's time to make a toast."

After their glasses were filled, Lovey raised her glass. "First, here's to the newly single, and very handsome and eligible, Addison Peyton Randolph, the third. While I do wish Jana the best, I'm so very, very happy for you today." Trip raised his glass towards his cousin, and they all clinked their flutes together.

"Thank you, Lovey. God knows it was a long time coming. She's walking away with a ton of money she doesn't need, but I don't regret a single penny." He smiled and leaned over to give April Anne a kiss on the cheek. He hoped he would not stay single for long, but it was just too early to tell with April leaving to live in another part of the state. For now, they would be in a long-distance holding pattern.

Lovey then continued. "And congratulations to the uber successful April Anne Adams. Her new book will be another bestseller, and a TV sensation." Again, the crystal goblets chimed around the table. "We are going to so, so miss you."

April blushed and looked around the table at her friends. There was no doubt she was in love with Trip, and her most ardent wish was that their relationship would remain strong and solid while she settled in her new home. Lovey was just like a sister to her, and she had come to think of Baylor in those same, familial terms. These three were the best friends she had ever had. Holding up her napkin she pinched the bridge of her nose tightly. "I refuse to cry," she said, holding back the tears. "I will miss you all as well. We'll get together often. I promise to visit Savannah and come back next summer to Highlands. And Lovey, I can't wait to see you and Lachlan at Honey Ridge Ranch. I swear."

Baylor spoke up with his sense of play and humor. "Pray tell where is our invitation to South Georgia? When you showed us the house plans, it looked like there were plenty of guest rooms, hint, hint," he said, dramatizing with two big winks. Baylor's question made Trip tense up. He was anxious to hear April Anne's answer. While she had invited him to meet her family on a cruise, no such invitation for a visit to her hometown had been extended. April Anne waited half a breath to answer, but the hesitation was not lost on the other three. "Baylor, I'd love to have you all down in 'my neck of the woods' as they say. I hope to have everything finished and in place by Christmas. Let's see how busy everyone is after Lovey and the new hubby get back from their Parisian honeymoon." Changing the subject, she continued looking on at the younger Randolph brother. "I so wish you were coming with us on this cruise. My folks would love to meet you."

Baylor winked at her again. "I don't want your folks thinking you caught the wrong Randolph. You know Brother refuses to have his picture made next to me, don't you?" He laughed and then said more seriously, "But I need to stay and help Lovey and Mom with the wedding plans. They'll have me toting and fetching 24/7 over the holidays."

At this point Lily and Dr. Lockwood entered the dining room, just arriving back from their third date. Lily's two attentive sons stood and gave their mother a kiss on the cheek, while Jackson shook their hands and gave a movie-star smile to Lovey and April Anne. Baylor turned to the doctor after all the pleasantries and slapped the older man, a bit hard on the shoulder. Jackson winced but managed to grin in good humor. "So, Doc," the big athlete said, keeping his hand gripped in place, "this is, what? The third time out for dinner in two weeks? I certainly hope you have good intentions towards our sainted mother," he said in a very serious tone, looking the man dead in the eye.

Before her date could answer, Lily spoke up. "Baylor, stop with your silly nonsense and sit down." Looking at Jackson, she said with a shrug of the shoulders, "My 'little boy' has an unusual sense of humor, and most of the time he is the only one that gets the laugh."

Baylor chuckled and gave the man a bear hug, and then held him out at arm's length. "Just kiddin,' doc. We're thrilled you and Mama are dating. Keeps her attention off of me and Brother."

Everyone laughed while Lily rolled her eyes. "Jackson, I had a lovely evening. Thank you again." She raised her cheek to let him give her a kiss. "Tomorrow night is my treat. I'll just meet you at the Club at six. Does that sound good?"

"Absolutely. Thanks for inviting me." Looking at his watch, he said, "I'll see myself out. It's almost 11 already. "You all have a nice night," he said and waved gamely to the group.

"I'll walk you to the door, Jackson," Lily said and looped her arm in his. "I'll be right back," she said looking at Lovey. "And I'd love a taste of that cobbler and maybe some decaf."

"Absolutely, coming right up." Lovey retrieved another spoon and bowl while Baylor went to the Keurig machine and made a quick cup of coffee.

Lily returned and sat down just as Lovey placed her dessert on the table. No one spoke as Lily stirred her cup. "What?" she asked, realizing that the four were looking expectantly at her. Lovey rolled her eyes. "Oh, Lily, come on. Tell us. How was the date? You two have been out three times already, and tomorrow he's escorting you to the Fall social." She clapped her hands together and followed enthusiastically with her signature line, "This is all just too much for words!"

Lily gave a small, indulgent smile. "There isn't anything much to tell, my dear. We just enjoy one another's company. And let's face it," she said, with a short tinkling laugh, "he isn't hard on the eyes, is he?"

Trip and Baylor exchanged quick, wondering glances. The elder brother spoke up before Baylor could offer up one of his asides. "Brother and I are very happy for you, Mama. It is good to hear you, well, giggle." Lily arched an eyebrow and became serious again. "I do not giggle, and you know that. Let's change the subject, shall we?" Looking at April Anne, she said, "I really wish you would stay for just one more night, dear. The party tomorrow is the last big hurrah before everyone heads home for the holidays. I know there will be any number of folks there that want to tell you goodbye."

"I very much appreciate the invitation, Lily, and I know it will be a fun party. But my Mom and Dad return home tomorrow, and I want to be there to greet them. Too, the contractor wants to meet with me to do a walk-through of the site. I hope to start moving in later this week."

"I understand, dear. What time do you leave?" Lily responded as she took a bite of the cobbler. "Well, I'm packed and hope to get on the road in the morning right at daylight. It's a 400-mile drive and will take me about 8 hours. I want to get there before dark."

Lily noticed her eldest as April Anne spoke, and though she knew he was trying to be stoic, he appeared to her like a little boy whose best friend was moving away. Which, she supposed, was true. It almost broke her heart. "Well, drive safely and make certain you call and let us know that you made it home without incident."

Trip looked at his Mom when she finished speaking and asked, "Did you bring it?"

"Yes, darling. Remember, patience is a virtue," she smiled as she reached beside her and pulled a slender, rectangular gift box from her purse. She silently handed it to Trip who then placed the gift on the table in front of April Anne

"Oh, my, Trip," April Anne gushed as she looked down at the beautifully wrapped package. "This is so sweet. Thank you." She stood up to give him a kiss on the cheek.

"You'll need to give everyone a kiss, hon. The present is a going away gift from all of us." He motioned with his hand, "Open it up."

April Ann carefully untied the bow and wrapping, took out the jewel box, and snapped open the lid. Inside was a triple-linked gold bracelet with six exquisitely made charms attached. Holding it up to admire, she found two Labradors, a golf club, a trout sporting amber eyes, the roman numeral 'VI,' and a thistle with dark green enamel petals and a lavender bloom. She was at a loss for words. Each piece spoke of her hosts: the labs from both Trip and Baylor, as well as the golf club and trout, the thistle was all Lovey McGregor, and she guessed, correctly, that the number six was from Mrs. Randolph. "The boys wanted me to have my charm be a replica of the motel sign, but I flat put my foot down about that. Hopefully this classier 'six' will still remind you of your time here." Lily stood and gently squeezed the younger lady's shoulder. April Anne had come to think of this past summer as her season of healing, and almost a rebirth. The incredible friendships formed had taken her from the aftermath of a bitter divorce to a spot to where she knew she was ready to move on with life and face the next chapter with eagerness. But the realization of how much she was going to miss seeing Lovey and Baylor, even Mrs. Randolph, who she liked and admired, was just overwhelming. And, knowing that she would not wake up next to Trip for quite some time, brought on an avalanche of tears. Through her waterworks she managed to finally say, "This is the most thoughtful and wonderful gift I have ever received." She turned around into Trip's arms and buried her head in his chest.

"Oooh, honey, don't do that, don't do that." Lovey exclaimed as she, too, broke down into tears. "I just cannot bear it." Baylor, who was misty-eyed himself, grabbed one of Lovey's fluttering hands and held it tight. He was going to miss the hell out of April Anne. Lily looked on for a moment, taking in the scene. It made her heart happy that her eldest had found what seemed to be true love after all of these years, but it also ached at knowing Trip was going to hurt until he and April Anne could resolve their relationship. She had vowed to stay out of it, and she would keep that promise, she told herself. At least for the time being, anyway.

Chapter 40

Patrick's morning began in the midst of the group gathered on the pebbled courtyard to see April Anne off. The new Subaru Outback had been loaded with her luggage, computer, and a number of locally crafted items she had bought over the summer to use in decorating her new home. She drove away amidst waves and tears at 7:00 a. m.

After the goodbyes, Lovey was able to drive herself to Lachlan's to spend the rest of the day as her license had recently been reinstated. Baylor had a number of tennis lessons to give through the afternoon and departed for the country club. Patrick then spent the remainder of the day with Lily and Trip

Patrick was in his last semester at UGA with only one class to complete. He had stayed on in Highlands at the invitation of Trip after his chauffeuring duties with Lovey were no longer needed; the once-a-week commute to Athens each Wednesday was an easy drive. Patrick was drawn to Trips work with the family foundation, and through several discussions about conservation and community health initiatives, he started evaluating various funding proposals and other requests to help with the workload. The process came rather naturally to him, and he and Trip had discussed a full-time position after the upcoming graduation. Trip would need someone to work alongside him as his clientele increased at Haddock & Mason. Lily had joined them that morning and helped read through the accepted applications for grants for the coming year. Together they would divvy up the more than fifteen million dollars to distribute in early January. Later that afternoon, following a five-mile jog and a quick shower, he drove the three of them to the club for the autumn celebration, arriving right at 6 o'clock. They were greeted by Jackson in the parking lot, and all walked in together to join the party. Whitt, Brantley, and their two wives arrived a few minutes later, as did Lovey and Lachlan. Patrick excused himself early on and made his way to the buffet table after grabbing a Michelob at the bar. Lunch had been a light meal at noon, and the jog left him famished. He spent a good quarter-hour grazing on the plentiful selection, making small talk with other members as he consumed two carved beef tenderloin sandwiches, several chicken fingers, and a plate of chilled shrimp with cocktail sauce. After finally moving away from the food, he plucked up another beer and meandered back toward the bar. He found himself standing several feet away from Lovey, Lily, and Lily's two sisters-in-law, who were animatedly talking together in a circle. As he quietly sipped his beer, not wanting to intrude in on their conversation, two more women and a gentleman approached. Patrick was close enough to hear the conversation.

"Ladies, hello, there. It is so good to see you. Harold and I wanted to introduce you to our friend; we're placing her and her husband up for membership here at the Club." She then motioned to the woman standing next to her. "Heather, I want you to meet our dear friends," she said, as she pointed in turn, "Lily Randolph, Eloise Baylor, and Leigh Anna Baylor. These three elegant ladies are all sisters-in-law. And this," she continued on, pointing, "is Lovey MacGregor." Then gesturing to her guest, she said, "Let me present Heather Bedford. Heather's husband, Adam, is a new partner at Harold's firm. They just moved to Atlanta from Dalton, their hometown." Pausing for a quick moment, she then looked at Lily, and added, "I actually think they are neighbors of yours, their place is just a few doors down from your tower."

Lily was standing facing directly towards Patrick, and he could tell a slight change in Mrs. Randolph's expression. Her look was discerned, too, by the two Baylor wives and Lovey. Lily tilted her head slightly and tapped her wine glass with a perfectly manicured nail. Before she could respond, Heather spoke up, her voice carrying to Patrick clearly, even though her back was turned to him. It sounded, as Lovey would describe later, piss elegant pretentious.

"How nice to meet you. Of course, I've heard all about each of you. You certainly are all known in the very best of circles." Turning to Lovey, she said, "And I've seen your work in all the right magazines. I'd love to have you come by and give me some advice on our new condo. It's a quaint little place, just under four thousand square feet." Lovey started to reply, but Heather interrupted. "We are so very excited to be able to join this wonderful Club. We plan to rent a house the coming season while we have ours built; we purchased a lot in Old Sayers Mill." Looking back at Lovey, she added, "Perhaps you could lend me a hand there, as well?

Not stopping to catch her breath, she sallied onward to the group, "What a lovely time I had here today. Margaret and I," she said, gesturing toward her hostess, "played two sets of tennis this morning. We even took in a session by a handsome and dreamy sports pro. That sort of service is certainly an amenity." Not catching the rather bland and non-committal looks she was getting from her small audience, and before her hostess could save her, she added, "Oh, speak of the devil. There is that dishy tennis pro over in the corner; it looks like he is having a cocktail." Patrick could not see the look on the young woman's face, but the tone of her voice was just shy of condescending. "How quaint that the Club allows hired help to mix and mingle during socials. I suppose it drums up business for golf and tennis."

Patrick could see Margaret and Harold Greene's embarrassed faces. Margaret reached out to grab Heather's arm to walk her away from the group. Before she could do so, Lovey, who in future stories about the night would say that she didn't like Heather Bedford before she even opened her haughty mouth, said rather archly, "Why Heather. Were you not introduced to that dishy pro?" She paused for a second. "You didn't catch his last name? Hmmm?" Lovey waited again for effect. "It's Randolph," she finished, gesturing with her head slightly toward Lily. Margaret let her hand drop from Heather, while Harold backed up and hurriedly left the group, making his way towards the bar. Margaret would not speak to him for several days afterwards for leaving her behind.

Patrick thought the newcomer must be as dim as she was snotty because she could not make the connection. "I'm sorry. I don't know what you mean." This time Leigh Anna spoke up. Whittaker's wife was known for frank observations, and her sense of directness increased with alcohol. Taking the last drink from her second appletini, she said, "His last name is Randolph. As in Baylor Stephens Randolph. The son of Lily Baylor Randolph. And my nephew as well as Eloise's. He inherited more in one trust fund than your hubby will ever make as a law partner at Harold's little practice." She had added in the last remark to be catty towards Margaret; neither woman liked the other and their husbands' firms were bitter business rivals.

By now Heather realized she had made a serious faux paux. She replied, rather lamely, and with a bit of a defensive tone. "Oh. I see. Well, you can't blame me, I didn't mean anything untoward. I just knew he was an employee here, and certainly didn't realize he was related to anyone that was a member."

Lovey chimed back in at this point. "Well, Heather, that employee actually *is* a member here, as is his Mother, and his Grandmother, and all of his close relatives, me included."

By now Margaret was mortified, and she again put her hand firmly onto Heather's elbow. Mouthing silently to Lily, "I'm SO SORRY," she hurriedly pivoted to her left, and almost knocked over the man who had just seconds before came to stand behind her and Heather. He spoke to them both. "Margaret. Heather. I was just coming to look for you two. I can't seem to find Harold." Margaret rolled her eyes. *That's because the coward is probably hiding out on the toilet.*

Both Lily and Lovey had recognized Adam Bedford's name when it was first mentioned, and upon seeing the fellow in front of them, they knew for certain it was Baylor's ex. Lily had seen his photo in her son's apartment all those years ago, and Lovey, upon learning about Adam earlier in the summer, had googled him and found his photo on Linkedin. Lily spoke up, putting her hand out towards Margaret. "Wait a moment, please, Margaret dear. This must be Heather's husband, Adam." She coolly looked the man up and down. "I believe you were friends with my son, Baylor." The attorney smiled and gave a puzzled look. "I'm sorry, I don't think we've met. I'm Adam Bedford." He offering out his hand toward Lily to shake. Eloise, Lovey, and Leigh Anna all three lifted eyebrows. A gentleman does not extend his hand to a lady unless she offers hers first. Margaret shook her head at the entire lamentable scene and moaned inwardly. *What in the hell has Harold gotten me into?*

Lily ignored the gesture. "No, we've not met, but I know who you are. Baylor told me about the friendship the two of you shared in Atlanta, years back. You do remember meeting my son, Baylor Randolph? He's there, over in the corner." Lily pointed with her wine glass toward her youngest son, who was still oblivious that he was being discussed. Adam turned to look in that direction. Lovey sensed where this discussion would go, and quietly moved Eloise and Leigh Anna away from the group without a word. Watching them leave, Lily spoke to the two women standing beside Adam. "Margaret, why don't you take Heather to the buffet and give me and Mr. Bedford a moment to chat about the Club. Since I'm on the membership committee I can give him a run down on expectations." She gave Heather an icy smile, and Margaret almost ran at the chance to get away, pulling the younger woman along with her.

"Well, now, Adam Bedford. I finally get to meet the pathetic ass of a man who treated my son so badly," Lily said, not raising her voice and smiling for those who might glance her way. "That boy loved you, and you treated him like dirt. I won't even begin to tell you what you put him through, because I don't believe you'd care. Not one bit."

Adam started to speak, but Lily cut him off. "No, no, I don't need to hear anything from you, save your breath. Just let me say you should be glad I didn't have you hunted down and have your knees broken." The man blanched at Lily's words; the demeanor she evoked, her tone, and the steel in her eyes were dead serious. Adam glanced nervously around to make sure no one was listening and gave another embarrassed look towards the unawares Baylor.

Lily took a step closer to Adam, and Patrick heard her distinctly as she continued. "I hear you and your pompous, silly little wife want to be members at Highlands. Is that so? Well, let me explain something to you. My brother Brantley is the chair of the membership committee. My grandparents helped found this club. And it will be a cold, cold day in hell before you ever get an invitation to join here."

Slowly twirling her wine glass, she went on with an additional social blow. "I understand you all just moved to Atlanta, too. Let me save you some time with your ambitious social climbing. There is absolutely no need at all to apply for membership at the Driving Club, or at Cherokee, for that matter. I'll make sure you're blackballed from both with my most earnest and utmost pleasure."

Stunned, Adam was speechless. Lily reveled in his discomfort. "In fact, when I'm done with you, Adam Bedford, you'll be lucky to get an invitation to join the local Moose Lodge."

Smiling with satisfaction, Lily turned on her heels and left the shamed man staring at the wall in front of him; Patrick could clearly see his hands were shaking. After a moment, Adam looked again at Baylor, then started across the room in his direction. Patrick stood still, watching. As the attorney made his way through the crowd, Baylor finally looked up in his direction. He blinked twice, and recognizing his former boyfriend, backed away toward one of the sets of French doors leading onto the patios below. He was through the opening in a blink, with Adam following right behind. Patrick waited for a moment trying to decide what to do, then finally walked out the side entrance and circled around to the terrace.

It was a cold night, and the club had not opened the outside areas for the party. With the stealth of his former training, he silently approached and stepped into the evening shadows of an enormous rhododendron. Adam had caught up with Baylor, who whirled around and with a voice Patrick had never heard from him before, coldly ask, "What the fuck do you want, Adam?"

Adam placed his hands in his pants pockets and rocked back and forth to ease some tension. With a short laugh, he said, "Is that any way to greet an old friend? It's been what, almost twenty years since we've seen one another?"

Not getting an answer, he continued, "You're certainly looking good. You're even more handsome now than I remembered." Patrick's stomach turned over in knots at the personal comment between the two men. Baylor answered in disgust. "You left me, Adam, not once, but twice. You broke my heart, and I actually prayed that I'd never lay eyes on you again."

"I'm sorry, Baylor, I am. But we were kids. We didn't know what love really was, or what it meant." He shrugged his shoulders to indicate his lack of concern of the situation.

"Bullshit. You were full of bullshit then, and full of it now. Just go the fuck away." Anger boiling over, Baylor turned so that he didn't have to look at the asshole any longer.

"Ok. I realize it was hard on you when we broke up, but you knew what we had wasn't permanent. I had my career to consider, and there was no place for us in society. Gay couples are a joke, no one takes that shit seriously." Adam had a touch of scorn in his voice as he talked to Baylor's back.

Baylor turned around and shook his head. "God, how I ever loved you is beyond my imagination. Now what do you want? Why are you here? I have absolutely nothing to say to you."

Adam's temper and arrogance, which had not diminished with age, could be heard in his voice as he answered. "Look. My wife and I are moving here for the summers, and we want to belong to this club. Many of my firm's clients are members, and I need to be a part. And your bitch of a mother just told me that she was having me blackballed. She even threatened to have us blackballed at the Driving Club and the Cherokee Club as well. My partners won't understand why I can't get in, and I'll lose my job, you dense jock."

Baylor froze in place for almost a count of three. He then stepped forward, and with his massive right hand back slapped Adam so hard the man fell to his knees on the flagstone floor. Standing over him, Baylor quietly said, "Don't you ever, ever call my mother a bitch. Now get out of here. You can kiss your precious membership wishes bye-bye."

Struggling to his feet, Adam turned viciously to him. "I'm going to sue you for assault and attempted murder. You could have broken my neck. I'll take you for everything you own. You won't get away with humiliating me like this."

"Go ahead. Sue away. I won't hold my breath. You'd be the laughingstock of any law firm in the South."

Adam rubbed his jaw, which was throbbing, and hobbled up the set of stairs towards the club's main floor, glaring back twice.

Baylor watched him leave, and then turned to lean against the wrought-iron banister, taking in deep breaths to calm down.

At that moment, Lily stood at the top of the opposite stairs and watched her son collect himself. Worried, she had been looking for him after the altercation with Adam inside. She started down to the patio, but then stopped short as she saw Patrick emerge from the darkness.

Baylor noticed Patrick at the same time, walking silently like a sentinel. The young man was full of anxiety. The whole episode that had unfolded in front of him was beyond disturbing. It wasn't about the violence; he was a soldier. It was rather the exchange and knowledge of what transpired between the two other men which had him upset.

"What do you want, Patrick?" Baylor asked, his agitation obvious. "The last thing I need right now is your judgmental looks and attitude."

Patrick took a step closer towards Baylor and into the shine of the bright harvest moon and the lighting of the club's landscaping. He felt even more nervous as he stood there than he had facing enemy fire in Afghanistan. The words he needed to say were stuck in his throat, and he was unable to speak.

Baylor was a bundle of nerves himself. While he was totally over his former lover and had moved on with his life, seeing Adam's conceited ass was beyond unsettling. Too, the man's words about love and relationships infuriated him. With all that had just happened, Baylor had no patience for Patrick Hogan at the moment. Looking at him squarely, he said, "I asked you a question. What do you want, and besides, why are you spying on me?"

Moving a bit closer to the younger man, he continued on, his own temper rising again. "I have spent most of the summer tolerating your attitude, your refusal to talk to me, and I've ignored that sour look on your face anytime something to do with me comes up in conversation. It's evident you don't approve of me, and my being gay. So again, I ask, what do you want?"

When Patrick still didn't answer, Baylor turned and stepped back to the railing, placing both hands on the cold iron. His shoulders shook a bit, and he fought back tears of frustration. From where Lily was standing, she could see that he was utterly miserable. She watched as Patrick carefully approached close to her son. Finally finding his voice, he said, "That's not it at all, Baylor. It's, it's..." he stumbled with his words, "...just hard to explain."

Baylor turned to give him a cold stare. "What's hard to explain? You've explained plenty. We used to be friends, we had fun together, and then this summer you acted as if I were a pariah. When I came out about being gay, you completely turned your back on me."

Again, Patrick spoke nervously, not trusting himself to say the right thing. "No, no, I promise, it wasn't about you being gay." He hesitated for a moment. "It was hearing about all of those men you were dating." He stopped, not knowing how to say the rest.

"I don't get it, and frankly, right now, after all I've been through tonight, I don't want to hear any lame excuses. Please. Just leave."

Baylor walked several feet down to the other end of the patio to distance himself. Patrick worked up his courage and plowed on. It was now or never.

"Please, please listen to me." Baylor slowly turned his head with a look of tiredness in his eyes.

Lily thought, *Oh, sweet child, you never were too quick on the uptake.* She could tell what would probably come next.

The red-headed soldier, the one who followed his idol around like a shadow since childhood, finally let his story spill out. With eyes closed, praying for strength, he put his true feelings into words. "Baylor Randolph, I have loved you since the first time I met you. I can remember it like it was yesterday. My family had just moved back to town, and Lovey picked me up to take me swimming."

Laughing a bit, he went on, "Lord, even then she couldn't drive. I was scared we'd never make it to the pool where you were the head lifeguard. When she introduced me to you, I thought I had never seen anyone so absolutely beautiful. I fell in love with you at that very moment." He cleared his throat. "And ever since then, through all of these years, I still feel the same way." He then opened his eyes and looked adoringly at the fellow he loved.

Lily watched as Baylor's expressions changed from one of wariness to polite disbelief and then to a small, relaxed smile. *Baylor, my dear, dear boy. Life has just given you a wonderful present.* She said a silent prayer for God's grace, and asked Him, as she turned to go back inside, for a blessing on her son's and Patrick's prospective happiness.

Chapter 41

While Patrick and Baylor were looking at each other with different eyes in Highlands, Martha sat by her pool, listening to the crash of the waves on the beach, enjoying the warm breeze blowing gently through the dunes and palmettos. It was an unseasonably warm weekend for October, and she needed only a light sweater for comfort. The twins had been visiting with her since Thursday and would leave early the next morning. After dinner the two young men had Ubered into the village, making the rounds at the island pubs. Auggie, after a long day of golfing and a good bit of wine with dinner, had turned in early. Martha was alone with her thoughts.

The weekend had been serious at times and even tense at others, but in the end, the time together solidified further the warm relationship she had with her great-grandchildren. How she adored those boys. Trip and Jana might have had a disconcerting marriage, but they certainly managed to raise two wonderful children. Both were thoughtful and kind like their Daddy, and good looking like their Mama. Besides her looks, though, Peyton and Ray had also inherited the head strong attitude of their mother, which came through in some of their conversations.

However, Martha had to admit that gene had been carried down from her, and from their grandmother Lily, as well. Fortunately, the twins were also articulate young men, and able to explain their thoughts and feelings without coming across as obstinate. That gift of wording, though, didn't keep them from giving Martha as good as she gave over the weekend in regard to family matters. She had finally met her match, she thought, laughing quietly to herself. Ship Watch loomed big in their frank discussions, and while they didn't agree on everything, they understood one another. There was also a feeling of respect that permeated their talks together, and no regretful words spoken. She said a repeated prayer of thanks to the Good Lord for the weekend, and for all He had provided, even at this late stage. After decades, she was able to spend her life, in a way she saw fit, with the man she had loved since her teens. They had not spent a single day apart since arriving on Sea Island; both were determined to make up for all the time lost over the years.

She could not regret, though, the long period without Auggie in her life; in all honesty, it had been wonderful as well. She had been granted a solid marriage, graced with an incredible son whom she missed each and every day, and then blessed with Trip, Baylor, and the twins. The struggles she had faced were real, and had hurt at times, but overall, she considered herself one damn lucky broad. She took the last sip of her tea, and with cup and saucer in hand, headed back inside. If she died tonight, it would be with happiness and content.

Chapter 42

While Martha made her way back into her Sea Island cottage, April Anne wearily laid her head down in her parents' Winnebago. She bought the traveling behemoth for them last Christmas, and the couple had made their life-long dream of a cross-country trip over the summer. She had texted a photo of the motorhome earlier in the afternoon and sent it to Trip, Lovey, and Baylor. Her note read, "See. I told you they were at the Grand Canyon."

The renovation of her grandmother's tiny house was complete, but it smelled so strongly of paint and wood stain that she couldn't sleep there tonight. The weather forecast was for clear skies, so she raised all the windows and opened the old-fashioned doors with screens to let the place air out overnight. She also opened the sliding windows of the Winnebago, welcoming in the sweet smell of pine trees and the soothing sound of chirping crickets. The new addition of the home should be completed and done by the end of November. She certainly hoped so, because she had her heart set on a big, fine cedar to decorate. It would be just like the trees her grandparents had when April was a little girl, one cut fresh in the nearby woods and then decorated with opaque colored lights, tinsel, and hundreds of strands of icicles.

She was absolutely exhausted, both physically and mentally. She had held back tears as she left the Motel 6 that morning, but as soon as she rounded the curve onto the main road she cried like a baby. She had to pull over at a mountain overview because she could not see to drive. It took her a good five minutes until she could stop her bawling. When she did calm down, she returned to the road, listened to a number of podcasts and some of her favorite classical works, and made the long trip to Quitman with just a few stops along the way. Her mom and dad, as well as her sister and brother-in-law, had already arrived by the time she pulled into their driveway just after four p.m. that afternoon.

She was greeted with big hugs, kisses, and more tears. She and her sister were polite to one another and on best behaviors; it did them both good to see their parents after all of these months. Over a dinner of take-out barbeque with all the fixings, they sat around the dining table and listened to the stories of the trek through the western states.

She had talked to Trip twice that day and exchanged a few texts. She missed him immensely. As scared as she was, though, of being apart, she had to hold on to the faith that their relationship would continue to be solid. Nothing had to be immediate in terms of living arrangements. They could figure that out as they adjusted to where each were now in life: two recent divorcees in their forties and in love. As she remembered his last kiss, and that wonderful warm embrace from the morning, she was able to fall into a deep, dreamless sleep wrapped up in the comfort of being back home.

Chapter 43

Like his first night in Highlands back in May, Trip sat alone outside, smoking a cigar, and looking out on the stars in the autumn night sky. His Mom and Jackson were inside having a cup of coffee, and the two dogs were asleep on the front porch of his suite. Lovey was spending the night with Lachlan, and he wasn't sure where Baylor or Patrick were; they had not returned yet from the party at the country club. Frankly, he was glad to be alone, and not pestered with a bunch of questions about how he was doing.

He wasn't sure himself how he felt. It was a mixed bag of emotions. He was lonely already, and the thought of going to bed unappealing at best, not without April Anne there beside him. He was anxious, too, about how each would handle this time and distance apart. It would be a month before they saw one another again. Adding to his consternation was the fact that, before leaving, she had not invited him down to see her new house. Besides all of those issues wearing on his mind, there was also the looming suit between his mother and grandmother, and neither side was giving an inch of space. When the case eventually did get to the courts, there would be even more angst to deal with.

He had not seen Grand Martha since their row at Ship Watch, though he had kept up with her through the twins over the summer. She had extended a few phone calls as olive branches, but he was still reeling from her earlier disappointing actions of exclusion. There was one silver lining to be thankful for, though. His divorce from Jana was final, lifting a tremendous weight off of his shoulders. *Well, I guess we'll see how it all goes over Thanksgiving,* he thought whirling the two fingers of small batch bourbon left in his glass. After a few more minutes gazing at the night sky and being lost in thought, he finally went inside at midnight, the two Labs following at his heels.

They normally slept on the porch, but he was more than just a bit forlorn. The two dogs looked at him expectantly as he undressed and sat down on the side of the bed. When he patted a hand on the mattress and whistled, Tammy and George happily hopped up beside him. With moist eyes and a crack in his voice, he said aloud, "Well, it's just the three of us tonight," getting appreciative licks from both of them. It wasn't often the dogs were invited up on the king-sized bed, and they could sense that Trip was unhappy. When he turned out the light, Tammy curled right up on his left side, and George secured a snug spot on the right. With the comfort of the four-legged babies next to him, and the warmth of the bourbon in his veins, he soon was asleep.

All three snored gently through the night and remained in the same spots together until long past daylight.

Chapter 44

As her ex-husband made his way to bed at midnight, Jana looked out over the mid-town skyline of New York and marveled at how she loved the dynamics of the Big Apple. After the stifling constraints of Savannah, she relished the freedom of anonymity. She had received title to the flat in the divorce proceedings. After the twins had started kindergarten, she'd inherited a tidy sum from her father's eldest sister, who died childless. She used the money and paid for the apartment itself, while Trip funded the needed upgrades.

It wasn't a very large space, only two bedrooms and two baths, with a combined living, dining, and kitchen area. A small balcony facing West 56th Street could squeeze in four comfortably. The size was perfect for her, and the historic building was located in a desired area within a five-minute walk of Central Park.

She had flown in earlier after a long good-bye lunch with Bebe. Though neither one of them had planned for Buck to die, only wanting to humiliate and embarrass him, they toasted his demise anyway with a round of mimosas at The Olde Pink House. The two women knew there were many other ladies in Savannah besides them who were happy that Buck was no longer a threat.

The gossip was that no memorial service would be held. Buck's parents both were dead, and he had been estranged from his son and daughter for years. His in-laws, the Bishops, had closed ranks around the two Pearson children, and ignored the whole incident as if the accident never happened.

As Jana continued to watch the flickering lights, she realized that this was probably the first time in years that she felt content. The divorce was final, and she had safeguarded Ship Watch for the twins, if the transfer didn't go through to the Trust, though that was a big 'if' still at the moment. She would sell the island property back in Savannah, and at some point perhaps buy a small condominium in the building where Bebe lived. She could use the house on Sea Island she'd inherited from her Mom whenever she had a yen for the beach. New York would be her new permanent home.

She was excited, too, about Thanksgiving. Ray and Peyton would be with her for the extended holiday and stay on until Christmas, after which they would join Trip and his family at the Greenbrier. The three were to take in the Macy's Day parade, go ice skating at Rockefeller Center, see some sporting events, and she even persuaded them to join her for a matinee of the New York City Ballet's *The Nutcracker*. Jana had been mesmerized by Balanchine's original production since she was a young girl, and attending a performance at Lincoln Center was always the highlight of her Christmas holidays.

Her phone binged with the third text from Bernie that day. Like her, Bernie was a night owl. They exchanged several phone calls, texts, and emails since he left Savannah, and this week he had been very solicitous since learning of Buck's death. They had talked about the outcome of that day only once, and that was on the phone. The two did promise one another to discuss the details of what happened the next time they were together in person.

Bernie had actually invited her to visit him in Miami over Christmas and Hannukah. His self-deprecating humor, along with this sincerity, had charmed her. He told her that, while he would have a menorah, he always had a Christmas tree as well because 'he liked bright, shiny objects.' She was seriously considering his invitation; after the twins left New York, she might be ready for a change of scenery. She thought about it for just a moment more, re-read his latest text, and made her decision.

Her answer back to Bernie read, "I would love a stroll through South Beach to see the palm trees decorated with lights and tinsel. When should I arrive?"

Part IV

Thanksgiving and Christmas

Chapter 45

Trip had been on three cruises in the past. The first had been a transatlantic crossing aboard the old QEII celebrating his grandparent's anniversary, the next with his kids on spring break to the Bahamas, and the last an Alaskan adventure with Brother to spot whales and fish for salmon. The current voyage had proven enjoyable so far as well, though he had been rather anxious at the beginning about spending a week with four people he'd never met.

Their days were spent on their own doing whatever they might like while at sea or in port. Trip and April Anne had gone snorkeling in the crystal waters off St. Croix and visited the rain forests of the incredibly verdant mountains of Dominica. They'd spent one day on the French side of St. Maarten in the capital of Marigot, where April Anne helped Trip select Christmas presents for his Mom, Lovey, Baylor, and the twins in the upscale shops lining the city harbor.

During each late afternoon, the three ladies met at the spa for a hair styling session, massage, or some other sort of pampering. During that time, Trip bonded with April Anne's father, Frank, and brother-in-law, Stuart. At six p. m. the three gathered outside aft bar and enjoyed cigars and samplings of single-malt and bourbons. Mr. Adams was a serious man, and a bit introspective, but he warmed up greatly when talking about US history and fishing. Having served in the navy, he was fascinated by Trip's stories regarding the Randolph family business, which built war ships during WWI and WWII. Stuart was a full out sports fanatic, though thankfully not an obnoxious one, and between the three, conversations never lacked during their hour or so together. Afterwards, their party of six would take their places at a private table for the ship's second seating in the main dining room. Tonight was Thanksgiving, and the menu had at the center the traditional Tom turkey, though they all shook their heads that the side was described as 'stuffing,' and not 'dressing.' After taking a bite, April's sister observed, "Well, it's not what you would have made, Mama, but at least we don't have to clean the dishes." Mrs. Adams, who insisted Trip call her by her first name, Joyce, replied with a smile. "No cornmeal to be found in this dish, that's for sure, but it does have a good taste to it." Trip thought about the three family women. April Anne favored her mother, who was a pretty, petite lady with eyes that always seemed to smile; she generally could find something good in any situation. Jenny Lynnette, Trip could tell, was never the prettier of the two sisters. She had probably been attractive in high school, inheriting her father's big blue eyes and ash blonde hair, but unfortunately, her genes carried his solid build as well, and after giving birth to two kids and working on her feet as a nurse, gravity and age had not been kind. He could understand how conflict in April and Jenny Lynnette's relationship over the years would have evolved. Sometimes her barbs were aimed at her sister, and more than once he had seen April bristle under the scrutiny. Toward the end of the meal, talk turned to the upcoming Christmas holidays. During the conversation, Jenny Lynnette turned to Trip and asked, "Will you be coming down to Quitman for Christmas? Mama puts out one incredible spread. You've never seen so much food."

Trip put his fork down, having taken the last bite of his pumpkin pie. Looking at Mrs. Adams, he said, "I'm sure it will be a feast; I'm sorry I'll miss it." Then to the table, he added, "Since my ex has my boys for Thanksgiving, they'll be with me during Christmas. We'll spend the week at the Greenbrier in West Virginia; it's a tradition my family has had for as long as I can remember."

Mrs. Adams wistfully said, "I've always wanted to visit the Greenbrier. I heard that during Christmas it is just spectacular. Do they really have sleigh rides for the children?"

"It is beautiful during the holidays, Joyce. There is a yule log burning in the big fireplace in the main hall, carolers providing entertainment, and they will even put a decorated tree in your room if you ask. And yes, there are always the sleigh rides, both for kids and adults."

"Well, it just sounds lovely, Trip." She started to say something else, but Jenny Lynnette spoke up first.

"Well, Trip, if you aren't coming at Christmas, when are you coming down to visit?" She cut her eyes to her sister, looking for a reaction.

Trip, without thinking his answer through, and regretting later he hadn't, said, "I don't know. I've not been invited yet."

There was a short silence at the table. "What? You've not been asked to come see us?" Her question had a mocking tone. "April Anne, are you embarrassed to bring your rich Savannah boyfriend down to our little country crossroads?"

April Anne's eyes flashed, and she answered in a steely voice. "Try not to be daft, Jenny, though everyone realizes you can't help it. If I were embarrassed to bring Trip to Quitman, would I have him here sitting with us now?"

Knowing how arguments could escalate between his two daughters, Mr. Adams made a short, loud tap on his coffee cup with his spoon. All eyes turned to him. He quietly but firmly said, "Watch your manners. Both of you."

The two sisters sat in stony silence for a few moments, fully admonished. The other dinner companions continued on in conversation about plans for the next day's port visit to St. Kitts. By the time the dishes were cleared, all was back to normal, and the three couples made their way out of the dining room and to their staterooms. When April Anne and Trip got back to the suite, they silently changed clothes, put on shorts and t-shirts, and went to sit on the balcony. The sea was calm, and the ship moved slowly toward the next port of call. Trip spoke up first. "I'm sorry I said what I did. I really wasn't thinking."

April Anne looked at him guardedly under the soft glow of the balcony lights. "Yes, I'm sorry, too. My dear sister will use any excuse to throw a little fuel on a fire."

Trip thought a moment, and though he didn't want to argue, he felt he needed to clear the air and get a straight answer. "Again, I'm sorry.

But April Anne, why haven't you invited me to visit your home? I mean, I begged you to move in with me in Savannah, and I've yet to get a simple invitation for a weekend in Quitman." Not getting an immediate answer, he asked the same question Jenny Lynnette had put forth. "I mean, are you embarrassed to have me see where you live?"

April turned in the lounge chair and said, "I figured you knew me, and loved me well enough, to know the answer to that inane question. First of all, though we love each other dearly, we both recently shed two long and very stressful marriages. I haven't been able to process yet getting back to who I really am. Let me move into my house, and settle back into my family life in Quitman. I've been gone for two decades."

Taking a breath, she went on with a bit more conviction. "And no, hell no, I'm not embarrassed to have you visit my home. I'm extremely proud of my parents, my family, and even my consistently inconsiderate sister. I'm proud of my entire heritage." She paused, still looking at him.

Trip knew there was something else she wanted to say but was holding back. "Talk to me, April Anne. I hear you in all that you are saying, and totally understand the need for time and space to get yourself re-established back home. And fine, you're not embarrassed for me to visit. What is it, really, then?"

He watched as she gathered her thoughts. The sky was lit with the Milky Way, and it glowed overhead as she spoke. "The worry I have, the real, knot-in-the-stomach worry, is the differences in our lives. You have made no bones about your willingness to come to Quitman, maybe even move there, but you've never spent time in such a small town, or that sort of rural area. I readily admit Highlands is small, as is Cashiers. So is Sea Island. But trust me, those places are just like little bitty Savannahs. They are nothing like my hometown.

You live in a city where you belong to four, count them, four, private clubs. One where you can go yachting. Another for golf, and two for parties and dinners. That doesn't even count the clubs in what, Highlands, Sea Island, Atlanta, and Lord knows how many places elsewhere? You grew up in one of the most famous houses in the

South, and own a huge cottage at the beach, not to mention access to all the other residences you have with your family. In Savannah you are invited to the best parties, formal balls, you are seated at the best tables at the best restaurants where every maître d' knows you by name. People defer to you in that town as if you're titled nobility, and that is not an exaggeration."

After another deep breath, she continued. "Where I grew up is charming, and the people warm and wonderful. The countryside is breathtakingly beautiful through piney woods, slow moving creeks, and the thousands of acres of plowed fields of cotton and soybeans that stretch on forever." She had tears by now forming in her eyes. "But it is a world away from yours, Addison Peyton Randolph, the third. My worry, my fear, what I'm so afraid of, is that you'll come to Quitman, try your best to fit in, but eventually decide that being there simply won't work." Through more tears, she added, "And then you'll go back to Savannah, and stay there, and what we have together will fade and go away."

Trip handed April Anne his handkerchief. He was at the same time both touched and annoyed at her confession. He gently cupped her cheek with his hand. "I had no idea you possessed such worries and reservations. All of your hesitancy about where we might live, or even me seeing you in South Georgia, came across, honestly, as having serious doubts about our relationship."

He went on after a moment's searching look. "You mentioned earlier how you thought I knew you and loved you well enough to understand what you needed." He shook his head slightly. "Well, darling, the same is true here. I thought you knew me, in my heart, and realized all those trappings mean so very little. How could you compare the love we have to a silly club membership, or a particular seat in a fancy restaurant?"

April answered with a bit of exasperation in her voice. "I don't know, Trip, maybe I don't trust my judgement, at least not when it comes to love. And think about it, you kept asking over again that I move to Savannah with you, which seemed as if you needed, and

247

intended, to stay back on the coast. So yes, I had my reservations and serious doubts about how you'd react to being in Quitman and what it would mean to our relationship."

Trip needed time to process this whole conversation. Hopefully it was all just a comedy of errors in communication, but he was too tired to think through anything clearly by this point. "Look. We're both exhausted. It's been a long day, and we need to get some rest. Let's talk about this later." Reaching over, he gave her a light kiss. "Come on to bed."

She kissed him back. "You go on in and brush your teeth and take your shower. I'll be there in just a bit."

Trip squeezed her hand and walked through the balcony door, closing it quietly behind him. April looked out over the sea, which parted lazily as the big ship made its way through the waters. *Where do we go from here,* she wondered. She waited for several minutes, doing her best to meditate on all her blessings, until she felt settled enough to make her way inside.

Chapter 46

Baylor could not figure out how, but his Mother and Lovey knew that something was going on between him and Patrick. Both women seemed to have an intuition that was eerily accurate; from the time he was a child he could never tell a lie or mislead either of them or get away with it. It was actually unnerving and irritating at times, but the fact that The Lil and Lovey loved and protected him so much made up for what he felt was mental intrusion.

What he didn't know, nor would he ever, was Lily's witness of his and Patrick's exchange at the country club. Lily, understanding the closeness of Lovey with both Patrick and Baylor, had confided in her son's cousin. After a long discussion, they decided to sit back, watch, and hope that things would work out for the best for the two young men.

After Patrick's confession to Baylor, and what the younger man had said finally sunk in, they decided that they needed to talk more, lots more. Patrick took the car keys to Trip and asked him to drive back to the Motel 6, using the excuse that he wanted to escape the crowd early. He and Baylor then got into Baylor's BMW, and drove to a private wooded area on the edge of the Randolph property, away from the main house. There they sat, talking, and listening, until almost 3 a.m.

Since that night, they had been in constant company. The two men came to realize that they needed time alone with one another, at least for a while, away from the knowing eyes of Lily and Lovey. Thankfully, his mother didn't protest when he told her that he would not be joining the Baylor clan at her new penthouse in Atlanta for Thanksgiving. She just gave a small smile and told him to enjoy himself, not asking any questions about his plans. Patrick's Mom and Dad were a bit disappointed that their son would not be in Savannah, but with seven other children, and eight grandchildren, they would be very much occupied on Turkey Day.

Free to roam where they chose and wanting to be in a spot far from home, they rented a bungalow on a side street in old Key West. It was outrageously expensive because it was a last-minute booking during the holiday, but Baylor didn't care. He could afford it, and he had always wanted to visit the island. The rental was a small, white clapboard house shaded by towering palms and a huge Banyan tree; bright pink bougainvillea grew rampant along the old wooden fence and on top of the backyard pergola. The couple ventured out to see the sites and take in some of the tourist attractions, dined in the local eateries, and spent most afternoons by the small plunge pool in the lushly landscaped yard.

A true ginger Scot, Patrick had to be careful about his time in the sun, and Baylor smiled as he glanced over at his new boyfriend, who wore a broad-brimmed straw hat and an outrageously colorful silk shirt they had purchased at one of the island's shops. The younger man lay under the shade of an enormous umbrella, dozing. Baylor beamed as he lay back, his happiness knowing no bounds.

It had taken a week or so to fully comprehend, but he soon realized that all he had hoped for in a partner had been under his nose the entire time: someone into sports, with a good sense of humor, hard-working, and kind. The compact young red head had the body of his soldier training, and with his piercing blue eyes and squared chin, looked like he had just stepped down from the Scottish Highlands. It was the entire package, and Baylor was thrilled at his happiness. Their week had been so relaxing that he had asked the real estate agent to extend the lease for another ten days.

As he reached over to grab his Tervis mug full of spring water, he saw that he had missed several calls and texts. He had turned his ringer off to let Patrick sleep. He picked up the phone, read the messages, and hopped up from his chaise, in shock. He walked over and gently shook Patrick by the shoulder until he woke. "What, you big hunk?" he asked sleepily, stretching, and smiling up at Baylor. Baylor answered somberly, "Get up, fella. I'm so sorry, but we have to go home to Savannah. Now."

Chapter 47

The Green-Meldrim Mansion, which faces Madison Square in Savannah, is one of the finest and most ornately appointed examples Gothic Revival architecture in the country. Built in 1850 for an English shipping and cotton merchant, Mr. Charles Green, a relative of the Randolph family, it showcases richly carved black walnut woodwork, elaborate stucco crown moldings, silver plated doorknobs, and marble mantelpieces. The home, famously, or infamously according to how you viewed the situation, served as the headquarters of General William T. Sherman during his occupation of the city in 1864. Today, the structure is the parish house of St. John's Church in Savannah, a religious bastion of old Savannah families.

The mansion overflowed with guests for the wake held there on this late November afternoon. Even two hours after the reception began, there were still over a hundred people nibbling from the never-ending platters of tomato sandwiches, chilled shrimp, and exquisite petit fours. Trip, Baylor, Ray, and Peyton had been standing in the entrance the entire time as the official mourners. Next to them, on an enormous wrought iron easel, was the life-sized portrait of Grand Martha that had hung at Ship Watch. The family matriarch had died in her sleep six days after Thanksgiving. Auggie had gone to wake her for breakfast and found her unresponsive. He told her family that she looked very much at peace, and even had a slight smile on her lips. He didn't tell them that he sat by her side for an hour and cried like a child. He was not one to share emotions, with the exception of his beloved Martha. Her ashes would be interred within the family vault at Bonaventure Cemetery after the New Year in a private ceremony. Her mortal remains now sat in a polished mahogany box on the table next to her portrait. Trip, the closest to the door, at last was able to turn to his brother and sons and say, "There is no one else in line. Mrs. Faison looks like the last through."

Right at that moment Lovey walked up with April Anne, each carrying two plates of food. Handing the china to the four men, Lovey instructed, "Y'all take a moment to eat something. You've been here on your feet for an eternity." April Anne gave Trip a small peck on the cheek and squeezed his hand. Keeping her hand in his, Trip looked at his brother and sons, and said, "Excuse us for a minute." He grabbed two canapes off the plate and led April Anne out the doorway, eating the sandwiches along the way. He didn't realize until that moment how hungry he was. The two walked over to a private corner of the wrap around veranda and stopped. Trip gazed down at April Anne and said, "Thank you again for coming. You don't know how much it means to me."

"Of course I came. It was the least I could do." She paused and said thoughtfully, "How are you doing? Are you holding up all right? I know you and Martha had been at odds for quite some time."

He was both tired and mournful. "It's all just so unreal. Grand Martha was someone," he paused as in disbelief, "who you just thought would always be around. She was a force to be reckoned with, but God, how I loved her." Thinking for a moment, he added, "We hadn't really communicated since that exchange in May. That was my fault, and I'll always regret my refusing to take her calls over the summer."

April Anne's face was full of concern and love as she tried to give what she hoped to be honest reassurance. "Don't censure yourself for what was or wasn't said. You were terribly hurt by your grandmother's actions, and no one blames you for having felt hurt, or even bitter, for that matter." She intertwined her fingers in his and pressed warmly. "But Martha never stopped loving you, and in your heart, you know that. You have over forty years of wonderful memories with her. Hold on to those times and try your best to let go of what was just a short break in an otherwise extraordinary bond."

Trip gave a half smile. "You really are an astonishing wordsmith, Miss Adams. You've made me feel better already." He stooped to give her a kiss on the forehead. April Anne sincerely hoped that he did indeed feel better. It was heartbreaking witnessing all that he and his family were going through. "What about the twins, how are they, Trip? It sounded like they all had a remarkable time together this summer with Martha. What a gift for all three of them."

"They dearly loved their Grand Martha, and those couple of months on Sea Island brought them even closer together. Both boys have had their cries and are still rather in shock, but they're holding up well." Changing the subject, he asked, "Are you headed back to Quitman today, or can you be with me for a while longer?" He had hoped that she'd stay through Lovey's wedding, which was two weeks away.

"If you don't mind, I'll stay tonight, then leave in the morning. There are still some details the builder is working on, and I want to stand over him while he finishes. But I'll be back in a week. I've got to return to help Lovey with her last-minute items, and then there's the bridal luncheon I'm giving for her with your Mom." She read the disappointment in his eyes but wanted to finish what she planned to say before someone came up and interrupted them. "Speaking of your Mother, I need to let you know something. Lily and I were standing inside earlier talking with Lovey, mostly about wedding plans. Well, Auggie was in a small group of people right behind us; your Mom had her back turned to him. Somehow, Ship Watch was mentioned, and Lily made a comment — now mind you it was not catty or unkind — about how the whole ownership situation could now be easily resolved. Her insinuation was that without Grand Martha to push the transfer forward, the contract could be declared null and void." Taking a quick breath, and looking around to make sure no one was approaching, she then said, "Well, apparently Auggie heard her comments and took a step over to where we were."

She stopped there for a moment as Trip looked over her shoulder to smile and wave at a guest who was leaving. "Go on," he said, turning his attention back to her.

"In his very patrician voice, Auggie let your Mother know that he was representing Grand Martha's estate, and that he had every intention of seeing her wishes through in regard to Ship Watch and the National Trust."

Trip was mentally and physically exhausted. While he grieved deeply for his grandmother, he had silently hoped that matters about the plantation could now be put to rest. He desperately wished he was back at the beach house, taking a nap, instead of having to hear what April Anne was about to say. With a look toward heaven, an extended sigh escaped. "I'm almost afraid to ask what her reply was. Tell me anyway."

April reached up to place her hand on Trip's forearm, and gave it a sympathetic pat. "She said, and I quote, "Well, then, counselor, I suppose I will see you in court.""

Chapter 48

Lovey had scheduled her wedding for a Friday night so, in her words, "people would have the rest of the weekend to recuperate." It was a wonderful celebration, Lily thought as she sat sipping a cup of tea in her suite at the DeSoto Hotel. Trip, Baylor, and her two grandsons would arrive soon to wish her goodbye before she headed back to Atlanta. Room service had just delivered a tray of scones, croissants, and fresh fruit for them to enjoy as a mid-morning treat. Settling herself into a wing chair in the living area, Lily recalled how the wedding had gone off so well. A radiant bride, Lovey looked stunning in her cream-colored dress that complemented beautifully her dark blonde hair and flawless skin under the glow of candlelight. Her grandmother's large and exquisite thistle brooch, hand carved in 18kt gold, pinned a silk sash of MacGregor green and red plaid on her right shoulder.

The decorations inside First Presbyterian included a small forest of Scotch pines of varying sizes, each draped with tiny white lights and strings of shiny red cranberries. Wreaths made of local cedar, boxwood, and English ivy adorned the ends of each pew. The evergreen circles on the bride's side of the church were tied with bows matching Lovey's sash, while ones on the right of the aisle sported the blue, green, and yellow plaid of the Campbell clan.

Lily sat in the front of the church along with Jackson, her date for the festivities. Trip and Baylor gave the bride away, and Lily's heart swelled with pride and love as her two handsome sons, dressed in black tie and kilts, escorted their cousin to the altar. After the two Randolph men sat down beside her on the pew, she watched from the corner of her eye as Trip stared intently at April Anne, who served as Matron of Honor.

An elaborate reception for the 200 guests followed. The bars featured more than two dozen selections of Scottish single malts, two fountains of Veuve Clicquot champagne, and case upon case of exquisite French wines. The buffet of gourmet foods had rich samplings such as whole, smoked Scottish salmons, carved tenderloin of lamb, oysters on the half-shell, and a charcuterie of imported cheeses and cured meats that stretched out the length of the parish hall.

Two hours into the party, the food tables were moved to the sides of the church banquet hall and a six-piece band began playing. Lovey's favorite scene from *Gone with the Wind* is Scarlett and Rhett dancing to the Virginia Reel. The Reel is rooted in the Scottish folk celebrations, and a week prior to the event, Lovey emailed all guests a tutorial of the dance. When it played, with Lachlan leading Lovey to the floor, the entire crowd came to their feet. It was so popular the song was repeated two more times that night, along with a variety of other music including Carolina shag, disco, and big band. Lily had not danced so much in years.

Just before midnight the food tables were put back in place, now laden with a Southern breakfast of buttermilk biscuits, country ham, cheese grits, and scrambled eggs. With so much whiskey and wine flowing, Lovey and Lachlan figured they should feed their guests, again, before folks started on their way home.

A few minutes before 10, the doorbell rang, and Lily rose to let in her guests. The men all came in single file, each giving a Lily a kiss on the cheek. She led them into the living room and gestured toward the room service cart. "Help yourselves. There's coffee, tea, water, and juice, and those croissants have a chocolate filling. They are all delicious." Pointing to her grandsons, she said, "Ray, Peyton, go ahead."

The twins made their way right to the food, stacked their plates, and grabbed bottles of water from the iced bin on the table. After Trip and Baylor poured cups of coffee and helped themselves to some pastries, Lily made herself a fresh cup of tea and sat in the wing chair, facing her sons and grandsons. "You look lovely as always, Mother," Trip said, lifting his coffee cup in a gesture of cheers. "That sweater is especially charming on you." Lily was dressed casually in dark red cashmere top and charcoal-grey wool trousers; gold knot earrings and a very fine Italian gold rope necklace finished her ensemble. The other three joined in with various compliments until Lily held up her hand and laughed, "Stop. You four are too much. You're going to make me blush." She then eyed them all quickly, one at a time, and said, "And you all look strikingly handsome. I take it you are headed to the golf course after I leave town." Each of the fellows had on long-sleeved knit polo shirts stitched with the Savannah Golf Club insignia and lightweight sports pants. Knowing Lily's views about hats worn indoors, they had left their caps in the car.

Ray answered, "Yes ma'am. We have a one o'clock tee time."

"Well, y'all enjoy yourselves. It's a bit breezy and cloudy today. I hope the weather holds for you." Looking out the window, she added, "And for me. I hate to drive in the rain."

Baylor looked up from his coffee. "I thought you and Jackson drove down here together." Glancing around the room, he continued, "Where is the love doctor this morning, by the way?"

Lily closed her eyes for a second as if praying for patience and then cut them back at her youngest son. "You do know that you exasperate me, don't you?" When the boys all laughed, she just shook her head. "We did drive down together, but he is flying from here to Washington to visit with his sister for a few days."

Ray spoke up. "You and the doc did look rather dashing last night on the dance floor. He's a nice man, Grandmother. I hope you both have a good time together."

"Thank you, dear. And yes, we do enjoy each other's company a great deal." Then looking at Trip, she asked, "How long will April Anne be here? What is the latest on that front?" She worried that the two, who were obviously meant for each other, would somehow bungle their relationship through some meaningless misunderstanding. She admitted that her eldest was indeed a smart man, but at times rather oblivious to the obvious.

"She's helping Lovey pack for the honeymoon. I'll see her for dinner tonight and then she'll head back to South Georgia in the morning." Placing his coffee cup on the table next to him, he sat back in his chair and crossed his legs. "Before I forget, Peyton and Ray have something they want to talk to us about." Looking at his sons, he asked, "What's on your minds, fellas?"

Peyton spoke first. "It's actually about Grand Martha." Ray then added, "Along with the lawsuit regarding Ship Watch. We're both very concerned about what is happening here."

Lily and Trip exchanged glances. They had agreed to leave the twins out of the legal proceedings, hoping to protect them from the drama. Neither had spoken to either twin about the subject.

Lily leaned forward in her chair, and said in a serious but caring tone, "Don't you two worry about the lawsuit. Or what will happen to Ship Watch. I'm taking care of it. No one is going to take your inheritance from either of you."

The twins looked at one another and Ray nodded his head toward his brother. "Go ahead. You first."

"Grandmother, we love you and we respect you immensely." Ray nodded in agreement, and Peyton continued. "And we appreciate greatly what you've tried to do for us. We truly do."

Lily looked on warily. "Yes, I'm listening."

Ray nodded. "We don't want to upset you, but we don't agree with your decision of a challenge lawsuit."

Lily wasn't sure she heard correctly. "Let me make certain I understand what you're saying. You mean you don't agree that I should keep this legacy in the family for the two of you?" She was astounded, and she could feel her blood pressure skyrocket.

Peyton said in a respectful but firm tone. "No, we do not. We don't like how this whole situation has played out and want you to drop the lawsuit."

Lily sprang to her well-heeled feet. Looking down at the two young men, she said, "So how did this all come about? I simply don't understand. I have done my very best to make certain you will not lose your rights to the property which has been in this family since it was built. You two are the rightful heirs, as will be your children, and their children. I could not stand by and let your great grandmother just give it away." Putting her hands on her hips, she bore down at them with a look that meant serious business. Baylor was silently grateful he wasn't at the other end of the stare but prayed that the twins would hold their ground. Trip was thinking along the same lines. "So I take it over the summer Martha spent her time wining and dining you while you were on Sea Island, and coaxed you around to her half-truths?"

"No ma'am, that is not what happened. In fact, we never had one single conversation about Ship Watch with Grand Martha until just before she passed away," Ray said quietly, still very much in mourning for his great-grandmother. "No word of the lawsuit was exchanged the whole time we were at the beach this past summer. I swear."

Lily stayed in place and looked back and forth between the two. She could tell they were not lying. Her perceptivity with them was as strong as it was with her two sons. "All right. I believe you. But why come to me with this now? You do understand that Martha made this decision all on her own. She didn't consult me," and then pointing at Trip, she added, "and she didn't take the time to ask your father, either. That arrogance of making such an autocratic move was just like her. She always did as she pleased, when she pleased, without regard to how it would affect others. It was infuriating."

Baylor at this point did catch his mother's eye, and he gave her a very subtle look that read, "Careful, Mama." Lily took a moment to realize that the twins had never heard her speak with such irritated fervor before, and certainly not to them. She turned and sat back down, trying to regain her temper. Ray spoke up again. "Yes, we both agree. It was infuriating. We told Grand Martha the same thing. Both of us let her know that it was extremely presumptuous on her part and that it had caused a huge rift in our family. One that we were worried would not heal." Ray fought back tears. "And now," he said, wiping his eyes, "she's gone."

Peyton took over speaking at this point. "But it was just as presumptuous that neither you, nor Dad, came to the two of us and asked what we felt should happen after Grand Martha made her announcement. You never gave us a choice. Just like Grand Martha, and I mean no disrespect here, you just plowed forward, never taking counsel, or getting feedback from either Ray or me. You filed a lawsuit, a very public one, on our behalf, and never even took the time to let us have a say in the matter. Sorry, but that's the pot calling the kettle black."

Lily was stunned and upset to the point her hands trembled slightly. "I filed that suit to do what I thought was best for this family."

Ray answered her. "And that is why Grand Martha did what she did. She thought it was what was best for the family."

A moment of silence lapsed. Trip spoke to his sons. "We're sorry it upset you, and you're right. Your grandmother and I should have spoken to you and brought you into our confidence. It was a mistake, and I'm sorry." The twins nodded at their Father and accepted his apology. Lily continued to remain silent as her mind raced. Both grandsons loved her without reserve and hoped that the issue could be resolved without bitterness. Peyton spoke. "Grandmother, we know you want what you think is best for us, and we love you for it." Looking over at his twin, and back at Lily, he went on, "but Brother and I don't know when, or if, we'll ever move back to Savannah. When I finish school, I hope to live in New York, or London. I'd love to explore the Asian financial markets and work in Tokyo someday. This one," he pointed with his thumb, "will be bumming around the globe with his golf clubs."

Ray smacked his brother on the arm. "You play with your numbers; I'll play with my golf balls." Then looking at his grandmother, he went on, "Not that we don't appreciate our heritage, but we don't want to be saddled with a museum to take care of, at least one where we probably will never live. And the costs are astronomical."

Peyton nodded at his Dad. "You know how much it costs to run that estate: hundreds of thousands of dollars a year. There's what, two groundskeepers, three security guards, a full-time housekeeper, and a chef?" Trip nodded, and Peyton continued. "You told me last year that the insurance with Chubb was over a hundred grand, and the taxes almost as much. That doesn't include physical maintenance; the trim alone has to be painted every two years because of the saltwater and humidity. How much is that?"

Trip looked at his Mom and then back at Peyton. "Last year the invoice was just over $60,000."

Peyton went on, explaining their reasoning. "We both have trust funds, yes, and we're extremely well off. Yet I don't want to spend that kind of money on a place where I won't ever live. I hope you understand, Grandmother."

Ray shrugged and looked on hopefully at the lovely woman in front of him. "Think about the Swan House, and Hills & Dales." He referred to the expansive, popular mansions of two other old Georgia families. "Those are both open to the public, yet everyone will always know and remember that they were built for the Inman and Callaway families. And Ship Watch will always be because of the Randolphs, even if the National Trust owns it."

Lily looked up; for the last few moments she had been staring at her lap. "Humph." Baylor could never recall his elegant mother give out anything even close to a grunt. She was either defeated or ready to unleash some flying monkeys. In truth, his Mother's emotions were somewhere between those two extreme ranges. Lily was devastated that she had gone to such extremes and that her efforts were utterly wasted. She was still furious with Grand Martha and mad as hell with herself. But she could not, and would not, be angry at Peyton and Ray. She grudgingly realized that there were some definite silver linings to this dark cloud.

She would never have moved back to Atlanta if fate had not forced her, but would have remained, forever the proper widow, living in the shadow of the Randolph's on the coast. And she was now exceedingly happy in her return to the home of her youth and being surrounded by her Baylor family and childhood friends. She also admitted to herself, in turn, that she was quite pleased being on the arm of Jackson Lockwood

Peyton gave a half smile at his Grandmother and hoped this last bit would get them through the discussion. "You should know, too, that the conversation we had with Grand Martha was a good bit louder, and with more colorful language than this one." He looked over at Ray.

The other twin laughed. "When we told 'the old broad' as she referred to herself that she was overreaching and imperious, she slammed her martini glass down on the table so hard it broke."

"And she called you an 'uninformed little shit,' if I remember correctly." Peyton laughed again, recalling the exchange.

Baylor's eyes got big. "You actually called her 'imperious' and 'overreaching' to her face?"

Ray looked over solemnly. "Yes, and apparently she just took it the wrong way." That last statement made the two younger brothers double over in laughter at the memory, and the humor of the moment became infectious. Even Lily laughed, thinking how she wished she could have been a fly on the wall.

Trip cleared his throat and tried to get serious; he certainly hoped that the twins and Martha had parted on good terms. "So how did you all leave it with your Great Grandmother? When you left from that weekend visit?"

Ray said with a smile and gentle tears in his eyes. "It was fine. She understood where we were coming from. She just didn't expect a couple of 20-year-olds calling her hand on anything."

His brother smiled, too, and added, "It ended with her telling us she was glad to see that we had inherited some of her gumption and spunk and those traits would serve us well later in life. We hugged; we each cried a little bit when we said goodbye. There aren't any regrets on our end, and there were none on her part, either. It was a very good last visit for all three of us."

Baylor, who had not joined in on the conversation, spoke to his nephews. "It's good you got to say goodbye. I'm sorry I didn't get the chance. I hadn't seen her since she left for Sea Island."

Trip agreed. "Those memories of this summer are wonderful gifts. You certainly had one helluva Great-Grandmother." He then turned and smiled warmly at Lily. "And you've got a class act beauty for a Grandmother." Pausing for a moment, he said, "What do you think, Mom?"

"Think about what? Your assessment of my being a class act? Well, yes, I suppose that's true."

Seeing that the ice was broken, the fellows all breathed an inward sigh of relief. Trip smiled and looked toward the twins and then back at his Mom. "I'm glad you agree. I was sincere about the beauty part as well. But seriously, Peyton and Ray have told you what they think, and feel should happen. What are you going to do?"

All eyes were on Lily, who remained silent for a few seconds. "You two boys do know that I went through this whole ordeal because to protect what is rightfully yours?" The two nodded in assent. "Well then, there's little else to be discussed. I'll call Whittaker as soon as you all leave and withdraw the suit."

Ray spoke for them both. "Thank you, Grandmother. We love you."

"And I love you, too." She then looked down at her watch. "I don't mean to rush you all, but I've got a four-hour drive to make and a dinner engagement at seven."

They all started to stand up except Trip, who held up his hand. "Hold on, y'all, please, for just a minute." The four others sat back down and looked on expectantly.

"What is it, Brother?"

Trip wore a hopeful expression. "Well, after such a colossal issue is settled as the one with Ship Watch, what I have to say shouldn't be a problem at all. I need to talk to you all about Christmas."

Chapter 49

On Christmas Eve April Anne sat in the great room of her new home with her Mom and Dad, enjoying the warmth of the flagstone fireplace and nibbling on Joyce's freshly baked sausage balls and homemade Chex Mix. On April's old turntable, Lawrence Welk's orchestra played while the Lennon Sisters sang about a white Christmas and dashing through the snow. The eight-foot red cedar stood in the corner decorated with her Grandmother's Shiny Brite ornaments, gold and silver tinsel, and strands of old-fashioned icicles. The large, multi-colored strands of lights glowed like a Christmas rainbow. It would be a quiet holiday for the three of them. Jenny Lynnette and Stuart had left yesterday to spend the week with Stuart's family at their cabin up in the Blue Ridge. And while several of her parents' brothers and sisters had invited them to dinner, Joyce and Frank insisted they simply wanted some quiet time at home with their daughter, which suited April Anne fine; she wasn't in the mood for a crowd.

However, her Mother had still cooked as if feeding an army, April thought as she passed by the kitchen earlier in the afternoon. A variety of covered dishes sat waiting to be warmed for supper, and a 15-pound turkey was in the oven as well. She guessed they would be eating leftovers for several days. She'd not seen Trip since the Sunday following the wedding, and those two weeks seemed like an eternity.

After she helped Lovey get herself together for the trip to Paris, she and Trip had enjoyed a quiet dinner alone at the beach house, and a beautiful night together. It was all she could do to break away the next morning and make the drive back to Quitman. He kissed her through the window of her car, then waved a solemn goodbye as she drove out onto Highway 80. She would not see him again until after New Year's; he and his family were already ensconced at the Greenbrier. The two had talked by phone a few times since she left Tybee and traded texts each day. The notes from him sounded a bit stiff and hollow, though, and his messages were vague as well. Maybe she was just reading too much into what he said, or rather what he didn't say. It was just very hard being away from him at Christmas.

Things had been busy for her in Quitman, thankfully. With the construction finished, she kept herself engrossed with decorating her new home, holiday shopping, and visiting with extended family and friends she had not seen in years. When she wasn't occupied with something to do, though, her mood would shift to quiet melancholy. April Anne found the nights to be extremely lonely and more than one evening she had cried into her glass of wine. Her sister had been particularly solicitous since they'd returned from the Thanksgiving cruise; April Anne supposed they both had matured a good bit over the past decade. Though they didn't always get along, they did love each other, and Jenny Lynnette knew that her sister was struggling with her emotions.

As dusk started to settle that afternoon, with the skies rosy and pink through the windows, April Anne was about to doze off in her recliner when the bells on her gate chimed. She had installed the sensor to give notice when a car pulled onto the dirt road entrance a half-mile drive up from the house. Joyce and Frank both looked toward the door. "I wonder who in the world that would be?" her father asked, glancing at his wife. "I don't know," she said as she stood.

April peered over at her parents. She couldn't put her finger on what it was, but they just sounded a bit strange. April moved the lever to let herself up from the recliner, and her Dad did the same. Together they walked out onto the large front porch and watched as a large white SUV and a Mercedes sedan made their way down the drive. April could not believe her eyes; of course, she recognized the cars, but the owners were supposed to be four states away.

After parking in the shadow of one of the yard's ancient live oak trees, Trip emerged from the SUV with Peyton and Ray, while Baylor and Lily exited the sedan and made their way to the porch steps. They were all smiling from ear to ear, tickled to see the surprise on April

Anne's face. Words failed her. Her Mother spoke first. "Trip, it is so good to see you again. And we are so pleased to finally meet the rest of you in person. We've heard so much about you."

The group made their way onto the porch and Trip introduced his family to Mr. and Mrs. Adams. He then turned to April Anne, who still had yet to say anything, and said, "Surprise." April stood still for a millisecond, and then wrapped her arms around his waist, reaching up to give him a kiss. "Oh, my goodness. This is a surprise." She gave another appreciative brush on the lips, then let go to hug and welcome the rest of the newly arrived guests. After all the greetings were finished, Joyce said to the group, "Please come on inside. Let's get you all something to drink and I have some hot sausage and cheese balls that just came out of the oven." Frank held the door open, and the group went inside except for April and Trip. "Daddy, you go on in. Trip and I'll join you all in just a few minutes." Her father winked at the two and closed the door behind him. April hugged Trip again. "I cannot tell you how happy I'm to see you." Trip hugged back and gave her another kiss. "But what in the world are you doing here? I thought you all were at the Greenbrier."

Trip took off his blue blazer and draped it across April's shoulders. "Here, it's getting chilly. Sit down for a second and let's talk." They then sat in two of the eight, oversized wooden rocking chairs lining the porch. "Truth is, I've actually been in the area for almost a week now."

April blinked her eyes a couple of times in disbelief. "What? Here in Quitman? What do you mean? And why didn't you let me know?"

"I understand this is kind of a shock." He reached over and took her hand. "Just give me a moment and I'll explain." He stared into her eyes and smiled. He was so glad he had made this decision. "Well, the day after Thanksgiving, after our talk, I was honestly out of sorts. I knew in my heart that we needed to be together — yet it was apparent that you weren't ready to come back to Savannah, and very reluctant to have me join you down here. So," he said, smiling, "I decided to come to Quitman anyway. I went to the ship's business center, got on the internet, and searched for a house to rent in the area. And found one."

April was trying to take all of this information in. She could hardly comprehend that Trip was sitting in front of her, let alone he had rented a house in Brooks County. "I wondered where you wandered off to; I didn't see you from lunch to supper time," Thinking back on that Friday, the port of call had been St. Kitts, where she and her mom and sister spent the afternoon shopping. "And did I hear you right? You've rented a house. Here?" She said the last word in total puzzlement.

"Well, not exactly next door. The place is actually about ten miles west on the road to Thomasville. It's the caretakers lodge for the old Round Pond Plantation. Sits right on the Aucilla River, has a dock, and is completely furnished. I have it under lease with an option to buy."

"Trip, sweetheart, this is all wonderful, but you have to give me a minute to digest this news. Not only are you leasing a house, but you've also put in an option to buy?" Again, her disbelief shown through, as she asked again, "Here?"

"Hey, after I saw the property, and the owners gave me a price, I knew it was a good investment. It's a wonderful structure from the 1920s, full of knotty pine paneling and two fireplaces, and it has been totally upgraded. I can't wait for you to see it."

"I know the house well, Trip. The father of one of my best girlfriends growing up was the general manager of the plantation and lived in the lodge. I've visited dozens of times. It is a lovely place."

He took her hand up and kissed it. He happily noticed she was wearing the charm bracelet given to her earlier that fall. "My intention is to be wherever you are. Whether it is in Savannah or Quitman, Georgia. I love you, and I want us to be together. Always."

April was beside herself with emotion. It was too good to be true. "I love you, too, Trip, with all my heart. Thank you. Thank you for seeing what I couldn't because of my fears and worries." Her mind then went to Trip's beloved Tybee cottage, and the anxiety returned. "You aren't going to sell your beach house, are you? That place means so much to you."

He shook his head and gave a short laugh. "No ma'am. Even if we moved to Butte, Montana, or some other spot across the globe, I would not part with my place at the beach."

They both rocked for a moment, and then April asked about his family. "How in the world did you get Lily and the rest of the family to give up a holiday at the Greenbrier and come here instead? I mean, I'm thrilled to see them, don't get me wrong, but that is one big change in plans."

Trip warmly relayed what happened. "Actually, it was The Lil's suggestion. I told them about my intentions to come here, and why. They totally understood. When I showed them pictures and described the property, Mama said, "Well, if it has four bedrooms, why don't we all just join you? We've been to the Greenbrier plenty of times." The twins and Baylor all thought it a great plan. Mama adores you, and Baylor thinks of you as a sister already. The twins are happy that *I'm* happy, and they think the world of you." He smiled at how it all had turned out. His heart was just full of joy. "We even put up a tree at the Lodge. Mom ordered it from one of those high-end decorator shops in Thomasville. Your Mom gave her the recommendation."

April gave a quick turn of her head. "You mean Mama knew about this all along?" She looked toward the door and back at Trip. "No wonder she fixed so much food and brought it over tonight, and that's why she turned down all the invites we had for family dinners at my aunts' and uncles'. She and Dad were in this all along?"

Trip smiled from ear to ear. "She and your Dad actually came with me and looked at the Lodge when I did the walk through."

April laughed and shook her head in amusement. "Well, you all certainly pulled the wool over my eyes." She got out of her rocker and put her hand out to Trip. "Come on, let's go inside and see what everyone else is up to. I'm guessing they are getting a good 'haha' out of all this." She then stopped just short of the doorway. "Wait a second. I don't want to step into holes, so to speak. How are Baylor and Patrick doing, and where is Patrick?"

Trip was happy to answer. "Talk about two peas in a pod. Brother and Patrick seem just perfect for one another. Patrick had promised his family he'd spend Christmas with them this year. He's got seven or eight nieces and nephews that just love their Uncle Pat. So, he is busy with them."

April answered, "Wonderful. They just seem so comfortable with one another." She glanced at the door. "And what about your Mom and Jackson? Are they still an item? I don't want to ask about him and learn that they're no longer seeing one another."

Again, Trip had good news. "April, if you had told me six months ago that my mother would be seriously dating someone, I would have had a good laugh. She and the doc get along famously, as it turns out, and it is the first time I've seen her relax in years, since before my Dad died. Jackson's spending the holiday with his kids and grandkids. By the way, Mom is planning a birthday dinner for him in Atlanta for New Year's Eve. She's going to invite you to attend, so be prepared to have a little 'Lily' pressure applied for the trip up."

April smiled as she looked through the windows into the great room. She could see Lily and her Mom admiring the Christmas tree, while the four men gathered by the fireplace talking and enjoying a cocktail. Aside the man standing next to her, it was the prettiest site she'd seen in a long, long time. "Of course, I'll come up for the visit. There isn't any way to resist your Mama when she sets her mind to something. And truth of the matter, I can't think of a better way to spend New Year's Eve." She reached up to give him a kiss on the cheek.

"Oh, one more thing before we go in. Is it OK to release the Krakens? Tammy and George are in the Suburban." Trip motioned toward the cars.

"Yes, oh my gosh. Are those precious babies here? I can't believe they haven't been barking their heads off to get outside." April's eyes danced with joy. She had missed the two Labs as well as the people she had left back in Savannah.

"I gave them two huge chew bones right before we turned into your driveway. They're in the car gnawing away." Trip went down the stairs and did a half jog over to the SUV, opened the back door, and whistled. The two big, blonde dogs jumped down and smelled the ground. They immediately picked up the scent of their long, lost friend, and looked up toward the porch. April Anne sat quickly down on the top step, gave a whistle, and clapped her hands. The dogs took off like lightning and bounded upwards, barking until they both reached April Anne, whining with joy as she grabbed them one under each arm in an embrace. Trip followed up from behind and took a seat as well. He leaned over to give April a kiss amidst all the dogs' lickings and affection. "We're all so glad to see you, darling."

April smiled with glee, still hugging the dogs. "And God, I'm so glad to see you, too, Trip Randolph. You are the love of my life."

Behind them six sets of eyes looked out through the windows from indoors, having heard the commotion of the dogs. Lily and Joyce reached out and squeezed one another's hands. Frank gave his wife a peck on the cheek, and Baylor, Peyton, and Ray all 'high-fived' one another. It was going to be the best Christmas ever.

Epilogue
One year later

Lovey had always romanticized there wasn't anything as pretty, or splendid, as a Christmas wedding, and she was so very happy to be a part of the one tonight. She stood aside the altar of the Church of the Incarnation in Highlands, waiting for tonight's six o'clock nuptials to begin. An early seasonal snow fell gently outside, greeting the guests as they arrived. The interior of the historic house of worship flickered with candlelight against the stained-glass windows.

Her mind raced with happy thoughts. She had survived cancer, found a wonderful husband, seen a pair of cousins fall in love despite the two men's miscommunications, and now her best friend, and her dear, lovable Trip, were about to be married. Lachlan caught her eye from the front pew and gave her a lewd wink. She blushed three shades of red and gave him an admonishing look. He smiled back broadly with a pair of slightly raised eyebrows. *God, how I love that man,* she said inwardly, giving a quick prayer of thanksgiving for her good fortune. Turning her thoughts back to April Anne and Trip, she ruminated contentedly as the musical trio played a soft, seasonal yuletide prelude. All had worked out perfectly with Trip's part-time residence in Quitman. He found southwest Georgia and northern Florida to be a sportsman's paradise, and spent his time there fishing on the large, spring-fed lakes and off the flats of the Gulf when not working.

The two lovebirds managed to sort out their living arrangements with ease. Trip had kept the caretaker's lodge and recently decided to purchase the property. It was a perfect spot to set up an office for his investment and foundation work. April Anne needed her privacy to write, and so they ended up in two places a mere ten minutes from one another. And while they might spend their days apart, they were always together at one place or the other at night. The couple also divided their time between Quitman, the beach house, and Highlands. They had spent all of July and August at the Motel 6, escaping the heat of South Georgia.

It was there, under the brilliance of a starry night, that Trip had proposed to April Anne. She had worn Grand Martha's enormous diamond solitaire every day since, alongside which tonight a simple gold band would henceforth accompany. Lovey beamed over at Baylor, who was standing as best man. She then took in the sight of her precious Patrick, who she had so unfortunately misjudged. He sat with Lily, Jackson, and the twins, and together they made an extraordinarily happy family. Patrick and Baylor were planning a wedding of their own come summer and had moved together into Grand Martha's townhouse. Eurelia's blue trimmed home next door would house the twins when they visited Savannah. Not for the first time, Lovey thought what a striking couple Lily and Jackson made. They each had such incredible style and bearing. Lovey had asked Lily if she and Jackson would tie the knot. The answer, with a raised eyebrow, was a short, "Of course not. We're too old." However, Lovey knew for a fact, through mutual friends who lived in Lily's building, that Jackson could be seen leaving the penthouse on many an early morning. *Never say never, Lily,* was going through her mind as Trip caught her eye. He winked at his cousin, and mouthed, "Love you."

And in the very back row she spied Auggie. She was so very glad that he had made the trip up to Highlands for the wedding. With him sat his and Martha's cousin from England, Anthony, who had accepted Trip and April Anne's invitation. Lovey was certain Martha was smiling down from heaven on the entire scene.

At that moment, the trio stopped for a count of five, and then streamed in flawlessly to Pachelbel's "Canon." The melodious and classical music of the violin, bass, and baby grand piano filled the church as April Anne and her father made their way down the aisle. Trip had never looked happier, and both his and April's faces glowed with sheer joy. Lovey had promised herself not to cry during the service, which of course was a vow she could not keep as she dabbed her grandmother's lace handkerchief to her eyes. Giant tears of tears of gratitude and happiness poured forth for her cousin and best friend. And, in her joyful and grateful mind, she thought happily in her signature sing-song Lovey voice that, *This is just TOO much for words. It is simply just TOO, TOO MUCH for words!*